AS IT IS

Written

MICHAEL EVANS

ISBN 979-8-88616-462-6 (paperback)
ISBN 979-8-88751-512-0 (hardcover)
ISBN 979-8-88616-463-3 (digital)

Christian Faith Publishing
832 Park Avenue
Meadville, PA 16335
www.christianfaithpublishing.com

Printed in the United States of America

CONTENTS

1

The Bishop Is Dead

Francis had his head bowed as he slowly maneuvered through one of the stone tunnels under one of Rome's basilicas. The corridors were covered in shadow with evenly spaced candles providing just enough light so one could travel from candle to candle without being in complete darkness. Francis, a humble priest of Rome, loved the solitude of the corridors because they helped him to meditate. He was aware that others in the past had loved the corridors because they helped them to conspire. He questioned how such a thing could be. How could one place produce the qualities of Christ to one individual and the characteristics of the devil to another? The thought occurred to him that Christ prayed in the garden while incredibly the devil attacked him in the same garden. A life set apart brought out the best and also the worst. As he came around one corner, another priest was rapidly moving toward him with his head also bowed down, however, not in meditation but in agitation. Both men were lost in their distinctly different thoughts when they collided. Francis nearly fell backward, but the hand of Benedict reached out and steadied him.

"Oh, Francis, please forgive me. I was hurrying. Are you injured?"

"Nonsense, Benedict," answered Francis as he smoothed out his robe. Benedict smiled in relief. There were many who would not take such a fault as graciously as Francis. The church in Rome was rife with those always looking to take advantage of one's mistakes. Though he felt that his convictions and habits did not live up to the saintly behavior of Francis, it would be helpful if others possessed the same gracious spirit Francis always seemed to exhibit. But such thoughts must remain only thoughts. The role of the priest was to obey and trust God.

"My brother, is something troubling you to cause you to be in such a state?" asked Francis, who by now was steadied and had placed one hand on Benedict's shoulder.

Benedict paused at the question. He was not sure if he was allowed to confide in Francis. He had been instructed by the bishop to be a support witness to His Excellency, but he hadn't been told that he could not speak with someone else. He was not eager to let His Excellency know what he had witnessed, but he was dying to communicate it to someone he could trust. Francis and he had come from small towns in Bohemia and had a common geographical kinship. If there was anyone he would choose to confide in, it was Francis. God forgive me for gossip he silently prayed, not sure if he would be sinning but not wanting to take chances. He gently pulled Francis to the outer wall of the corridor, so that if anyone approached the corner, he would be able to see in both directions.

"Francis, can I count on your discretion?" asked Benedict.

"Of course, Benedict. I would hope that you knew that of me by now. Please be at liberty if it will bring you relief."

Others often came to Francis to informally confess their sins and thoughts. He knew he had a reputation that he could be trusted with a fault. For those who confided in him, he took the responsibility and the obligation to pray seriously. He assumed that Benedict was about to do the same. He had no idea that what Benedict was about to say would forever change their lives.

Benedict's eyes appeared suddenly lit with fear as the words tumbled out. "The bishop is dead! He attempted to use the writing tool for the benefit of His Excellency, but it took his life from him. I saw it with my own eyes."

There was a deathly silence as both men looked into each other's face. For a moment, Benedict could feel the hand of Francis tighten on his shoulder.

"Benedict, what are you saying? Which bishop are you referring to? How did he die?"

Benedict looked down each darkened hall to confirm no one was approaching. His voice lowered to a faint whisper as he pressed his mouth toward Francis's ear.

"Bishop Speso attempted to use the writing tool for His Excellency in order to try and stop the Bohemian heretics. I alone was witness. Bishop Speso said that if it was successful, he wanted a witness when he met with His Excellency."

Francis had never seen the writing tool, but its existence and legend were known to those who were privy to be part of His Excellency's service. Only a few had seen it and Francis had never actually heard of anyone using it outside of the unverified fabled stories accumulated over the centuries. Rome had many artifacts accompanied with fanciful legends. He, like many, hoped for miracles and manifestations of God's power in such possessions and while he would never publicly disparage the stories or the articles supposedly producing such miracles, he secretly and quietly questioned the adoration they received. But Benedict was not known for tales, and he clearly was troubled about the event.

"Tell me, Benedict, what happened to the bishop?"

Benedict pulled his head back a little but still kept his voice low.

"His Excellency has been meaning to execute a papal bull against the Bohemian heretics. Bishop Speso thought that he would try to use the writing tool, hoping that he could simply eliminate them through its power."

Francis frowned. Through the years, he had seen many trying to manipulate their way into recognition.

"And?" asked Francis.

"I watched the bishop as he wrote. He seemed quite pleased with himself when he finished. I think he actually saw what he wrote but...Francis, nothing was written down. The scroll he had written on was blank. He turned toward me as he set the pen down. I think he was going to say something, but I could not take my eyes off the scroll. The bishop looked back at the scroll and suddenly froze with a look of terror in his eyes. I asked the bishop if he was ill, but he just stood there. His eyes fixated on something—I do not know what."

Benedict started to tremble.

"The whites of his eyes reddened. Then his skin turned fiery red. I could feel a great heat coming off his body. I stood back as he opened his mouth in horror. His skin started to burn like a pig on a spit! Oh, Francis! It happened so fast. In only a moment, he became a pillar of burnt charcoal, standing with his mouth still opened. Then he turned to ash and crumbled to the floor."

Benedict looked toward the ground as he relived the horrifying experience.

"The ashes just fell to the ground. Just like the words on the paper, he did not exist. I don't know what to do. If I say anything, they will either accuse me of killing the bishop or think I am possessed. Please pray for me, brother. And please do not confide in anyone."

Francis stood stunned, his hand still gripping Benedict's shoulder. He thought for a moment before speaking.

"You have my word, Benedict. Say nothing to no one. If what you say is true, the bishop's disappearance will remain an unsolved mystery. No one could even conceive of what you just told me. Go in peace."

Benedict paused for a moment, feeling a strong desire to never leave the spot. Then he was off, disappearing into the darkness of the corridor. Francis was left alone with his meditations, the subject of those thoughts having drastically changed.

His Holy Excellency was Pope Martin V, the first pope to be elected after the Western Schism, a period of nearly forty years when the Catholic Church claimed as many as three separate popes at the same time. Born Oddone Colonna, he rose through the Catholic religious ranks and in 1417 at the age of forty-eight became Pope Martin V. On March 1, 1420, Pope Martin V took a quill to issue a bull proclaiming a crusade for the destruction of all Wycliffites, Hussites, and other heretics in Bohemia. To make it official, he used a leaden stamp with the image of the apostles Peter and Paul on one side and the name "Pope Martin V" on the other. The writing implement of the day was the quill which like all writing tools had the potential to express great thought and produce even greater action. When the pope took quill to parchment, it was considered by many to represent the thought and desire of the Almighty. If the pope was the vicar or representative of Christ, then his declarations too had to represent the thought of Christ. The problem in 1420 was that some, including scholars, were beginning to question the authority of the pope to stop what the pope considered was their subversive behavior.

Unbeknownst to all except Francis and Benedict was that one of their own, Bishop Speso, had just attempted to exercise omnipotence with a mysterious instrument. What the bishop learned, like many before him, was that omnipotence had its own will and those who did not understand that eternal truth paid the price.

In the mid to late 1300s, John Wycliffe was a troublemaker to the Roman Catholic Church. He sought reform by proclaiming the then audacious truth that the pope and the church were second in authority to the scripture. He believed Christians should have access to the scripture in their own language and declared that the practice of indulgences, or the selling of forgiveness, were a blasphemy. His followers were called Lollards, a derogatory term for those who followed Wycliffe, whom the Holy Roman Empire felt lacked any credentials. The scholars who followed Wycliffe were politely called Wycliffites, though they were just as despised by those not interested in reform. It was the beginning of a movement and even though Wycliffe was dead, his followers were also included in the papal bull of Pope Martin V. The movement started by Wycliffe was unmistakable, and the fear of its success was strong enough so that forty-three years after Wycliffe's death by stroke, his body was dug up and burned just to prove a point.

Reform was like a fire that slowly starts in one room and then quickly crosses the hall into another room. Wycliffe was an Englishman. Less than forty years later and eight hundred miles to the east, the Hussites, followers of Jan Hus, who had been a church reformer until he was burned at the stake in 1415, had also been officially declared heretics by Pope Martin V. By the spring of 1420, a holy army was raised from the Holy Roman Empire to bring the unholy Hussites to their knees. The Hussites, like their now martyred leader, had spent much time already on their knees, and the result was a desire to hold their ground in Prague, the home of their leader and their movement. God's man for the hour was Jan Žižka, and he was about to be introduced to the one instrument that could not be controlled by man.

After his conversation with Benedict, Francis left the corridors of meditation and sought the isolation of prayer. He was strangely bothered by what he had heard from Benedict. He detested wild fables and had often witnessed priest and layman alike exaggerate stories both modern and ancient. In many ways, he was a silent skeptic. He preferred fellowship with God to fancy and fiction. But as he spent the night in prayer, he became convinced by morning that he had to investigate the matter for himself. After morning prayers, he slipped away and discretely headed back through the darkened corridors and down two flights of stairs into a dungeon-like room. He had not been there for a number of years and could not remember if it was kept lit at all times as were the hallways. As the room was seldom visited, he assumed it was not, so he brought a candle with him, hidden in his robe, and when he passed the last candle in the hallway, he lit his own and walked into the damp room.

In the dim light, he made his way along the right side of the wall, past the collection of martyrs' bones, reported pieces of the cross, and various artifacts used by the catalog of saints through the years. Stubbing his toes on the uneven surface and occasionally bumping into old saints he eventually found his way to the back of the room. Up against the back wall was a single table no larger than four feet squared. On the center of the table was some parchment. To the right was the writing tool. Francis crouched down with candle in hand and examined the floor. A pile of gray ash lay on the dirt floor. Curiosity tempted him to touch the ash, but he restrained himself. He had only met the bishop twice, and while he had never felt comfortable around him, he honored his position.

Francis moved the candle around the floor area. It was clear that there were two sets of fresh prints on the dirt floor near the table. There were three sets of prints to the right of the table which would account for not only his own set of prints but also those of the bishop and Benedict. He moved the candle along the floor to the left of the table. There was one set of prints which had to be those of Benedict. A set of prints went up to the front of the table and appeared to be mostly buried under the ashes. He could see what looked like a partial front of one shoe imprint extending beyond the ash. The set of prints that Francis assumed was Benedict's moved away from the table along the opposite wall, back toward the exit. Francis followed the prints toward the door. At first, there seemed to be one large print spread out, but as he moved closer to the exit, Francis could see the large print separate into two distinct shoe prints. Initially they were very close together, but as they came closer to the door, they spread further apart.

Like a detective, Francis attempted to piece together what had happened. Benedict and the bishop had entered the room walking down the right side. There were no diversions in the path which would indicate that the bishop knew where he was going, but probably Benedict was simply leading the way with the candle for light. When they had reached the table, Benedict continued past to the left while the bishop stopped in front. Francis suddenly had an idea and went back to the table. Extending his arm, he directed the candle closer to the surface of the table. There on the corner was a small drop of wax. Benedict must have set the candle down on the table. After the failure to use the writing tool and the combustion of the bishop, a shocked Benedict must have shuffled about dumbfounded, a reaction anyone would have had, before he stumbled his way out along the wall opposite their entry. By the time he had reached the door, Benedict had picked up the pace and hurried out, moving at the same speed he had when the two had collided in the hallway. Francis looked solemnly at the ashes and said a prayer for the soul of the bishop. He then looked back to the table. The parchment was indeed blank as if nothing had touched it. Hesitantly, Francis turned his eyes toward the writing tool.

Jan Žižka was no stranger to battle which was one reason he was elected along with three other Hussite leaders to be military commanders. "One-eyed Žižka" was born into the ruling class, yet as a Hussite, he had a strong connection with the peasants. The Hussites were divided into two groups. There were the more radical Taborites, many of whom came from the lower ranks of society and there were the Utraquists, which were more moderate and attracted the ranks of nobles and those from universities. Žižka sided with the radicals, though his credentials might lead others to believe he might be moderate. Like many who were great in battle, he could be misleading in appearance. The patch over the bad eye and the wild hair were intimidating, and as a soldier who had a ten-year history of battles before 1420 Žižka could display the roughness and bluntness of a soldier. But Žižka was more than a soldier; he was a leader with a brilliant mind for tactics. He knew how to strategize, and he knew how to organize and train the simple Hussite peasants.

By 1420, the battle lines of Bohemia had been drawn. Skirmishes between the Catholics and Hussites had forced Pope Martin V to give Sigismund, the new king of Czech, permission to take the kingdom by force and drive out the Hussites. With the power of Rome behind Sigismund, Žižka was faced with overwhelming odds if he were to help save the Hussites.

Francis felt as if he had been standing at the table in the room of relics for hours. Once he felt confident in Benedict's account of the bishop's fate, he intended to leave and keep the matter to himself. But as he stood at the table, he became mesmerized by the writing tool. He had silently and secretly detested those who worshipped artifacts yet he almost felt as if he should be bowed down in reverence before the instrument. The feeling caused him to do what he had learned over the years when he was conflicted. He bowed his head and prayed.

Francis had developed the habit that whenever he started praying he would begin by worship. He found that as he did, the direction of his prayer seemed to find its own way to the matter that was most important. As Francis worshipped, he slowly began to think of the factors at hand. First there was the pope's desire to do away with the Bohemian heretics through a written bull. Then the heretics themselves were brought to his mind. He was silently sympathetic to some of their convictions, yet to break with the church and the Holy Father was unacceptable to him.

It seemed that the doctrinal divisions between the church and the heretics were drawing to an unavoidable physical separation. Compromise seemed to become increasingly out of the question. He knew that there had been violence on both sides. In prayer, he brought these thoughts before the throne of God. What did the writing tool, which he felt unexplainably drawn towards, have to do with these matters? What power did this device have that it could turn a man into ash? It did not seem evil to him. There was a presence felt in the room that reminded him of times when he had felt particularly near to God.

He knew enough about the bishop to know that his primary intentions were to please the pope for his own recognition. If the writing tool could take a side, would it side with His Excellency or with the heretics? The death of the bishop suggested that it did not side with either the bishop or possibly even the desire of His Excellency regarding the papal bull. As he thought on these things and continued in prayer, he realized that he was in a conflict of conviction that had been secretly dogging him for years. If he was forced to take a side, would he side with His Excellency or with the heretics? His very call and presence in Rome said he was siding with the pope. His lingering presence in front of the writing tool said he was considering the alternative. After seeing the bishop's remains slowly become part of the dirt floor, he knew he would not attempt to execute the pope's will the same way the bishop had done. But what would he do? What should be done? In the end, he came to a decision. He would give himself to the will of the writing tool. A wave of joy swept through his soul. He lifted his hands and sang out.

"All praise be to thee Father through thy Son Jesus Christ. Let your ways be known and your name magnified."

2

The Heart of Jan Žižka

Jan Žižka had been a busy man. Tabor, almost fifty miles south of Prague, was the home of many of the Hussites. After securing Tabor from any remaining loyalists to the Catholics, Žižka went west in hopes of building up his meager army. But he was kept busy by local Catholics who kept him pinned in at Plzen. Knowing that Sigismund was on his heels, he quickly made a truce with the locals. Even though they soon broke the truce and attacked, Žižka was able to flee with his small band of men back to Tabor. While he was there, he prepared his men for what seemed certain to be an imminent attack by Sigismund.

While his army included some mounted and armed nobles, the majority of his force was infantry equipped with agricultural tools such as flails, billhooks, and axes. Žižka had come up with the innovative idea of converting peasant wagons into war wagons and loading them with armored drivers. However, if he had any hope of victory, he would have to move his army to Prague. Even though the Castle of Hradčany on the west bank and Vyšehrad had been captured by royal troops, Prague would provide protection and offer some advantage to a bold plan Žižka was forming in his mind. Fortunately, before midsummer of 1420, Žižka was able to get his people to Prague. It was there that he would meet an army superior in almost every way.

For Jan Žižka, a man who showed no fear and exuded confidence to all who fought with him, he was deeply troubled as midsummer, 1420, approached. Certain that Sigismund could attack at any day, he knew that his plan was sound but contained possibly catastrophic risks and the conclusions would depend on where and how the enemy would attack. Žižka was conscious of the numbers Sigismund possessed and that they far outweighed his scant cadre of fighters. He also knew that while his men possessed a will to fight like none he had ever known, their abilities and weapons overall were far inferior to the king of Bohemia.

Žižka thought that though the Castle of Hradčany and Vyšehrad were under Sigismund's control, that Sigismund would use them only as diversionary points and that Sigismund intended to attack the city from the other side. Žižka chose to place his defense at three main points, hoping to draw the enemy in and then flank them, forcing them to the river. Because the numbers and experience were in Sigismund's favor, Žižka knew that if he was wrong about Sigismund's intentions, then they would have no hope of stopping the overwhelming force. While he had great confidence in the will of his men and the God that was with them, he found himself on his knees before God presenting his concerns. As he was doing so one night, a voice was heard outside his tent.

"Commander, may I enter?"

Žižka stood. "What is it?"

"We have caught a priest. We thought him to be a spy, but he claims to have travelled from Rome and has brought something for you. He has requested to meet with you," replied the voice on the other side of the tent.

"As long as he is not armed, he may enter," answered Žižka.

"Very well, Commander." The tent flap opened, and the soldier ushered in the priest. The soldier then walked to Žižka with a parcel wrapped in a tattered brown piece of cloth and set it on the table.

"This is the item the priest wished to give to you. That and only a small piece of bread were all that he was carrying." Žižka nodded to the soldier, and he left through the tent door. The priest and Žižka stared at each other until finally Žižka spoke.

"You understand that I cannot let you return, as least not until I am certain that you are not a spy. Even then, it is possible that you will not be allowed to return."

Francis stood silent for a moment before answering.

"I will not be returning. You may do with me as you wish. I only desire the opportunity to present to you something I believe God has chosen, at least for the moment, for you to possess."

Žižka sat down on a simple bench he had in front of the table. He motioned for Francis to sit opposite him. Francis sat down while Žižka watched with a quizzical expression.

"So what is wrapped in that torn piece of cloth that caused you to travel all the way from Rome, risking your life, and I sense now alienating you from the power of protection that rests in the pope?"

"Please see for yourself, Jan Žižka. Do you mind if I finish the piece of bread?"

Žižka nodded at Francis and as Francis chewed on the bread Žižka unraveled the cloth. He cocked his head to the side so that his good eye was able to view the tool. It was a straight thin rod made of a metal unfamiliar to anything Žižka had ever seen. It was slightly smaller than a forearm's length with the width of one of Žižka's thick fingers. The width was in the shape of an equilateral triangle, both ends tapering to a dull point. One end of the instrument had a small gold ring around it just below the tip. The tip of the tool on the ring side was gold. At first, Žižka thought the instrument to be a deep blue, but the color was deceiving. He could not tell if it was the light from the candle or the change in angle when he moved his head. At times, it appeared to be dark blue, and then it seemed to be more of a silver shade. And at one point it, seemed to be reddish green. He looked up at Francis, who was intently watching Žižka as he examined the writing tool. Žižka had come to be distrustful over the years with the priests who represented Rome. Many of them seemed in his estimation self-serving and inept when it came to truth and the practicalities of daily life. This man in front of him, in spite of his disheveled appearance and gaunt look, was different. He possessed a poise and quietness about him that was intriguing to Žižka.

"What is this that you have brought me and why have you risked everything to do so?"

Francis finished his last bite of bread and looked about, hoping that there was something to drink. His last drink had been from a brook a day earlier, and his throat was so dry that it had been difficult to get the bread down. Žižka saw him look around and sensed what Francis needed. He went to a corner of the tent and poured some ale from a bucket into a wood cup. He walked it over to Francis and handed it to him.

"Many thanks, kind sir," said Francis as he took a drink. "This will help me greatly in explaining the tale I have and answering your questions. I will answer the second one first if you do not mind."

Žižka nodded for Francis to continue.

"As to why I have risked everything to come here, I can only say that the object itself directed me to come."

Žižka's eyes opened a little wider as he cocked his head questionably at Francis.

"This?" he queried with one eye brow lifting slightly as he pointed to the object. "This directed you to come to me? And just how did that happen?"

"That," answered Francis, "leads us to the tale which I hope will answer your first question." Francis downed his drink and set the cup on the table.

Francis then told Jan Žižka of how Bishop Speso had attempted to use the writing tool. Žižka had heard many elaborate tales of relics with magical powers. Had any other soul been telling this story Žižka would have given them the scorn he felt they deserved. However, as Francis spoke, Žižka could see that Francis himself did not believe many of Rome's fables about the power of religious relics.

Žižka looked down at the writing tool and looked back at Francis.

"The pope intended on using this tool against us?" he asked.

"No, I don't believe so," replied Francis. "While His Excellency executed the papal bull, I believe he had no involvement in the tool."

"Why do you defend His Excellency?" said Žižka sneering, with an emphasis on the words *His Excellency*.

"I am not defending him," answered Francis calmly. "I am simply telling you my conviction. I agree with you that had the pope the ability to use the tool he may have done so. But what happened to the bishop is an example of what we know about the history of the tool. Most of the stories of the tool's history end in destruction, so much so that it has seldom been used. The instrument cannot be controlled by man. It has its own will, and I believe that will is the will of the Almighty."

"Yet," said Žižka. "If the tool brought you here, then apparently you have used it and lived. That part of your tale has not been told."

Francis looked at the writing tool. He remembered when he had first held it in his hand. As it lay motionless, cradled in his palm, he could sense life flowing from one end of the tool to the other. That life seemed to seep into the skin of his hand and run through him—testing him, knowing him, seeing what manner of man he was. Francis felt that the nature of his heart was being opened like a knapsack with all the content's being exposed, as if the writing tool was peering intently, examining the contents to see what it contained. Francis also saw what was in his heart. He saw belief and unbelief, sincerity and insincerity, deeds good and bad, righteousness performed and righteousness ignored. Of all these features, Francis felt the tool was also searching, combing through them, not to find the deeds and character of Francis but to know what Francis's will was regarding the tool itself. It was brushing aside everything else as if the outcome of those things would be decided by another. The tool was looking for what concerned itself. It was looking for the hidden motive of Francis heart.

"It is true," answered Francis. "And though I am here because of its will, I believe that there is a history of death with the tool. I do not believe it was ever meant for man to use, especially for his own purpose."

Žižka rubbed his chin. He picked up the writing tool and let it roll in his palm. It felt light yet the metal was something he had never seen before. The thought occurred to him that the tool could not be easily snapped or bent.

"So tell me what this has to do with me?"

Francis leaned forward.

"I am not a man given to superstition. I serve the living God, and in all things, it is His will that I seek."

"I have found that can be unusual for a priest," commented Žižka.

Francis leaned back and smiled. "I know that there are disreputable priests. I am sadly aware at the manner in which many serve their call. But I believe that you are a man who could say the same thing about yourself that I have said about me. Let us put the others aside."

Žižka gave a slight nod of his head. "Tell me what you know of this thing and of your experience."

"Legend has it that before Lucifer uttered the five 'I wills' mentioned in the book of the prophet Isaiah that he had written them down with the writing tool that is before you. It is believed that the writing tool is one of three used by God. It has been speculated that this particular one has the power to execute whatever it writes. Lucifer presumed that the writing tool would bend to the will of the user. But he did not know that the writing tool is more than just an instrument of enforcement. It is an extension of the will of the Almighty. It does not operate apart from the will of God.

"When Lucifer penned his 'I wills' with the intention that they come into existence, he was penning his own downfall. It is said that after he penned the 'I wills' that he declared them before the angels. One-third of the angels sided with Lucifer before he noticed that the writing on the paper had changed. Though there is no recorded history of what was written, the tale says that the five wills of Satan became the three wills of God. Satan looked at the paper and saw the words *fallen*, *cast down*, and *pit*. As with Satan, so has it been proven in the case of the bishop. The instrument has its own will or I should say that the writing tool cannot write what God does not allow. As Lucifer plunged from heaven he fell along with the instrument. In his fall, the instrument was lost to him but it landed on earth. At some point, possibly by Adam and Eve in the garden, the writing tool passed into the hands of man.

"During the span of time, numerous tales have been told regarding the writing tool. Some believe that in Daniel chapter 5 when Belshazzar was having his feast that the writing on the wall was written with the instrument. Some believe that John wrote his revelation with the writing tool on the Isle of Patmos."

"Who kept the tool during those times?" interrupted Žižka.

"It appears," said Francis, "that the instrument kept itself. There is no record that the Jews kept it with their sacred items. We only know for certain at what point it came into the possession of the church."

"When was that?"

"You are familiar I am sure of the story of Constantine and the vision of the cross."

"It is a papal classic," answered Žižka with some sarcasm.

"It has been alleged that Constantine sought the will of the tool and was given the words *In hoc signo vinces* or 'In this sign conquer.' The cross was also written by the tool on the same scroll, and then later, Constantine claims to have seen a vision of the cross. Whether you believe that or not, the church since then has had possession of the writing tool and kept it with their many relics. Others have attempted to use it through the years but it has developed a reputation of being more of a curse than a blessing."

Žižka listened intently and then replied, "And yet, as I mentioned before, in spite of all this, you have chosen to not only use the instrument but to bring it to me. Maybe the pope sent you to kill me the same way the bishop was killed."

Francis grinned at Žižka.

"Spoken like a true man of war. I myself would never have considered such a thing. I agree that there are those who would attempt such an unholy deception, but you will have to take my word for it that I am not one of them. Because I am not superstitious, and because I serve my Lord with my whole heart, there was no fear when I gave myself to the will of the writing tool. I had no agenda when I attempted to write with the instrument other than to allow the tool to do as it willed. When I wrote, I saw the original words on the parchment that I had written. Those words declared that I was giving myself to the will of the instrument for the purpose of serving the Lord of all creation."

"Do you have the parchment that you have written upon?" asked Žižka.

"I do," answered Francis. He lifted up his robe, and at the base, he tore the stitching open where he had created a secret place to store the parchment. He pulled the parchment out and handed it to Žižka.

Žižka unfolded the parchment and read aloud. There were three separate lines of writing with spaces between them to indicate that they were three separate sentences. There was no punctuation or capitalization.

go to jan zižka in bohemia and give him the tool

the seed sown will blossom into a great tree and bring many to salvation

glory

Žižka, puzzled, looked at Francis.

"The words are different than the ones you penned."

"They are," answered Francis. "They are the instruments work."

"Did you know of me before you wrote this?" asked Žižka.

"No," answered Francis. "But I am sure that the pope does."

Žižka looked at the last word.

"What does glory mean?"

Francis gazed down at his hands. There was a jagged scar along the left hand that ran from the base of his thumb across the palm and around the back. He was six when a dog had attacked him. He remembered his mother fighting the dog back with a stick. He could still recall the fierceness in her face as she fought and the tenderness in her eyes when she cleaned his hand and wrapped it.

"It means that I am to die soon. I do not know when."

"How do you know this?" asked Žižka.

"To know its words is to know its mind," Francis replied simply.

"I see," said Žižka as he looked at the instrument. A long silence ensued before Francis spoke.

"You have asked of me many things Jan Žižka, and rightly so, for the tale is strange. May I ask you one question?"

Žižka looked back at the priest and nodded, knowing already what the question would be.

"Why does the instrument want you to seek its way?" asked Francis.

Žižka stood and began to pace back and forth behind the bench. He seemed to be almost having a conversation between himself, debating not only how much he should tell the priest but whether he should use the instrument. Francis sat and patiently waited. After a few minutes, he stopped pacing and turned to face Francis. The fight within had come to an end and he had made up his mind.

"We are outnumbered, and we face an enemy with superior skill and weapons. I have a plan, yet if I am wrong, our movement is lost and many will die—seasoned warriors and simple peasants alike. So much is at stake. I am torn. If I knew my plan would not succeed, I would change my tactics and do what I could to protect the people God has entrusted to me."

Žižka sat down and stared at the instrument before him. There was no need for any more questions. The only one remaining was whether Žižka would use the instrument. An hour before, he had been on his knees praying. Was this an answer to his prayers? It certainly was not what he was expecting. He stood and went to a trunk sitting at the base of his tent and pulled out some parchment. Slowly he sat down on the bench and picked up the writing tool. He looked up at Francis only to see that Francis was on his knees praying.

This is an honorable man, Žižka thought. *I could use more like him.* He started to write.

"I love my people. I love my Lord. I only wish to know whether the plan I want to implement will be successful for the sake of those who trust me. I submit to the Lord God Almighty and to the will of the instrument."

When he was done, Žižka closed his eyes expecting that at any moment he might die like the bishop. But nothing happened, and he opened his eyes, looked down at the parchment, and then grunted.

"Hmph."

Francis heard Žižka and rose from prayer. He walked back to the table and looked at Žižka. Žižka turned the parchment around and pushed it toward Francis who sat down on the bench and read.

> victory
> victory
> glory

"Is that what you wrote Jan Žižka?" asked Francis.

"No, as it was with you, it is only the answer."

"Do you know what it means?"

"The first answers my question. The last is similar to yours. The second is like unto the first. However, I do not know the details, but I will later."

The two men looked at each other, and then out of relief broke into laughter.

"Well, you did not suffer the fate of the bishop anyway," said Francis.

Žižka sighed and ran his hand across his forehead.

"This has been a strange night, my friend. I do not wish another like it. My mind is at ease and I have peace about what will happen. I even have peace about the last. I should be afraid, but I am not. Is that how you felt?"

"It is," said Francis with a smile.

"What will you do?" asked Žižka. "Will you return to Rome?"

Francis shook his head. "No, my direction has changed. Until the Lord calls me unto Himself, I would like to serve the people here if I may."

Žižka nodded enthusiastically. "Of course. I will give explicit directions that you are with us and you are to be honored. We can use a noble priest. I do not think I need to tell you this, but what happened here tonight should stay between us."

Francis smiled. "Frankly, I have no desire to repeat it."

Žižka folded the writing tool back into the cloth and pushed it toward the priest. Francis stopped Žižka's hand.

"It is yours now, Jan Žižka. Keep it to yourself the best that you are able. However, should you lose it, do not fear. I believe that the tool cares for us more than we can care for the tool."

Two weeks later, Sigismund's men attacked. Jan Žižka's plan worked perfectly and a superior army was sent running by a group consisting mostly of peasants armed with simple tools. Francis spent the two weeks prior to the attack tirelessly and joyfully serving the people of Prague. He heard confessions and administered the sacraments. He helped with common chores, often singing praises as he worked. When the day of battle came, though he did not take up a weapon, he helped the wounded by pulling them out of the battle and harm's way. Toward the end of the battle while the enemy was being routed, an errant arrow found its way to his heart and he died instantly. In two weeks, he had won the hearts of the Hussites, and Jan Žižka wept openly at his burial.

In the winter of 1421, Žižka again found victory in spite of overwhelming odds when he faced Emperor Sigismund at Kutná Hora. In 1424, Žižka was taken to heaven to meet his Lord and reunite with his friend Francis. Emperor Sigismund lost every battle he took on against the Hussites. After being beaten by the Ottoman Turks in 1428, he decided to leave the fighting to others until his death in 1437. Žižka never again used the pen. Eventually, the Hussite movement fractured into five different factions, spending much of their time squabbling with each other. However, the seeds had been sown. On October 31, 1517, Martin Luther nailed his ninety-five theses to the door of the Wittenberg Castle Church, and the beginning of the tree blossoming began to take place in the Reformation.

3

---◆●◆---

The Road to Prague

Francis had left Rome the day after using the writing tool. While his absence was not noticed for a few days by anyone other than Benedict, the bishop's absence was noticed the next day by the pope. Inquiries were made, and Benedict was requested to meet with His Excellency. Benedict was particularly nervous because shortly after Francis had gone to investigate the bishop's death, Benedict had also returned to the room of relics. It had occurred to him that others might discover the same thing Francis had found, which was the damning evidence of footprints. Benedict thought that he should sweep the area of the footprints and of the bishop's ashes. He was petrified that as the bishop's aide he would most likely be the prime consideration in any perceived foul play.

Upon entering the room of relics, he soon discovered that not only were there additional footprints but that the writing tool was missing. After sweeping the floor free from dirt and ash, he searched frantically for Francis to no avail. In spite of the scant possessions that Francis kept in his room, it was clear that he had left Rome. While Benedict was unaware that Francis had used the instrument, he correctly assumed that Francis had gone to Prague to warn the heretics. He envied Francis's strength of character. It was what drew him for counsel and confession. Francis would always do the right thing no matter what the consequence. Knowing this about Francis also irritated him because Benedict knew himself to be a coward and an opportunist. Even as Francis had been aware of his inner conflict between the pope and the heretics, Benedict was aware that there was a battle being fought in his soul and that he was being pressed toward a side. "*Choose you this day whom ye will serve.*" Benedict was being pushed toward that moment of decision as he was summoned later that day to meet with Pope Martin V.

He was not sure what to expect when he entered the office of the pope. It was more of a large hall than office and felt even larger by the fact that no one else was in the room except the pope, and he was sitting on a chair in the distant corner of the room. There was an empty chair beside him. The pope appeared to be waiting patiently for Benedict to arrive. Once Benedict was in the room, the pope made a slight gesture with his hand that Benedict was to sit in the seat beside him. The walk toward the pope seemed interminable. As each step brought him closer, Benedict could feel himself shrivel like a wilting plant. He dreaded the confrontation that would follow and wished that he could spend the rest of eternity just walking and never arriving. By the time he reached the pope, he could feel the moisture on his forehead and sweat running down his back. After kneeling and kissing His Excellency's ring, Benedict sat and stared nervously at the pope. Pope Martin V, the vicar of Christ and successor of the Prince of apostles, warmly smiled at Benedict.

"I agree with you, Benedict," said the pope sympathetically.

Benedict's throat was dry, and he was confused by the pope's opening statement. He said, "Excuse me," but it came out high and choppy. Benedict cleared his throat.

"Excuse me, Your Excellency?"

"The heat," answered the pope. "It is much too hot for this time of year. Can I offer you something to relieve you from your discomfort?"

"Oh, no, thank you, Your Excellency. Yes, the heat. It is much too warm." Benedict looked at the pope's face which seemed very cool and relaxed.

The pope leaned forward and placed one of his hands loosely on Benedict's wrist. His eyes peered into Benedict's, and while there was warmth in the look, there was also steel.

"Please do not be nervous, my son. We are all brothers serving the Lord, are we not?"

The pope patted Benedict's wrist a couple of times and leaned back in his seat.

"Yes, Your Excellency. Of course," answered Benedict.

In spite of the fact that the pope had never met Benedict, it was clear to him that Benedict would tell him everything he needed to know.

"Very good, Benedict. We are more than servants. We are brothers. Benedict, did you know that I have a brother? His name is Giordano."

"Yes, Your Excellency. I have heard that, though I have never had the pleasure of meeting him."

The pope's eyes widened. "Oh, I hope someday that you will, Benedict. It would do me a great honor."

"I'm sure that the honor would be mine, Your Excellency," replied Benedict weakly. The pope smiled.

"When Giordano and I were boys, we told each other everything, Benedict. We had no secrets. He was my brother, but he was also my truest and most loyal friend. That is a true brother, would you not agree, Benedict?" One of the pope's eyebrows arched slightly at the question. Benedict swallowed and looked down at his hands resting uneasily on his knees. It was then he realized he never had a chance. He would never be a Francis. He would never lose his life. The words tumbled out of Benedict's mouth.

"Your Excellency, Bishop Speso asked me to accompany him to the chamber in which the relics are stored."

Benedict flustered about a bit trying to figure out how much to say and how to say it. The pope rested attentively, like a cat waiting for a cornered mouse to make his move.

"And why is that, my son?"

"He wanted to be of service to you, Your Excellency, by seeing if there was a way in which he could help resolve the problem of the Bohemian heretics."

Benedict stopped, naively hoping that this would satisfy the pope and he could be mercifully dismissed. There was a long silence, awkward for Benedict but enjoyable for His Excellency.

"Please go on, Benedict."

Benedict felt like a child being forced to finish telling his parents the painful details of what he had done wrong. He put his hand to his mouth and coughed lightly.

"Well, Your Excellency, as I mentioned, he…ah, heard about the difficulties with the heretics, and he…ah, thought that maybe, he…ah, might help by using one of the relics stored in the chamber to…um…help."

"Is that so," replied the pope, now expressing some genuine interest in what Benedict was saying. "Bishop Speso has always had the interest of the church at the forefront of his mind. Just which relic was he attempting to use to help us in our problem with the heretics?"

Benedict had his head down while he had been speaking. At the pope's question, he lifted his eyes just enough to peer at the pope.

"The writing tool of Flavius Valerius Constantinus, Your Excellency."

Without displaying any emotion, the pope sat shocked. He had assumed that the bishop had gotten himself into some minor trouble and that his lackey Benedict was simply caught in the middle. He knew the nature of Bishop Speso. The bishop, if given the opportunity, would do whatever he could to gain power and control. The bishop had presumed that wiping away the heretics would have given him greater favor in Rome, and it probably would have, thought the pope. The writing tool had legendary powers, but he had never heard of anyone using it successfully or without coming to a tragic demise. Secretly, while he thought the bishop a fool, he had to admire his courage to risk everything in order to gain favor. However, knowing the bishop's thirst for power, it was also possible that Bishop Speso was attempting to use the tool against him.

"And how exactly do you know this?" asked the pope.

"He told me. He wanted me with him when he attempted to use the writing tool so that I might be a witness."

The pope's eyes widened a little.

"And what, Benedict, was it that you witnessed?"

Benedict looked around the room wishing that there was a way of escape. He caught the pope's eyes and realized that the pope no longer seemed congenial but was extremely serious.

"His destruction," was all Benedict could say.

The pope leaned forward, his elbows resting on his knees and his hands clasped.

"Tell me how," he said eagerly. He knew Benedict was not the type to kill the bishop and make up such a tale. Benedict was a fool, but he was not a murderer and the bishop had chosen Benedict for that reason. The bishop had needed someone who could do his bidding without trying to undermine him.

Benedict explained everything that had happened while in the chamber. The pope was fascinated by the details and asked him to repeat them after he had finished. After the second rendition of the tale, the pope leaned back in his chair and rubbed his chin. As Benedict squirmed, the pope thought about what he should do about the bishop's disappearance and Benedict's involvement. The pope did not want wild stories regarding the bishop consuming everyone. There were many ways he could explain the bishop's disappearance. As for Benedict, he would simply ask him to be silent for the time being. He was also very curious about the writing tool. The pope looked at Benedict who was sweating so much it looked as if he had just bathed. He might be useful to me, the pope thought. He reached his hand out and placed it encouragingly on Benedict's shoulder while giving him his most comforting smile.

"My dear son, please do not be anxious. I believe you. Bishop Speso, though he meant well, should not have attempted something so foolhardy. For now, let us keep the matter between us. I think that would be wise, don't you?"

The last line was said in such a way that Benedict couldn't tell if it was a suggestion or a threat. Either way, he was relieved that the pope was not blaming him for the death of the bishop.

"But, Your Excellency, what should I say should someone ask me about the bishop?"

"Just say that he is in service of His Excellency. It is doubtful that anyone would pursue you with questions, but if they do, please refer them to me. For now, it will be our secret."

Not only had a huge weight been lifted off Benedict but now he was being asked by Pope Martin V to help him. Somehow his misfortune had completely changed.

The pope smiled at Benedict and motioned that Benedict could leave. Benedict stood up and kissed the ring of the pope and started to walk away.

"Excuse me, Benedict," said the pope casually. "But could you please bring me the writing tool from the chamber? I wish to take a look at it."

Benedict froze, his back to the pope. He suddenly felt very nauseous. Slowly he turned and looked down. He did not have the nerve to look the pope in the face.

"It is gone," was all he could say.

"Where?" answered the pope with some irritation in his voice for the first time.

"I believe it has been taken by a priest named Francis."

"For what purpose? And how do you know this?"

"When the destruction of Bishop Speso first happened, I came across Francis in one of the hallways. I was frightened and told him. I was afraid that I would be accused of killing the bishop. I have confided in Francis in the past. He is an honorable man, and I knew he would believe me."

"And where is Francis now?" asked the pope, the irritation in his voice turning into controlled anger.

Benedict hesitated.

"I said where?" shouted the pope.

Benedict thought he might be sick. His skin was pale, and he clutched his hands to keep them from shaking.

"I believe he has taken the writing tool to the heretics."

The pope stood quickly and walked up to Benedict. He leaned forward, and his face almost touched Benedict's right cheek.

"Then you will go find him and bring the writing tool back to me," growled the pope through clenched teeth, who then abruptly turned and briskly exited through the door, leaving Benedict alone in the room.

For the next two days, Benedict readied himself for the trip. He was allowed a travelling aide named Antony to accompany him. He was a simple farm hand who had made trips north before and had a good reputation for discretion and direction. Benedict was given a letter to the church in Bohemia should he be questioned. It was a personal word from His Excellency encouraging them to be strong in the faith and to resist all heresies. Along with this cover letter, Benedict was also given a letter direct from the pope stating to any church that they should provide shelter for Benedict and his aide. He was told by one of the pope's assistants that he was not to return until he had completed the pope's mission.

It was an ominous directive, and a great depression filled Benedict as he trudged away from Rome toward Prague realizing that the probability of ever returning was unlikely. All the things that he was facing were beyond his capacity. He simply was not the type to be on such a mission. Could he even find Francis? How could he convince a man like Francis to either give him the writing tool or to return with him? What would he do if he could not find Francis or secure the instrument? Was he to be a priest in Bohemia? Would others pursue after him if he wasn't successful? He silently cursed Bishop Speso for getting him into this complicated mess. It wasn't fair. Had Antony not been with him while they were travelling, Benedict might have considered killing himself. With Antony around, Benedict was not even allowed the luxury of feeling sorry for himself by having a good cry.

With the pope's letter to the church's regarding the traveler's welfare, Benedict enjoyed for the first time in his life a sense of importance. The letter opened a whole new world of feeling privileged. Upon reading the pope's letter, any bishop or local priest immediately flung open their doors and whatever Benedict or Antony requested was at their disposal. Benedict had thought that the trip would be arduous and tedious, but with the treatment and attention they received, Benedict never wanted the trip to end. If the letter was not dated and had not stated that they were journeying specifically to Bohemia on the pope's behalf, Benedict thought he could spend years just travelling from city to city enjoying the lavish hospitality and attention.

A subtle change began to take place in Benedict. He had always been a bit of a weak, sniveling placater. Now, as he walked onward toward Bohemia and Rome became farther and farther behind, he could not only feel his muscles strengthening but a sense of self purpose developing. He had always served at the will of others because he had never known his own will. The thought of being his own man with his own purpose had never been entertained, but now as he joyfully trekked along the hills and valleys, he began to consider what he really wanted.

He was surprised to discover that he did not want to return to Rome. All that awaited for him in Rome was servitude, whether it was to another bishop or the pope himself. The image of the pope's face with its sense of superiority and disdain was something that Benedict never wanted to suffer again. He had been a dog who licked the scraps off the floor and was kicked when he let down his master. He was sick of being the dog. He did not know what he could master, but he knew it would never happen in Rome. But what to do about his errand, he wondered. As Benedict walked, a desire and a vague plan began to form, and it centered on the writing tool. The instrument represented power, and even with his new outlook, it was what Benedict lacked to make anything happen. Somehow the writing tool was the answer. He would just have to figure out how.

Benedict had grown so accustomed to the warm receptions and honor he received from the many cities that he was shocked when he entered Prague and was immediately accosted by peasants. They demanded to know why he was in Prague and where he stood in regard to the doctrines of Jan Hus and the actions of Sigismund. Benedict was completely caught off guard, stuttering and stammering that he was visiting from Rome with papers. Using the word Rome was all that was needed to seize both Benedict and Antony and throw them into prison. Benedict could see that preparations for a battle were taking place and that he could not have come at a worse time. He and Antony were separated into different chambers.

As an experienced traveler, Antony seemed to take the imprisonment in stride, feeling at home with the peasants of Prague as they seemed to know that he was just a hired guide and that Benedict was their main concern.

Benedict sat dejectedly on the damp floor. His confidence and high plans evaporated in the foul stench of the prison walls. The piece of paper that had been his passport to importance was now his death sentence. Gone were the praise and abundance of victuals. Instead he was left with his own miserable thoughts and stale bread.

Those thoughts centered mostly on his fate. He was no longer under the comfort of Rome's blanket of protection. Benedict had never actually given much consideration to the Bohemian heretics. They were a distant irritant to Rome's upper echelon and had little to do with Benedict other than to entertain him through idle gossip and speculation. Even when Bishop Speso set out to eliminate them with Benedict as a witness, Benedict's only interest was in how he could increase favor with the bishop.

Now he was in the hands of a group of people who clearly despised all that he represented. While in Rome, Benedict had grown accustomed to being unremarkable, but being hated and the symbol for all that was wrong with the world was new to him. And they definitely hated him. Benedict could feel it and hear it in the whispers from the guards and even the other prisoners. To them, he was worse than disgraced. He was a disgrace, based solely upon his relation to Rome. It seemed so unfair to Benedict, particularly since he had no convictions one way or the other regarding the heretics. It was just days earlier that he had dined sumptuously on roasted pheasant with a local bishop and now he was picking the maggots out of a piece of bread. Yet, as he sat in the darkened corner of his prison, that was not the worst of Benedict's present concerns.

Benedict felt certain that he would be executed, or at the very least, tortured. Until then, he had no idea how far the heretics had departed from Rome and what they were willing to do. After travelling through cities friendly to Rome, it had come as a shock to see just how real the pope was an enemy to the heretics. As a young boy growing up at the turn of the fifteenth century, torture and execution were not uncommon sights to Benedict. He had seen public confessions garnered through the use of branding irons. Benedict could be demanded to recant his loyalty to the pope or make some type of confession, true or untrue, regarding his reason for being in Prague. The branding iron had also become a way of marking someone for their crime so that all could see and be warned.

There was an infinite amount of ways to produce pain to get what one wanted. Benedict had also seen the boot used to gain a confession. He was never quite sure just how it worked. A metal casing went over the prisoner's foot and screws were tightened. He had seen a man in the town center, accused of robbery, and tortured repeatedly with a boot in order to give up his accomplices. Benedict never forgot the screams and distorted grimaces of pain on the man's face. Eventually he would pass out from the pain, only to be revived and tortured some more. There was no reason for Benedict to believe that he would escape something similar if his captors thought he had anything to offer or wanted to make an example of him. It was unlikely he would be lucky enough to get just the stockade.

Whatever torture they decided to use on Benedict would work without any resistance. Benedict had no convictions other than self-preservation. He would say and do whatever they wanted if it kept even the slightest threat at bay. But that was not what kept Benedict awake at night as he shivered on the cold stone floor of the prison. It was the thought of a grisly drawn-out execution that plagued him. No recantation or confession could stop the vengeance of a righteous multitude, and there were any number of ways a man could be put to death, none of which were guaranteed to be short and painless. The most so-called compassionate way would be death by guillotine or simply having one's head cut off. Another might be burning at the stake. Those, however, were usually reserved for royalty, those of renown, or woman. He would not be given such a merciful end. There was little comfort in knowing that even a beheading could be protracted if the blade was dull or the executioner was not a good aim.

Forgers, especially those of coins, were sometimes boiled alive. Benedict had never seen anyone executed in this manner, but he had heard horrid stories, often told by those who reveled in telling them, of how long and gruesome the death was, especially if the water or oil had not been completely brought to boiling. While it was unlikely anyone would doubt the authenticity of his letter from Rome, the idea of the punishment was nevertheless disturbing.

Perhaps the best he could hope for was immurement. He would be placed in a coffin-sized prison and left to die from starvation. It could be done discreetly so that Rome would be none the wiser. It would be out of public view, and only the guards would know of his death. Or his immurement could be done publicly like a trophy being displayed in the streets. He would be hoisted up in a cage for all to see as he rotted away. He would beg for food only to have rocks thrown at him, and in the end, the birds would pluck away at his flesh. It would be very public and the message would be clear to Rome. This was a form of punishment that Rome had given out at times to those who expressed heresies. The Bohemian heretics might consider this a fitting dose of Rome's own medicine. Benedict wondered if the pope would do anything about one of his priests being executed by the heretics. In the end, it would be only if it was in Pope Martin V's best interest and not because the pope felt any loyalty to Benedict. Benedict knew that whether secretly or in public, he would not die nobly. If immured, he would suffer and die dishonorably, knowing he had seldom expressed anything in his life other than self-interest.

All these tortures and more plagued Benedict's mind as he wallowed in his possible outcomes. But the worst was the one he had seen as a child and one which had left him with nightmares the rest of his life. A local man, convicted of being a traitor, was drawn by horse throughout the woods and into town, where a noose awaited him. Benedict's father had insisted that Benedict witness the event so that he would see how serious it was to be a traitor. By the time the man had reached town, he seemed nearly dead to Benedict. A rope was fitted around his neck and he was hung briefly. His executioners, who seemed to know how to hang a man so that he would not die, removed him from the rope and laid him out on the public square. It was then that they began to cut the man and remove various parts of him. Benedict tried to turn his head, but his father said that he must see what happens to the Judases of life. At some point, the man mercifully died or passed out from their deed, never to awake. The men then cut off the dead man's legs, arms, and head. His head was left on a post in the center of town to be eaten by the vultures until all that remained was his cracked skull. The rest of his body was dispersed about to other towns as a reminder of what happened to traitors. It didn't help Benedict to know that this form of execution might actually have been the quickest and least painful. The man had seemed barely conscious after having his head banged about from the drawing of the horse. It was the ghoulish memory of a lustful crowd of blood thirsty men and women reveling in the dismemberment of a body that haunted Benedict.

After three days of little food and anxiety-filled fears, Benedict lay listless on the floor. It was then that he heard the voice of Francis in the hallway.

4

Reversals and Departures

B enedict jumped up excitedly and rushed to the door, attempting to push his face as far as he could through the bars. Francis was at the other end of the hallway. It sounded like he was visiting each prisoner, encouraging and consoling them while offering them a small piece of bread. He could hear the joy in Francis voice as he conversed with each prisoner. Benedict couldn't wait.

"Francis," he yelled. "Francis, it's me Benedict!"

Francis heard the familiar voice of Benedict and hurried to his cell.

"Benedict? Is that really you? What are you doing here?"

"Francis, thank God you have found me. Can you please get me out of here?"

Francis looked at Benedict with a puzzled expression.

"Benedict, I will try but why are you here and not in Rome?"

Benedict wondered how much he should tell Francis. He now saw a ray of hope, and he did not want to ruin it by frightening Francis.

"I was sent by His Excellency. He said that he is concerned about you. He knows about Bishop Speso and that you have the instrument. He says that all will be forgiven if you return. He's concerned that the writing tool will come into the wrong hands."

Francis stepped back from the cell and looked carefully at Benedict.

"And you believe that if I return all will be forgiven?" he asked.

Benedict could sense Francis mistrust. He decided to change tactics. He looked down at the ground and then slowly lifted his head.

"No, Francis. I don't. He wants the instrument for his own purpose just as the bishop did. I could see it in his face when he sent me here to bring it back. He has no interest in you." Benedict lowered his head again and paused before meeting Francis's eyes and speaking.

"He has no interest in either of us. He is simply using me as a pawn. I cannot do as he demanded."

Francis eyes widened. "You are not returning? What will you do?"

"I don't know," answered Benedict truthfully. "What are you doing here? Why is it that you are not suffering the same fate as me?"

Francis told him of his experience using the writing tool and his commission to bring the tool to Jan Žižka. He did not want to tell Benedict about the purpose to which Žižka had used the tool because it was apparent that Sigismund would attack any day now and Francis felt some reservations about Benedict's behavior. He had seen the duplicity that some exercised in Rome and was not certain that Benedict was exercising some of that now.

"You used the writing tool?" asked Benedict who was genuinely shocked.

"Yes," answered Francis matter-of-factly.

"To what end?"

Francis said simply, "To know its will and to obey."

This piece of information was tucked away in Benedict's mind. The instrument could be used, but the condition was that one had to be submitted to the will of the tool. Perhaps there were other conditions or circumstances that would cause the tool to bend to the will of another.

"And, Francis, what was the will of the tool? Clearly it was not what Bishop Speso hoped it would be."

Francis pondered how much to let Benedict know. Was he being too suspicious, he wondered. Francis decided not to tell Benedict about the approaching events regarding the Hussites, so he only told him about two of the writings the tool had given him.

"Its will was for me to give the tool to Jan Žižka and…" Here Francis paused. He looked down the hallway to make sure no one else could hear him before continuing.

"And that I was to die."

"What?" said Benedict incredulously. "When?

"I don't know," answered Francis. "Soon."

The two men stared at each other, both at a loss for words. Francis heard a prisoner nearby groaning and looked toward his cell.

"I need to go, Brother Benedict." Francis sighed. "I will talk to Jan Žižka on your behalf. They are just being careful. I'm sure if I vouch for you that he will allow your release. I will see you as soon as I am able. Goodbye, my brother."

Benedict watched Francis as he tended to another prisoner. He seemed quite content ministering to those less fortunate. It made Benedict wonder why he himself had become a priest in the first place. He did not particularly care for the poor. They seemed so needy. He realized that serving the bishop in Rome had actually been quite an easy occupation. While Rome could be very political and kept one on their toes, for those who enjoyed power without effort, it offered the potential for great reward. Bishop Speso had known that to be true. He just made a fatal mistake in using the tool. Benedict saw that he was no different than the bishop, but he was determined that he would not make the same error. If he was to control the tool, he had to learn as much as he could about it.

Francis was right when he said to Benedict that he would die soon. The next day, Sigismund's army attacked and Francis was killed while attending to the needs of the wounded. After the battle, there was great joy in Prague. The Hussites celebrated after Sigismund's overwhelming numbers had fled. News filtered down to Benedict not only about the victory but also of Francis's death, and he knew that whatever he hoped to achieve was lost with his death. It would only be a matter of time before he too would be murdered with any other sympathizers of Rome. The next day after the celebrating, as he was dejectedly sitting in his cell, a man came to his door. Benedict stood, assuming it was either time for him to get some bread or that he was being called out for execution. The jailor unlocked the door, and Benedict's shoulders slumped. He felt his knees weaken as he started for the door.

"Jan Žižka would like you to be brought to him, priest," said the jailer with a sneer.

"Do you know why?" asked Benedict.

"No, I do not," answered the jailor. Then he smiled. "But it is not a good day to be a priest from Rome."

Benedict was led to Žižka's tent where he was ushered in by a soldier outside the tent door. Žižka was leaning over a table looking at some parchment. A long sword resting in its sheath hung loosely at his waist. Benedict's first impression of Žižka was that he looked like a wild man who most certainly was about to use the sword on Benedict. Then Benedict noticed the writing tool next to the scroll. He had an absurd impulse to grab the tool and make a run for it, especially since the prospect of being beheaded seemed imminent and certain, but the guard was standing at the door and Benedict would not stand a chance of escape.

Just then, Žižka looked up and to Benedict's surprise he smiled.

"You must be the friend of Francis," said Žižka kindly.

Benedict silently breathed a sigh of relief while nodding his head.

"We won a great battle yesterday, but I lost a friend," said Žižka sadly. "It is strange. It has only been a fortnight since we met and yet I feel as if he has been my friend for years. But he was your friend for years, and I am sorry for your loss as well."

"Francis died doing what he loved, serving the needs of others," replied Benedict. "Thank you, Jan Žižka, for freeing me from the prison. I am in your debt."

"I am only glad that Francis was able to reach me before he died. Otherwise, your fate would have been entirely different, especially after the papers we found on you. Had Francis not spoken on your behalf, you most likely would have been banished or executed."

Žižka looked Benedict over, trying to figure out what manner of person he was. He did not seem to be of the same nature as

Francis, but because of Francis, Žižka wanted to do what he could for Benedict.

"Francis told me that you would not be returning to Rome. In spite of your letter from the pope, he said that you also have become an enemy of Rome. If you are interested, I would like you to stay on and serve with us. Any time a priest sides with us, it is an encouragement to the people."

Before Benedict could speak, a small girl of six ran into the tent and jumped up into Žižka's arms. He laughed heartily as she buried her face into his beard, smothering him with kisses. Žižka looked at Benedict with laughter in his eyes.

"My granddaughter Andela," said Žižka proudly as he held her in his arms. While Andela was in Žižka's arms, she noticed the writing tool on the table and reached out for it while clasping and unclasping her hand.

"So, little one, you want to play with that, do you?" said Žižka to his granddaughter while giving Benedict a wink. Andela vigorously nodded her head. Žižka set her on her feet and picked up the writing tool and placed it in a leather bag to his side.

"I'm afraid not now, Andela. Why don't you go play with your brother while I talk with this kind man." Andela quickly forgot about the instrument once it was out of sight and ran outside the tent.

Žižka did not know how much, if anything, Benedict knew about the writing tool nor did Benedict know how much Francis had told Žižka, so both kept quiet about the instrument.

"So, Benedict, if you are willing to serve with us, that would be greatly appreciated. I also have a favor to ask of you if you are intending on staying with us."

"As I mentioned, I am indebted to you for releasing me. How may I be of service to you?" replied Benedict.

"I have a grandson, Jakub," answered Žižka, "who is almost twelve years old. We have given him what we can in regard to education, but I have been interested in finding someone who could help him further. I assume as a priest from Rome that you have a learned background in the major studies."

Benedict saw his opening to obtaining the tool.

"I do, Jan Žižka, and I would be honored to help. Once I am able to find some lodging, I would be most eager to begin."

Žižka smiled and walked toward Benedict. He put one arm out and rested it on Benedict's shoulder.

"You must stay with us, Benedict. You can teach my grandson without the burden of travel and in your free time serve as priest to our people. We would be honored, and I cannot think of a better way to honor the memory of Francis."

Benedict left Žižka's tent marveling how quickly his fortune had changed. Less than one hour earlier, he was certain that he would be killed and the instrument would be lost to him forever, but now he could feel that it was almost in his hands.

That same day, orders were given to help Benedict move to Žižka's residence, and the following day, Benedict began privately tutoring young Jakub. Andela and Jakub's parents had both died, and Žižka had been responsible for their upbringing. Jakub had a strong foundation in reading and writing, and Benedict, though he had never taught a child, did not find it difficult to build on the boy's foundation. In the late afternoons into the early evening, Benedict would minister to the peasants of Prague. He did this solely for appearances. Most came to know him as the friend of Francis, who had become even more revered and loved after his death. Because of his connection with Francis, Benedict could sense that they were expecting the same service from him. It was difficult work, and Benedict despised it. If it were not for the fact that most of Benedict's time was spent with Jakub, Benedict knew that he could not put up the charade for long.

One day, Benedict was informed that Jakub would be late for his mathematics study. He had been with his grandfather working on archery, and Benedict was told to wait at the house for his return. As Benedict was walking around the perimeter of the house, he came across Andela. She was sitting on a stone bench looking at something. The bench sat on a hill and had a beautiful view of the landscape. Benedict came up from behind and looked over her shoulder. Andela had the writing tool in her hand.

Benedict sat down beside her and smiled. Andela, now used to seeing Benedict around the house, smiled back and continued to draw on a piece of torn parchment, resting on the bench. Benedict was amazed that she was able to use the tool. He could see from her drawing that she was attempting the landscape. There were crude hills and valleys and some trees. Andela looked up at Benedict with a very serious expression.

"Please don't tell Grandfather about me taking his quill. I like it because I don't have to use the inkwell."

Benedict winked like a coconspirator.

"I won't."

"It is such a wonderful quill," said Andela.

"It is?" replied Benedict innocently. "What do you mean?"

"Watch," said Andela. She started to draw clouds in the sky. As she did so, clouds began to form in the sky. Benedict looked up in wonder as puffy white clouds suddenly appeared. He looked down at Andela who seemed pleased yet not surprised that there were actual clouds in the sky. It occurred to Benedict that the writing instrument could be used for one's own will assuming that the will of the user was innocent, such as a child's intentions. Benedict wanted another test. He winked again at Andela and smiled.

"I hope it doesn't rain today," he said.

Andela laughed and started drawing spots under the clouds. Immediately, rain began to pour down, and the two had to get up and run toward the house. Benedict told Andela that she should put the writing tool away before her grandfather returned and that she should probably not show him the picture. Just then, one of Žižka's housekeepers appeared in the hallway.

"Excuse me, Friar Benedict, but Jakub has returned from his archery lesson and is waiting for you in the study."

Andela, her hair matted down from the rain, smiled at Benedict and skipped off to her room.

"Thank you," answered Benedict. "I will be there shortly."

Benedict turned around and watched the rain come down. A plan for the instrument began to take shape in his mind.

For the next few weeks, Benedict went about his business of tutoring young Jakub and ministering to the needs of the community. He did not want to bring about any suspicion regarding the instrument for fear that Žižka would hide it or put it far out of his reach. It did not seem that Andela had said anything to her grandfather about using it, and Benedict waited for another serendipitous opportunity to begin the first stage in his plan. He now had a new piece of important information regarding the writing tool. In the hands of a child, the tool seemed to ignore the undecided will of the child in regard to the consequences of its use. A child would not understand what Francis had done when he gave himself to the will of the pen nor would a child understand someone like Bishop Speso who used the instrument for his own personal gain at the expense of another. The tool honored innocence. Andela would only retain that innocence so long. Benedict had to find an opportunity to use Andela before it was too late, even though he only had a vague idea of what he wanted to do with that opportunity. He was still mulling over how the instrument could best benefit him when he was informed that Žižka had to travel north to Kutná Hora. Benedict was told that Jakub would be accompanying his grandfather, so Benedict suddenly and unexpectedly found himself with some free time and liberty. He immediately sought out Andela.

"Andela, I remember your artwork of the hills and trees." Benedict was careful not to mention the clouds and rain.

"It was quite extraordinary. Since your brother is away and I have some time, would you like an art lesson?"

"Oh yes," cried Andela. "Can we go outside on the bench again?"

"That is a magnificent idea, Andela. I will get some parchment to write on, but what should we write with?"

Andela's eyes lit up. "I can get Grandfather's quill!"

"Oh, that would be fun," said Benedict. "Do you know where it is?"

Andela frowned and put her finger to her chin. "I think so."

"Well, Andela, I will bring some quills with an inkwell in case you cannot find it," said Benedict casually.

"Ugh," said Andela. "The inkwell is so messy. I will find Grandfather's quill."

They met on the stone bench, and Andela brought out the writing tool. Benedict smoothed out the paper.

"Andela, do you know what is the most important key for an artist?" asked Benedict seriously.

Andela's eyes widened. "No, I don't."

"You must believe that what you are painting or drawing is real. The greatest artists painted as if what they were painting was not just a picture but something living and breathing. That is the first rule of drawing that I want to teach you. Now before we begin, I would like to see how well you have mastered your letters. A good artist must also be an able master of their letters."

Andela listened intently to Benedict's words.

"I can write my letters, but I have not learned to read them yet," Andela confessed.

"No need to be anxious, Andela. We are only concerned about the smoothness of the stroke of your quill. Now I will say some letters to you, and you write them down."

Andela poised the writing tool on the parchment and waited intently. Benedict spoke each letter carefully, and when Andela was done, they both looked down at what she had written.

"Friar Benedict possesses immortality."

Benedict picked up the paper and with excitement and some nervousness quietly read the words to himself.

"How are my letters?" asked Andela, eager to move on to drawing.

"They are glorious, Andela," beamed Benedict, unable to take his eyes off the parchment.

"Can I draw a picture now?" asked Andela.

Benedict took the paper and rolled it into his hand.

"Andela, it is time for your meal," called a voice from the house. It was one of Žižka's maids.

Andela groaned but picked up the writing tool and headed toward the house. She did not notice that Benedict had kept the paper.

Benedict thought that he felt different, but he wasn't quite sure what immortality felt like, if it felt like anything at all. He was hoping to have another opportunity to get the writing tool from Andela but he sensed that the head housekeeper did not trust him. She had a suspiciously nasty habit of showing up whenever Benedict came near Andela and finding a reason to take her away. The thought occurred to Benedict that if he were immortal, then he should be able to snoop around and find the pen on his own without any concern for capture or even death. The problem however with any consideration about immortality was that his confidence could only be resolved through testing, and testing involved death. Benedict was not quite ready to kill himself just to prove he couldn't die.

Two days after the use of the instrument, Jan Žižka returned with his grandson Jakub from Kutná Hora. Benedict returned to his studies with Jakub while he continued with ministering to the needs of the community in the early evenings.

If I am truly immortal, thought Benedict, *the first thing that I'll do is stop the pretense of caring for these people.*

Other than that, Benedict had not given much thought to what he would do with unlimited time on his hands. This was one reason that Benedict wanted the writing tool for himself. He wanted to explore the instrument's possibilities and how to exploit them without turning into a pile of dust like Bishop Speso. In order to do so, it appeared that he would need an endless supply of young human guinea pigs to test the tool.

Three days after returning from Kutná Hora, Benedict was walking from his chamber toward the room used for Jakub's lessons when Jan Žižka appeared in the hallway. Benedict had not had the opportunity to see Žižka since his return. Although Žižka had always been cordial toward him, Benedict sensed that Žižka had reservations about Benedict and had it not been for Francis, he would not be tutoring his grandson. In all likelihood, he probably would be dead. In a way, Žižka was like Pope Martin V. He did not tolerate those whom he considered fools. It was for that reason that Benedict tried to always be as pleasant as possible when around Žižka. It annoyed

Benedict that all he had done by leaving Rome was to trade the pope for Jan Žižka. Benedict smiled warmly as Žižka approached.

"Greetings, Jan Žižka. I hope all is well in Kutná Hora. I am sure it was quite an adventure for young Jakub."

Žižka did not smile back. He stopped and glared at Benedict. Immediately, Benedict realized Žižka knew about Andela, yet as to how much, Benedict wasn't sure. He decided to play it as innocently as he could.

"Is something wrong, General Žižka?" asked Benedict.

Žižka did not feel like playing games with Benedict.

"What do you know about the writing tool Francis gave me?" he growled.

Benedict tried to look as if he were caught off guard by the question.

"The writing tool?"

"Do not play games with me, Friar Benedict. You knew enough about it to get my granddaughter involved. Tell me what you know!"

"Oh, that, Jan Žižka. It is nothing. Francis told me about some of the superstitions regarding the instrument. I personally never believed them. As far as Andela is concerned, I came upon her one day while she was using the writing tool. On another day, she wanted a drawing lesson, and I believe she had the same tool with her. We worked on her letters before she was called inside. I assume the instrument we are referring to was what was in your tent the day we first met?"

Žižka continued to silently glare at Benedict, unsure of how much Benedict was saying was true and how much he was holding back. His granddaughter had mentioned that it had rained right after she drew the clouds with Friar Benedict and that on another day, he had worked with her on her letters. Žižka wasn't certain what Benedict's interest with the quill was or even if the two had used the tool for anything other than harmless amusement. Žižka had always been a good judge of character, but he was beginning to realize that perhaps his affection and admiration for Francis had clouded his suspicions about Benedict.

"What brought you to Rome in the first place, Benedict? And don't tell me what was in that letter you had from the pope. That was just a cover. It is too coincidental that you and Francis arrived so closely together."

Benedict sighed heavily, as if he had just been caught in a large deception. Žižka may be able to judge someone's character, but Benedict had learned from Bishop Speso the art of misdirection. Better to sacrifice one deception to protect another. The bishop had often quoted Matthew 5:25 to Benedict: "Agree with thine adversary quickly, whiles thou art in the way with him; lest at any time the adversary deliver thee to the judge, and the judge deliver thee to the officer, and thou be cast into prison."

"It is true," he admitted. "The letter was a cover. I was sent by Rome to find Francis and question him regarding his disappearance and try to convince him to return. They were concerned that he was sympathizing with the Hussites. Francis was my friend, and I was concerned for his safety. I knew that if he returned to Rome, he would not stand a chance."

"And the tool?"

Benedict did his best to meet Žižka's cold stare, but for a moment, his eyes darted away and then back to Žižka's face.

"All I know about the tool," said Benedict with as much diplomacy as he could muster, "was that Francis had given it to you, though I'm not sure why. When I saw him in prison, he told me that he had met you and given the writing tool to you. I assumed at the time that it was a gesture of good faith to show that he indeed was sympathetic to your cause."

Žižka stood silent. Benedict could see the doubt in Žižka's face.

"Look, I risked everything coming here for my friend Francis. By not returning, I have burned my own bridges with Rome. They must now certainly consider me a Hussite."

Žižka was unimpressed. He knew Benedict was not the type to risk his position, even for someone as noble and befriending as Francis. Benedict may have burned his bridges with Rome, but it was not willingly. In all likelihood, he had been sent, and in all likelihood, he knew of the instrument's power and sought it for himself. On top of all that, Benedict probably had tried to use Žižka's granddaughter, and for that, Benedict would never be trusted. Francis was everything a priest should be, and Benedict was everything Žižka had come to loathe. Yet for Francis's sake, he would not kill the man. He leaned menacingly toward Benedict as a general would while confronting a possible deserter.

"Maybe you risked everything for Francis and maybe you risked everything for the instrument. I do not know for certain. I do know that Francis risked everything for me. I have known honorable men and I have known traitors. Often only time can tell which is which. For now, you should know that the writing tool has been removed to a place that you will not discover."

Žižka turned to go and stopped.

"I think that you should leave, Friar Benedict. You are officially discharged as Jakub's instructor."

5

———————•◦•———————

Enter Immortality

As Žižka's footsteps faded away, Benedict stood alone and unemployed. Ever since he was a child, he had been coddled and cared for with the only demand on his life being that of studying to become a priest. His father had been wealthy enough to get Benedict an education and connections to minister in Rome. From there, Benedict served briefly as an educator until Bishop Speso saw in him the potential to be his personal confidant, or in simpler terms, his errand boy. Much had been given to Benedict and little had been required. He had never completely been on his own or had to prove himself adept at anything other than someone's attendant. Now, as he turned to leave Jan Žižka's house, he was not only without employment and homeless but with no experience at making his way in the world. In a very short time, he had gone from having a secure position in Rome to becoming an enemy of Rome. He had also just lost his only possible support in Prague. He was alone with little money and no friends, yet possibly immortal. As he exited the house, a fierce rainstorm began, and Benedict tried to find shelter.

For days, he hopelessly wandered the streets of Prague seeking some type of employment. However, word had quickly spread that the hero of the Hussites had released Benedict from his service. Žižka never told anyone why, but rumor was enough to keep everyone at arms distance from Benedict. There was a selfless servitude to Francis that the people of Prague had instantly recognized and

46

loved. And though they would never have criticized Benedict for Žižka's sake, they also recognized that Benedict was perfunctory and insincere. He had become a pariah, rejected by a community loyal to Žižka. Benedict now found himself not only constantly hungry but depressed by how quickly events had changed. It soon became apparent to Benedict that he would have to leave Prague. He decided to head south, back toward Italy. Perhaps he could find someone along the way who remembered him when he had first left Rome. There might be an opportunity for a local priest who was neither known as an enemy of Žižka or a fugitive of Rome. He decided to head to Vienna where he had been warmly received.

The walk was arduous. Benedict did not have his guide, and while he was able to occasionally convince someone to put him up for a night and give him a meal, most of the time he was alone, hungry, and cold. He tried to save the few coins he had, preserving them if possible until he reached Vienna. Benedict was wary of the reception he would receive there because he wasn't certain what Rome knew of him and how they would respond. Hopefully he had been forgotten by the pope. However, he wanted to be prepared to leave quickly if needed.

One evening, just before sundown, Benedict was looking for a convenient place off the road to bed down for the night. He had just turned a corner in the road when he stumbled over a body. Benedict fell flat on his face with a grunt. He stood up and brushed himself off, thinking that he had either stumbled over a log or large tree root. As he was brushing the dirt off his robe, he turned and saw a man face down on the ground who appeared unconscious. Benedict tentatively leaned down and gently shook the man.

"Are you injured?" he asked.

The man did not move. Benedict wondered if he was dead. He repeated his question and then decided to roll him over. As he turned the man onto his side, a knife hidden from Benedict's view suddenly plunged into Benedict's chest. Benedict could see the devious smile on the man's face as he watched Benedict clutch at his chest. Benedict fell to his knees with his hands around the knife and his mouth opened in a silent scream of pain. He looked down at his chest, his robe quickly filling with blood. The man leapt to his feet and knocked Benedict to the ground. Benedict stared open eyed at the man with a confused look. It still had not dawned on him why he was being attacked. He rolled onto his side, sporadic bursts of breath coming out of his mouth, producing a slight hissing sound. He could feel his blood spreading across his chest, soaking his shirt. Out of the corner of his eye, he saw the man lean over him and with one hand rip his coin purse free from the rope around Benedict's waist and with the other hand pull his knife out of Benedict's chest. Benedict's eyes opened wide as he gasped.

"Thanks kindly," said the man. He had long scraggly hair and a hooked nose with a scar that ran down the side. When he opened his mouth, he revealed a surplus of emptiness and what few teeth he possessed were crooked and discolored. The man ran off down the road.

Benedict lay on his side watching the receding legs of the man. A puddle of bright red blood started to form on the ground in front of Benedict. He could feel an intense burning in his chest and thought that he was about to pass out. It had all happened so suddenly that Benedict was just beginning to understand that he was dying. That was his blood surrounding him. His eyes started to flicker and then close. He sighed heavily. Then he felt something within himself change.

Benedict opened his eyes. The pain had disappeared, and he was no longer gasping for breath. He sat up and then pulled his blood-drenched robe open and looked at his injury. His torso was covered in blood, but as he slid his hand over the wound, wiping away the blood, he discovered a soft pink scar. The dizziness and faintness was gone, and Benedict stood slowly to his feet. By the time he was standing, he felt just as well as before the attack. It was like a bad cold or flu that feels as if it will never end; then suddenly, the fever lifts or the nauseous feeling leaves and it is hard to even remember those miserable aches and pains. If it was not for his clothes soaked in his own blood, Benedict might doubt he had ever been stabbed. He decided to go after the thief.

It did not take long for Benedict to catch up to his attacker. The sun had set, and a full moon lit the road. They came across a long straight stretch in the road. The man had slowed to a walk, feeling secure that he was far enough away from any danger of discovery. Benedict quietly quickened his pace and eventually came to within ten yards of his assailant. A confidence and calmness settled on Benedict. For the first time in his life, he felt as if he were in control.

"I want my money back."

The murdering thief stopped immediately and swung his head around, surprised that someone else was on the road. He did not know Benedict's voice, and it was the last one he expected to hear. Unable to comprehend what he was seeing, the man staggered in disbelief. Fragments of protests came out, stifled by the incredulity of what was before him. Even in the moonlight, Benedict could see the blood drain from the man's face. Benedict stepped closer to the thief.

"I want my money back," he repeated.

The man started to raise his hand in protest, not in protest of Benedict's demand but in protest of what he was seeing. Before he could get any further, he fell to his knees clutching his chest. The crushing pressure on his chest caused the man to gasp as he looked one last time at Benedict in disbelief before collapsing face first onto the earth. Benedict rushed toward the man and turned him over for the second time that night. This time there would be no trickery, no knife play, and no sinister grin. The dead man's face was frozen in fear and bafflement. Benedict took his purse of coins and the remainder of the dead man's possessions which included the knife still fresh with Benedict's blood, some additional money in another purse the man was carrying, and a satchel of some hard bread. The man was dressed far above his station in life as a thief, probably due to the fact that he also stole the clothes of the men he robbed.

Underneath his bloodless tunic, which Benedict exchanged for his garment, was a silk undergarment, clearly at some time in the past a possession of nobility. To Benedict's surprise, under the silk garment, the man had a smaller satchel filled with various jewels. By now it was late in the night, but with the full moon, Benedict was able to see well enough to exchange clothes with the man and gather his possessions. When he was done, he pulled the dead man away from the road into some shrubs behind the trees. He smiled at the man, wondering if in eternity the thief was getting his questions answered as to what had just happened. He gave the man a smile, similar to the one he had received earlier.

"Thanks kindly."

He walked back to the road and looked up at the full moon. Any questions about the writing tool's power of immortality had been settled. Up until then, Benedict was just grateful that by using the writing tool, he had not suffered the same fate as Bishop Speso. His plan so far had been simply to wander, hoping to find a place to teach and not be found out by Rome. Now his outlook was completely changed. He was immortal. Rome could not touch him. He need not fear any man. Whatever he had read about God now seemed to be overshadowed by this simple fact. He could not die. He was no longer a mere mortal. He was like God.

Benedict threw his hands up, and looking to the heavens, he cried out, "*Death, where is thy sting, grave where is thy victory!*"

Rain started to fall and Benedict laughed out loud. There was no need to run or hide. The pope or Žižka and his followers in Prague held no fear over him. Benedict turned back toward Prague. He had unlimited time. He would find the writing tool and discover a way to add to his newly acquired power over death. The tool could hide. He could wait. Sooner or later, it would surface and he would master its power. He was a different man now. He may not be a better man but he was immortal.

As Benedict headed toward Prague, he began to think over what the possibilities were, or perhaps more importantly, what the limitations were—living as an immortal. He had survived a knife attack which clearly would have killed anyone within a matter of seconds. He wondered how it all worked internally within his body. Had the interior damage healed the same way, his skin had sealed up the tear? Occasionally, he would check the scar on his chest and it appeared to be thinning out. Would even the scar eventually disappear? This led to other questions. What if he lost a limb? Would it grow back? What if he was decapitated? Would he wander like some monstrous freak without a head? What if he suffered the same fate as Jan Hus? Was it possible to be destroyed and remain immortal? He entertained the idea of all the horrible ways of dying. He certainly wasn't eager to experiment, but he was curious.

There was one unnerving thought that began to push all other considerations aside. The moment he was stabbed, he had felt the searing pain of the knife as it plunged into his chest. He may be immortal, but he was not impervious to pain, which meant if someone wanted, they could torture him indefinitely. It never occurred to Benedict that even immortality could have its drawbacks. If he were to find the instrument again, he would have to find an answer to the problem of pain.

But how to find the instrument? It had stayed hidden in Rome for at least hundreds of years. Žižka said that he had hidden it and that Benedict would never find it. Well, Žižka would not live forever, and Benedict did not have to worry about time. He did, however, have to be cautious. The thought of being strapped down and tortured forever gnawed at this newfound fear. He could not simply storm into Žižka's place and start snooping around. Benedict realized that finding the instrument would have to be done patiently and without drawing unwanted attention to himself.

A plan began to form in his mind. He was no longer the priest from Rome. He had some money and jewels from the man who had tried to kill him. Time was now an unlimited resource; however, he needed to have freedom of movement and proper connections. He had learned that from his father and his time in Rome. That would require money. He could not be a bear in the public square. He would have to be the fox in the woods, waiting for its chance to get what it needed. He realized that he had some power, though not as much as he first imagined. Were he able to get back to that time with Andela, knowing what he knew now, he would have been more specific about what to write.

While he was walking, Benedict decided to head to the town of Plzeň instead of Prague. Plzeň lay to the southwest of Prague and was known as being unsympathetic to the Hussites. It remained close enough to Žižka so that Benedict could keep his ear to the ground regarding the instrument. He also needed a fresh start where he was unknown and would be untroubled with his association with Žižka.

It would be difficult to accumulate wealth and influence. Few were able to rise above their position given at birth. Royalty was always royalty, and the poor were always poor. Those in between had limited movement. However, they all lacked the one thing that Benedict now possessed, which were an endless amount of days.

It occurred to Benedict that if he were unable to die, then consequently starvation or death by any other means of extended discomfort would not affect him. As long as he could hold off the feelings of pain and the irritations of cold or disease, he would be unencumbered by the things which so easily drained one's income. He could wait out the deaths of Žižka and those who remembered him and return back to Prague and search for the instrument. For the moment though, immortality did not preclude the need for Benedict to rest. He found a small patch of grass under a tree about twenty yards away from the road and fell asleep.

Once in Plzeň, Benedict started to build his future. He pawned the jewels and began to lend what little money he possessed. A little amount with low interests brought small results, but eventually those small amounts developed into larger investments. Benedict discovered to his own surprise that he was a shrewd businessman. Though he had no leanings one way or the other regarding the controversy between the pope and the Hussites, out of convenience he sided with those in Plzeň. He no longer served as a priest and made up a false past in which he had inherited some money at his father's early passing. He grew a beard and dressed as well as his finances enabled him to dress. People who saw the clothes often did not see the man. In the late fall of 1424, word reached Benedict that Žižka was dead. The following spring, Benedict left for Prague.

In Prague, Benedict discovered that he had been quickly forgotten. It helped that his look was different. Without the dress of a priest, it never occurred to those whom he met that Benedict was anything different than what he claimed. Another advantage for Benedict was that the Hussites had become a divided movement. Žižka might have been able to keep them united, but without him, the disagreements became too fierce. Like many movements, the divisions with the Hussites centered upon doctrine and behavior. Of the five main groups that had splintered, Benedict decided it was in his best interest to side with the Praguers, a group despised by the others because the Praguers were considered worldly. Simply put, the Praguers decided that they were no longer going to be giving their money away for the cause. It was time to get on with living. For Benedict, the Praguers were the best ones to lend money to because they were the ones who could pay back. Within a few months, he had integrated himself into their group and was actively doing business. He decided to seek out Žižka's granddaughter.

Benedict discreetly made inquiries into Andela's whereabouts and found that she was now a young lady still living at Žižka's home. His goal was to find a way to speak with Andela and if possible discover the location of the writing tool. But there was a problem. He was no longer the priest with whom Andela enjoyed drawing but a businessman who had no reason for visiting the granddaughter of a now fondly remembered leader of an opposing sect of the Hussite movement. He wasn't sure how to go about visiting her without causing suspicion. He wrestled with many different possible solutions, none of which sounded convincing. In the end, luck stepped in and Benedict found himself face-to-face with Andela.

Benedict and a business associate named Konrad had been walking the streets of Prague when they came across a large stone building. Benedict remembered it from his earlier days as a priest being used to house the wounded during the battles. He had often visited it in his evening ministrations. It appeared that it was still being used, but since there was no longer an influx of wounded being brought in, he wondered as to its purpose.

"For what reason is this structure being used?" asked Benedict. Benedict was always looking for a way to make some money, and even though he had no definite plan regarding the building, it was his habit to be prepared by asking questions.

"It used to be a monastery prior to Jan Hus," answered Konrad. "During the wars, it was used as a hospital of sorts, housing the wounded, the faithful, and the poor. I believe it has returned somewhat to its monastery state though not in as formal a way as before. Would you like to go in?"

"Yes, I am curious," answered Benedict. He was anxious to visit the place where he had once spent many an uncomfortable evening participating in a charade of service. He felt a sense of superiority returning to the place now as a respected merchant instead of a lowly priest. Unbeknown to Benedict, Konrad was also eager to enter, desiring to speak to a man named Matej. Konrad was interested in Matej's sister. The two entered the building. Matej was just coming around the corner as they entered.

"Konrad," greeted Matej.

Konrad smiled warmly at the man.

"Matej, how are you my friend?"

Konrad introduced Benedict to Matej, who looked at Benedict curiously. Benedict remembered Matej and was now beginning to wish he had never entered the building. Fortunately, without realizing he had come to Benedict's rescue, Konrad pulled Matej aside.

"Matej, I would like to speak with you about a private matter if you have a moment. Benedict wished to tour the premises. Do you mind?" Konrad asked the question so that it was directed to both to Matej and Benedict. Both nodded their assent, and the two men walked off while Benedict was left to explore.

The entrance of the monastery from the street opened into the main room which had in the past been used primarily for mass. The foyer preceded the main room and was supported by thick stone pillars with arches leading the visitor toward the pews. In the main room to the sides of the pews were larger archways, the ones to the left surrounded wide doorways and the ones on the right led to open rooms. Benedict decided to walk along the right side and view the rooms. During his brief service as a priest, he had spent a good portion of his time visiting the now empty rooms helping the wounded and ministering to those who were dying. It all reminded him of the type of person he was back then and the sharp contrast to who he was now. He had gone through the motions then, but his heart was not in it. He knew the words to say, but he never considered whether he actually believed them. If it had not been for Francis, he probably would have assumed that all priests felt the way he did and he in all likelihood would have continued to serve in such a manner. In a strange way, Francis's selfless example of servitude had freed him from a life of pretentious labor.

The rooms which had in the past been filled with people were now mostly empty. Some rooms had beds with occupants, and there were a few women wandering about who appeared to be helping in some capacity. As Benedict came to the last room nearest the front pew, a young lady walked out, and the two nearly bumped into each other. Benedict stopped abruptly. The woman had one hand on the wall, and her eyes were averted upward and to the side. It was quickly apparent to Benedict that she was blind. The woman seemed to sense Benedict's approaching presence and calmly stopped.

"Please excuse me," said Benedict. He lowered his head and continued to walk past her.

The woman tilted her head slightly at the sound of Benedict's voice and then excitedly turned her head toward Benedict.

"Friar Benedict?" said the young lady. "I recognize your voice. Is that really you?"

It was Andela.

Benedict had his back to the woman when she had spoken his name, and his first reaction was one of panic. He had no desire to be associated with the man of his past, and until then, he had easily gone undetected. He turned and smiled, prepared to deny that he was Friar Benedict. It was then he recognized the face of Andela.

"Andela? Is it you? I'm sorry that I did not recognize you, but it has been some years. How wonderful it is to see you. But..."

Andela finished his sentence which had hung awkwardly in the air.

"But I cannot see you. It is true, Friar Benedict. I've been blind for a number of years. As a matter of fact, I am blind because of the inkless quill."

Benedict, stunned, sat down in a nearby pew. There was no sense in pretending about whether he was aware of the instrument's power. Andela spoke with an unquestionable certainty, and it was just a matter of how much she knew.

"How?" he asked.

"After you left, my grandfather told me that you had been called back to Rome. It was only later that I learned that you had been dismissed. I missed our few times together. The inkless quill was an innocent amusement to me, and I still remember the time that we made the clouds and the rain. I also remember another time that you asked me to write some letters with the quill on a piece of parchment."

Benedict could feel the blind gaze of Andela as she paused after the last statement.

"You used me to get something from the quill," she stated flatly. It wasn't a question, and there was no anger or bitterness in her voice. Benedict did not respond.

"I assume that you got what you asked for from the quill. I do not hold any bitterness toward you, Friar Benedict."

"Please, it is just Benedict now, and the people here in Prague do not know my past."

"Very well," continued Andela. "I will honor that. The reason I will honor your privacy is that I have learned from personal experience that the quill can only bring you misery, so whatever reward or whatever advantage the quill has brought you, in time, it will bring you something much worse. That something will far outweigh any benefits. The quill is not fooled because it is not from man."

"Thank you," was all Benedict could say.

Andela found her way to the pew and sat next to Benedict before continuing.

"After you left, we had some cousins visiting from Kutná Hora. One of them was my age. Her name was Pavla, and she was very beautiful and remarkable, even as a young girl. I was jealous of all the attention she was receiving from my grandfather even down to my closest friends."

Andela closed her eyes, reliving the experience and the feelings that had painfully yet beautifully brought her to the grace of God. Benedict could see a look of torment on her face and wondered if she were praying. He sat respectively waiting, and after a moment, some peace came back to Andela's countenance and she opened her eyes.

"I decided to use the quill against her," she said.

Andela leaned back in the pew and lifted her head back slightly as if she were looking at the ceiling while she remembered.

"Grandfather had hidden the quill before he left on one of his trips. I'm sure he eventually found a more secure place outside of the castle, but for a while, it was still within my reach. I scoured the castle and finally found it behind some books in his library. I decided to draw Pavla's face with horrid-looking features. If the quill could make the clouds and the rain appear, then it could also make her ugly and unpopular. It was of course an evil thing to do. It was then I lost my innocence."

"What happened to the girl?" asked Benedict, thinking of Bishop Speso.

Andela shrugged her shoulders.

"Nothing, but the next morning, when I awoke, I was blind. I knew at once that it was the result of my misuse of the quill. I told my grandfather what had happened. I expected him to be angry with me, but he was very kind and gentle. He said it was his fault for leaving it out. I don't think he ever forgave himself. Grandfather removed the quill, and I have never looked for it nor desired it since. I suspect however that you still desire it, which could be the only reason to come back to Prague and risk being detected."

Benedict stood and faced Andela. He took one of her hands in his.

"Andela, it is more my fault than anyone's, and I too will never be able to forgive myself. It is true that I came here to seek the writing tool. I have my reasons, but I see now that it is time for me to leave Prague and never come back. For what it's worth, you are more beautiful than you know."

Andela smiled.

"God has broken me. I live now to honor him and serve others. So it is a great thing that God has done. Whenever you cannot forgive yourself, please remember that."

Benedict turned and left the monastery, not bothering to find Konrad. The search for the writing tool would have to wait. There was no way of finding where Žižka had hidden the instrument. For the time being, it was lost to Benedict. Within days, he had gathered as much as he could take and left Prague. He decided to head east. He would travel to a major city, learn the language, and conduct business. He decided to spend no more than ten to fifteen years in one location. He never aged, and it was easier to leave than to entertain the curiosity about why he always looked so young. He spent fifteen years in Cologne, making a small fortune in the maritime trade before leaving to Brussels. From Brussels, Benedict went to London where he met and fell in love with Margaret, the last child of Catherine of Valois, once upon a time the young wife of Henry V.

6

Spain: The Spring of 1491

Matheo lived in a small village outside of Palos de la Frontera. At seven years old, he was the head of his family, which was a burden that weighed much too heavy on the young boy's shoulders. His father had died less than two years earlier while fighting at Baza in the Iberian Peninsula for Isabella I and Ferdinand II against the Emirate of Granada. The Moors were Muslim inhabitants who had lived at the south of Spain for over seven hundred years. In 1482, Isabella I and Ferdinand II began a war in which battles would continue off and on until 1491 when all that remained was a minority of Moorish inhabitants. As long as Matheo was alive, it seemed two things had been constant: Spain had been at war and Matheo was finding it harder and harder to remember his father.

Matheo, like most of the inhabitants who lived in Spain, was Catholic. His national view, much like his worldview, was virtually nonexistent. All he knew regarding the war was that according to his father, the followers of Islam must leave their country or convert and that was why his father fought. Matheo's mother was dying. No one knew what was wrong with her, and there were no doctors available. Even if there were, they probably would not have been able to diagnose her terminal lung cancer correctly, and even if they could, there was nothing anyone could have done to save her. Each day Matheo watched his mother lying on her straw bed, wasting away, sometimes with coughing fits that were so painful Matheo had to leave to find a place and cry.

In such a small village, there were few children the same age as Matheo. The older boys were also fighting so that Matheo's days were long and lonely. There was a younger boy named Alvaro, but he was lame in his legs and could not get out unless someone carried him. Sometimes he would go and visit Alvaro, and they would talk about the war and the Islams, as they called them. Alvaro had a vivid imagination when it came to war and the mysterious infidels.

"First, I would take my sword and cut off their hands. That way they couldn't hurt me."

"That's pretty good," replied Matheo. "But one clean strike to the heart will kill them right away. I wonder what they do if they capture one of our men."

Alvaro made a gruesome face and clasped his hands.

"They eat them. I heard that the Islams even eat their own children," he said.

Matheo thought for a moment.

"If they ate their children, then who would do the fighting when the parents got old?"

Alvaro sat still while he considered Matheo's question before his eyes widened with a new idea.

"Just the girls."

"I don't know, Alvaro. Then who is going to cook and clean and have more children to grow up and fight? Maybe they just eat the ones who can't walk."

Alvaro's face went from the excitement of thinking that all the girls would be eaten to the possibility that he might be the one they would cook.

Matheo laughed.

"I'm just joking, Alvaro. I don't think they eat anyone. Mama said they are people like us. They just don't believe in our God."

Alvaro looked relieved yet a little disappointed that the girls were not being eaten.

"I still think they have horns and a long tail," he said.

If it was not for Alvaro, Matheo's days would be unbearable. There were three men who still lived in the village. Two of them were too old to join the soldiers and the other, named Pablo, had been blind since birth. The three men, Matheo, and any abled women worked together to manage the farming. Fighting lasted from spring to winter, and then the fathers, if they were not too far from their homes, would return for a short amount of time. Those were times of mixed blessings as the village celebrated those who had returned and mourned those who had fallen in battle.

One hot day in June, Matheo was walking on a cart path leading away from Palos de la Frontera toward the Friary of La Rábida, which was less than a couple of miles from his village. He had wanted to go visit the Franciscan Friary since he had first heard of it a year earlier. Matheo had never seen an actual building outside of the simple huts in his village. His goal was to one day walk to the friary and back. Each time he walked the path, he would challenge himself to try and go a little farther than the last attempt. He had come to a point in the path that had a sharp turn surrounded by trees that blocked his view from the other side. This point in the road had become a major test for Matheo's courage as each time he approached it, he would inevitably stand, frozen in a state of indecision—continue or go back. The last four tries, after an agonizing period of wavering, Matheo would turn back and run home. This particular day in June had been a difficult one for Matheo's mother whose coughing had never been harder or lasted longer. Matheo felt that whatever danger existed around that bend could not be worse than running back home to endure the suffering of his mother.

Matheo walked slowly around the sharp bend, arching his neck to see as far ahead as he could in case some frightening monster or villain should cause him to turn and run. As he turned the bend, much to his surprise and delight, there were no monsters. The trees on the inside of the bend continued on, but on the right side of the path was a stone wall about a foot taller than Matheo. He ran his small hands along the weathered stones as he walked. After a few feet, he saw a larger flat stone on the ground at the base of the wall. He stood on the stone and was barely able to peer over the wall to an empty field. Matheo sat down on the stone, inwardly congratulating himself on his bravery. After a few minutes, he stood and tried to move the stone, but it was too heavy. As he stood, he noticed a solid, dark object no thicker than his thumb tucked between some of the stones. With his thin, little fingers, he was able to poke between the rocks and pull. At first, he assumed it was just a stick, but once he pulled it out, he wasn't quite sure what it was.

Matheo rotated it around his hand, looking at it from all angles. He had never seen a quill and like everyone in his village, knew nothing about reading and writing. Because of its uniqueness, Matheo reasoned that it must have come from the friary. As he twirled it around in his hand, the sun caused the strange stick to change colors. Matheo sat down and leaning against the stone wall crossed his legs. He waved the stick around like a wand, watching in wonder as it changed colors. After a few minutes, Matheo stared at the wand sadly. How could one thing be so beautiful and one's life be so sad, he wondered.

He thought of his mother and started to draw absentmindedly in the dirt with the stick. He often would pass the time using sticks to draw in the dirt and had no idea what potential he possessed as an artist. A day would come that Matheo would have the opportunity to explore his love for art, but for now, his only canvas was the ground. As Matheo sat cross legged, he drew a picture of his simple one room house in the shadow of a few clouds, with the sun in the upper corner shooting rays of light into the sky. He then drew his mother standing in front of the house with one arm in the air as if she were waving to Matheo. He drew her long hair and gave her a big smile. Around her feet and in front of the house, he drew her favorite flower, which she always called her yellow cups. Matheo stretched his legs out straddling the sides of his drawing. He leaned back and looked at his mother smiling back at him. The smile did not look natural to Matheo, and he realized sadly it was because he could not remember the last time she was happy and well. He dropped the stick and buried his face in his hands and wept.

After a few minutes, he dried his eyes and went to pick up the stick. The dirt drawing had changed! Matheo wiped his eyes again and lowered his head closer to the ground. Staring back at him was a drawing of two faces, one above the other. The one on top had a face with hands covering the eyes and the one below had a face with hands covering the mouth. Matheo picked up the stick and stared at it in wonder. It was as if the stick had spoken to him like a person. He immediately understood what the two drawings meant. The top picture was telling him to hide the stick out of others' view and the bottom picture was telling him not to tell anyone about the stick. Matheo felt that God was speaking to him through the stick and that it was very important to follow the stick's instruction. Matheo stood in a daze and placed the stick back between the rocks and walked home.

It took Matheo about thirty minutes to get back to his home. His house was on a little rise from the path, and he had to walk between some trees before he could see it. As he came out the other side of the trees, he stopped and stared dumbfounded. Standing in front of the house was his mother. She was broadly smiling and waving at him. It had been overcast when Matheo had drawn the picture and now the sun was shining brightly and there were beautiful clouds above her. At her feet and encircling the small house in about a twenty-foot radius was a full field of yellow cups. Matheo thought for a moment that he must have died and was now in heaven with his mother. He ran to her, and they embraced, tears flowing down both their faces.

"Mama, are we in heaven?" asked Matheo.

"No, Matheo," she answered. "But God has done a miracle and brought heaven to us."

Matheo was tempted to tell his mother about the strange stick and his drawing, but the image of the message from the stick helped him hold his tongue. Anyway, it did not matter how the stick worked, Matheo reasoned. His mother was well. That night he fell asleep with his mother brushing his hair with her fingers while she sang a Spanish hymn. The next day, Matheo's mother, whose name was Dorothea, visited everyone in the village and told them of the miracle God had done in healing her body and the flowers in front of her house. She said that she had been coughing so hard she was sure that day would be her last when suddenly her room filled with a bright light. She thought that she was about to enter heaven and only wished that she could see her Matheo one last time to say goodbye and comfort him. Then she felt a hand reach out and touch her head, and she heard the voice of Jesus say to her, "Arise." Dorothea stood and walked toward the doorway thinking that she was leaving this world. When she stepped through the door, the sun was in her eyes and she was standing in a sea of flowers. All the pain in her body had disappeared. She stood in the field of flowers still thinking that she had entered heaven when she saw Matheo walking toward her. She waved goodbye to him, thinking that she was seeing him for the last time. Then he ran to her and hugged her, and for the first time, she realized that she was still alive.

Word spread to other villages and some came to see Dorothea and the flowers. For the first time in years, there was rejoicing in the small village. One of the friars from La Rábida came to question Dorothea about the miracle. He wanted to know what she thought had brought about such a wonderful miracle, and all Dorothea could say was that God must not have wanted her to leave her Matheo alone, so he healed her. The friar took one of the flowers back with him to the monastery to keep in honor of God's gracious miracle.

After a few days of excitement, when life settled back to the routine of trying to get through each day, Matheo decided that he would see if the stick was still hidden. Until then, it had been hard to find time alone, with everyone so excited about his mother's healing. Matheo went to the spot around the bend, this time without hesitation, and found the stick still hidden between the rocks. He pulled it out and sat down. Matheo did not know much about prayer. He was untrained and confused about such matters. His prayer was simple.

"Thank you, God, for Mama. I want to help Alvaro."

Matheo drew a picture of Alvaro running, his curly black hair bouncing and his arms swinging in joy. When he was done, he put the stick back into the rock's crevice and looked back down to the ground. The picture of the two faces was back. Matheo knew it was an important reminder and the sight of it made his heart leap because he also knew that he would see Alvaro running. He did not know, however, how soon he would see him off his bed and on his feet. As Matheo started walking back up the path toward home, he heard Alvaro yelling and screaming Matheo's name. Coming down the path, Alvaro was racing as fast as he could toward Matheo, his arms flailing wildly and his long curly hair bouncing up and down.

"Matheo, look at me. Look at me! I can run! I can run like the wind!"

Over the next few weeks, Matheo went to the place where the stick was and used it to heal everyone in the village who had any ailments, including Pablo who got his sight back. Crowds of people began coming to the village, hoping to be healed of diseases, though not knowing the source of the power. Within a few days, all of Dorothea's flowers had been picked by the curious and hopeful, thinking that maybe the healing came from the yellow cups. Dorothea, in her generosity, was glad to let anyone take one, also hoping that it would bring the same relief that she had received.

After that, it was difficult for Matheo to get away from the crowds and use the stick. Also, the war was ending and fathers were returning to their towns and villages. The return of fathers helped draw many of the curiosity seekers back to their own homes. It also brought a painful reminder to Matheo that his father was not one of them. As life in Matheo's village started to settle back to normal, Matheo had a thought. He did not know why he had not considered it earlier, probably because it was the type of thought no one could consider. Maybe the stick had the power to raise the dead. If it healed his mother, Alvaro, and everyone in the village who was sick, maybe it would bring his father back to him. He had heard that Jesus had raised people from the dead. Was it possible for the stick to bring his father back? That night Matheo barely slept as he thought of his father returning. He intended on going out early in the morning as soon as it was daybreak, but his mother told him that some older woman needed his help in the fields. It was agony for Matheo as he worked. The minutes dragged on as he labored. Finally, toward late afternoon, the woman thanked him and said that he was no longer needed.

Matheo raced to the path that led to the stone wall. As he neared the bend in the road, he heard some horses. He quietly walked to the side of the road, trying to peer around the corner to see what was happening. When he had come around the bend far enough, he could see a carriage about ten yards past the spot where the stick had been hidden. There was a man sitting at the reins looking forward. There was another man standing in front of the rocks, about five feet to the left of where the stick was placed. Matheo got down low and hid behind one of the trees.

"It's in here. I know it," said the man looking through the stones. The man had long wild hair that was held back with a bandana. On his right eye was an eye patch. The eye patch forced him to cock his head as he looked between the rocks.

"Make haste," said the man at the reins. "I don't want my legs back in irons."

Matheo's heart was pounding. He thought of running quickly up to the rock and pulling the stick out. He could try to bring it back to the village. Once they knew what it was, they would not let the men have it. Then he remembered the warning he had received from the stick. What was he to do?

"Ah ha…there it is. I knew I'd find it."

The man held up the stick and viewed it approvingly with his good eye.

"Get in, fool. You can admire it on the way," growled the driver. The man climbed onto the carriage and the two horses sped off.

Matheo stood in the center of the road stunned. It was gone and so was his father. He started to run after the carriage.

"No, no. Come back, come back," he cried.

As the carriage pulled away, the noise from the horses and carriage drowned out Matheo's cries. He continued to run, tears streaming down his face as he called out to the men. Matheo forgot about how far he was from home. He kept running until he found himself collapsing on the steps of the Friary of La Rábida. The carriage was nowhere in sight. Matheo laid his head on the steps and cried. Why had he not thought of his father sooner? Why did the stick, which had brought such happiness back into his life, deny him the joy of seeing his father again? As Matheo wept, he eventually sensed someone nearby. He lifted his head to see the silhouette of a large man in a robe towering over him.

"Matheo, why are you so far from home?" asked the Franciscan friar.

Matheo did not have an answer. The stick was gone and so was his hope of seeing his father in this life. The friar, noticing that something very deeply was troubling the boy and also knowing that he would not get an answer, wisely decided to give Matheo some bread and something to drink before sending him back home. Matheo made the long trek back to his house, crying off and on along the way. By the time he got home, it was early evening and starting to get dark. Matheo's mother was standing in front of the house. She had been walking about the village looking for him and now was waiting, hoping that he would show up soon. As the sun was setting, she saw his shadow come through the trees with Matheo just behind. His head was down and his shoulders were slumped over. The last days had been filled with such joy, and it was strange to her to see her Matheo filled with sadness.

"Matheo, my son, what is it? Why are you so sad? Did you hurt yourself?"

Matheo stopped in front of his mother and looked up at her face.

"I will never see Papa again," was all he could say before he burst into tears. He grabbed his mother and clung to her, his head buried in her arms sobbing. Tears rolled down Dorothea's face. She did not know why Matheo at this time would suddenly be so affected by his father's absence, but she had been thinking the last few days of the burden her brave young son had to endure with his father's death and her illness. She had also been thinking about the miraculous events of the last few days, and though she could not imagine how, she suspected that somehow it was connected with her son.

"Matheo, we will see Papa again someday. He is waiting for us in glory. I know it because I have seen His glory. He is so proud of you. If he is not here with us, it is because Jesus wants him with Him right now."

Matheo had been looking intently at his mother while she spoke. Without knowing about the stick, she had managed to speak to Matheo as if the stick was answering. A great peace flooded his soul and he knew it was not his fault that he missed using the stick to bring back his father.

7

The Mortality of Love

In the summer of 1455, Benedict was on the London Bridge, where he conducted a majority of his business amid the many buildings that lined the thoroughfare. Designed in 1176 AD by Peter de Colechurch, priest, architect, and builder, it was finally finished in 1409 and dedicated by King John to Thomas Beckett, the martyred archbishop of Canterbury. Henry II, seeking to find cause to disassociate England from Rome, found an enemy in the priest. Beckett for years bravely withstood the king, at one point excommunicating two bishops and one archbishop for overstepping their bounds by prematurely crowning Henry II's son as junior king of England while Henry II still lived. In his frustration with Beckett, the king commented that something should be done with this onerous man. Those who heard the king decided that what he meant was what they wanted to hear. Four knights went to Canterbury and murdered Beckett, who by all accounts acquitted himself with the honor that the knights lacked. The action backfired on those who wished Beckett dead. He became venerated as a martyr and canonized in Rome by Pope Alexander III. When the bridge was complete, King John, one of the sons of Henry II, and now king, perhaps out of guilt and contrition, but more likely an act of appeasement, wisely dedicated the bridge to the saint. A chapel which had been built by Peter de Colechurch also became dedicated in honor of Beckett and would be used as a starting point for those honoring the saint on their pilgrimage to Canterbury to pay their respects at Beckett's shrine.

For Benedict, who cared little for the bridge's history, the site became a source of commerce for him with stores and apartments populating the approximately nine-hundred-foot bridge. It was there that he was able to meet with merchants and traders to discuss business. He had enough saved to not only keep an apartment above one of the shops but also a small estate which he acquired just outside of London. Benedict was an oddity of sorts to the merchants of London. It was rare to have someone who clearly had a broader relationship with the world than most who conducted business on the bridge. While in regard to fashion, he fit in with those around him of similar status, once someone spent any time with him they came away with the impression that while the well-travelled merchant had the appearance of a young man, he spoke and acted as though he possessed a maturity beyond his years. Benedict was aware of the fact that he came across much older than he appeared. However, he had no desire to act the age of a younger man since he knew he would eventually move on to another city.

He was cautious with those who made any attempt at friendship. He remained as cordial as he could for business sake yet kept aloof as much as possible. There had been one exception to the rule in London, and that was Marshall. Marshall Mac Giolla Rua was from Ulster in Ireland, and aside from not being trusted or liked by most, he was often not understood with his thick Gaelic accent as he attempted to speak the common English. Benedict found in Marshall a kindred spirit because they were both outsiders of sorts. He also enjoyed hearing Marshall speak. Over the years, Benedict had accumulated a love of languages and was trying to learn Gaelic. Marshall was a savvy businessman who, in spite of the fact that he was unintelligible and disliked by most, did a fair amount of business in trade. He was often willing to ship items that others refused and had found a niche market as the last option for those trying to move goods. He had been driven from Ulster by a prominent businessman seeking justice because he suspected (incorrectly) that Marshall had been having an affair with his wife. Marshall figured that the last place the ill-informed man would search was England, so he fled to London. Like Benedict, Marshall had found a way to adapt and fit in despite his curious manner.

It was an overcast Friday afternoon as Benedict and Marshall stood leaning against a wall opposite some stores on the bridge. They had been discussing the moving of some linen that Benedict had purchased. Benedict was the only one Marshall knew who bothered to use Marshall for shipment of standard items. Marshall appreciated this and usually gave Benedict a very good rate for shipping. Benedict could not figure out why others did not take advantage of Marshall's desire to be accepted.

"You'll never get a better offer," said Marshall. "And you know it!"

"I know, my friend," answered Benedict. "Say, what is the word for linen in Gaelic?"

"It's a tough one, Benedict. I don't know if you'll get it."

Marshall said the Gaelic word for linen, and Benedict repeated it a few times.

"Not bad, Benedict. But you trample over the words like a farmer ploughing a field. Gaelic is light, like a fallen leaf fluttering in an autumn sunset. But it's also wild like no other. Wild as a maiden dancing by the fire with the sparks flying high and her long red hair madly flowing in the full moon. Aye, Benedict, Gaelic is a mad beauty, not a hammer on a nail."

Benedict rolled his eyes. He had heard Marshall a number of times celebrating the beauty of his language. It had become a running joke between them.

"I'll try and remember that, Marshall."

Marshall smiled. "Oh, you'll get the hang of it. You just need to recognize beauty, and when you do, it will change everything. Speaking of beauty, who is that lovely lady over there?"

That was when Benedict first saw Margaret. She was standing across the bridge in front of one of the clothing shops. There was a manner about her that made him almost feel as if he were looking into a mirror. It wasn't that she looked like Benedict. Quite the contrary. Benedict, who was tall and gangly, never thought of himself as handsome, yet this woman was strikingly beautiful. She had braided red hair in two sections that wrapped over the top of her head, accentuating her long thin neck and pearly white skin. Her face seemed sturdy with a sense of determination yet soft and gentle. Her eyes were light sky blue with one eyelid a little lower than the other which gave Benedict the appearance of sadness, as if she lived with the constant knowledge of having lost something sacred and dear. As he watched, the woman's lips pressed together in a slight pout, evincing an impression of gloom, and then she suddenly smiled, and to Benedict, it seemed that the sky had parted after a heavy rain and the sun had burst forth cleansing away the shadows. Her face, which before had looked like a smoldering fire at sunset, now looked like the first day of creation. That was the mystery of her beauty, but not the mystery of what reminded Benedict of himself.

She was dressed simply but comported herself as if she was royalty, and it was here that Benedict saw something of himself in her. She was not who she appeared to be. There was a mystery about her. The common woman Benedict often saw on the bridge might have a natural beauty, yet it was usually a marred and unflattering attractiveness taken on by the arduous labor that was required to survive. This woman, like Benedict, fit in but did not fit in, and this, along with her beauty, captivated his attention.

There was a time long ago when Benedict assumed that as a priest, he would be celibate forever. Everything changed when he had left Jan Žižka's employment. His break with Rome and his dissolution with Žižka freed him from any restrictions with which he had previously been encumbered, but since becoming immortal, Benedict had avoided the idea of romantic involvements simply on the practical grounds that he would eventually be found out. Plus, he had never found anyone who interested him. This arresting woman before him not only took his breath away in a manner he had never experienced, it seemed to draw him into a mysterious kinship he could not understand. Yet, like many a man before him who had fallen in love at first sight, Benedict stood like a mute with cement shoes on, unable to move or speak, mesmerized and powerless as she glided away into a sea of patrons and shopkeepers.

For weeks, Benedict hung around the same shop hoping that he could once again catch a glimpse of the woman. He was not sure what he would say, but for the time being, he would be content to gaze upon her countenance. Suddenly, immortality did not seem as important as knowing more about the woman who had bewitched him. Those who did business with Benedict noticed how distracted he was as they attempted to barter or deal with him. Some, older and wiser, did not know who had consumed the young man's thoughts, but they had been around long enough to know why.

One late afternoon after spending a day mooning around the shops, Benedict stood at the bridge's stone rail looking at the river. The buildings had been set up so that there was ample space between structures. Fires were common, and after some major ones had occurred in the thirteenth and fourteenth centuries, merchants learned to leave spaces between buildings hoping the flames from one building would not leap across to another. As Benedict stood gazing into the sunset, the thought occurred to him that immortality had many more faults than he had ever imagined. For the first time, time was not on his side. A small rock was lying on the stone rail in front of him. He picked it up and dejectedly tossed it into the river below. It was then that he heard people screaming.

Near the end of the bridge, just past the shop where he had first seen the woman, there was a great commotion. He started to walk down the center of the bridge toward the noise and then feeling an unexplainable sense of urgency began to run toward the clamor. As he ran, he observed smoke billowing out of the windows, and when he neared the building, he could see the flames climbing their way up the walls. By the time he came close to the building, most of the crowd was running away from the fire toward the end of the bridge. One woman stood in front of the building imploring those fleeing to stay and help. Benedict stopped and for the moment forgot about the fire. It was her. She turned to him, and Benedict briefly noticed a look of recognition, almost as if she had been watching him earlier just as he had watched her. At the time, he did not even think that she had seen him, but the quick look on her face was unmistakable.

It lasted only a moment before her face changed to anxiety as she pointed up to the second floor of the burning building.

"There is a child on the second floor. I can hear its cry."

Benedict did not have time to admire the loveliness of her voice. He plunged himself into the building through the doorway which had become a wall of fire. He screamed in pain as the heat and the flames licked his skin. He faintly heard the woman call to him to come back, but by then, he was looking for the stairs. They were so nearby that he almost ran past them. He could feel his arms and legs burning and his lungs fill with the smoke. He knew he would probably soon be dead, but he was determined to find and rescue the child. He heard a whimper coming from upstairs, and he raced two steps at a time up the stairs. Flames were everywhere. As he moved across the floor, the boards creaked, and he could sense it would not be long before they collapsed. In the corner of a room sat a small girl cowering in the only spot that the flames had not yet found. He quickly ran over and scooped up the child. The child looked relieved yet horrified at the appearance of Benedict. Benedict did not know it, but most of the skin on his face was burned badly, and to the child, he looked like a smoldering dead man. His only thought was to save the girl. He turned and ran to the nearest window. He could barely see as he leaned out the window.

"Can you catch her?" he yelled.

"Yes," she answered loudly, her voice rising above the flames. Benedict could only hope that he was letting the child go in the right direction as he tossed her out. As the child left his arms, flames ran up his back and around his chest. He opened his mouth in agony. Smoke and fire filled his throat and lungs. Seconds later, the entire building collapsed, and Benedict was buried in a mass of fire and wood.

By the time the blaze had finally run its course, night was fallen and all that remained was a pile of ash and embers. Those that fled had either gone off the bridge to their homes or returned back to the remaining buildings that had not been affected by the fire other than being covered by floating ash and the smell of burnt wood and flesh. By four in the morning, the bridge was completely void of pedestrians and shopkeepers as a naked man covered in black soot slowly emerged from the ashes of the building. Finding cover in the darkness of a crescent moon, Benedict walked back to his small estate where he washed himself before falling into bed and a deep sleep.

Two days later, he was back on the bridge. He visited the area where the buildings had been burned down. The rubble had been cleared away, and men were already beginning to rebuild. No one had seen Benedict when he entered the burning building other than the woman. If he saw her again, he was not sure what he would say to her. Normally this was the type of situation that would drive Benedict to seek another city before being found out, and even though he knew it was foolish, he couldn't bring himself to walk away.

"Well now, how does a man plunge into a burning building, rescue a child while he is being burned alive, and come back two days later, dressed like a prince, looking as if nothing had happened? Now that is a tale I think I have a right to hear."

Benedict did not have to turn around to know it was her.

"You are a man, are you not?" said the woman with some reservation in her voice.

Benedict turned and bowed slightly.

"My name is Benedict, and I am at your service."

"Yes, I suppose you have proven that. Margaret," she replied shortly as a way of introduction.

"How is the child?" asked Benedict.

"You saved her life."

"I am glad to hear it," replied Benedict.

Margaret looked at Benedict, now quite perplexed. She stepped toward him and brought her face close to his. With a pained expression on her face, she struggled to keep her voice and composure under control.

"How are you even here?" she implored.

"I am immortal," Benedict answered simply.

Margaret stared intently at Benedict's eyes to see if he was playing games with her. She could tell that Benedict felt a sense of release from the burden of holding in the knowledge that he had just imparted. It was that sense of release that convinced her without further questioning that he was telling the truth, or at least that he believed he was telling her the truth. She stood back and looked sternly at Benedict.

"I believe in God the Father, His Son Jesus, the Holy Spirit, and the angels, faithful and fallen. But I do not believe in immortality outside of eternity. How is this even possible and what does it mean?"

Benedict smiled at Margaret. Every expression she made was like a brand-new day.

"Do you know, I was once a priest," he confessed.

"And I was once the daughter of the queen of England," said Margaret.

At first, Benedict could not tell if Margaret was joking, but the mystery of how she carried herself suddenly made sense.

"Margaret, daughter of Catherine of Valois, wife of Henry V? You are that Margaret?"

"I am. Not quite on the level of immortality, but still impressive, is it not?" replied Margaret, half out of jest and half with a twinge of bitterness.

Benedict looked at Margaret's eyes and realized that there was a sense of sadness and loss of many things. She had lost a mother, a reputation, and quite possibly a crown. Mostly, Benedict could see that she had lost a mother.

"I'm sorry for your mother's passing," was all he could say.

Margaret walked over to the bridge's railing and leaned on the stones while she looked out over the water.

"Very few people know what I am telling you," she said slowly. "There are some who would wish to ruin even what little I have left and there are some who wish to kill me."

"It seems we both have secrets," answered Benedict. "You are the first person I have told about my immortality. Most certainly some would also wish to harm me."

Margaret smiled ruefully. "But you're immortal. How can anyone hurt you?"

"I cannot tell you how torturous it was to enter that building the other day," grimaced Benedict. "Apparently there is nothing in the rule book about immortality being pain free."

Margaret looked at Benedict's face. He looked much older than he should. She shuttered when she remembered the face she saw, burned and almost unrecognizable when he threw the small child out the window.

"Immortality or not, that was very noble of you to save that child the other day."

"I have to confess," answered Benedict. "I don't know if I would have done it were you not there."

"You saved a child's life to impress me?" chided Margaret. "No wonder you are no longer a priest."

"You are closer to the truth than you know," confessed Benedict as he lowered his head and picked at the stone wall. He thought of Francis and his life of selfless sacrifice, a life which had caused Benedict to challenge his own motivations.

Margaret watched Benedict, almost as if she knew his thoughts.

"I think that you would have done it anyway," she said firmly. "I think that there is more to you than you know." Margaret laughed lightly. "There certainly is more to you than others know."

Benedict nodded to the sunset.

"To our secrets," he proposed.

"To our secrets," Margaret responded.

Later that week, Benedict confided in Marshall that he was in love.

"It is no surprise to me," concluded Marshall.

Benedict's eyebrows rose as he looked at Marshall in surprise.

"Really?" replied Benedict.

Marshall laughed. "The last person to see is often the one closest to the light. Most knew you were in love, but I think I was the only one who knew who the woman was. The moment I saw you look at her that day, I knew you had no chance. So what is the name of the one who has captured the Bohemian's heart?"

"Margaret," answered Benedict.

There was a frown on Marshall's face.

"She isn't the Margaret who is the daughter of Catherine of Valois by chance?"

"She is, but how do you know?"

"The same reason that I think you knew something was special when you first saw her. Though she dresses like a commoner, there is a sense of royalty about her. Her family is forgotten and disgraced, but I remember hearing that Catherine of Valois had a daughter named Margaret shortly before her death."

"We would appreciate it if you kept all of this to yourself, my good friend," confided Benedict.

"Benedict," replied Marshall. "You are the only good friend I have. I have no better friends that I would even be tempted to speak with. Now, when will you two be married?"

"We just met," answered Benedict with shock in his voice.

Marshall laughed.

"Like I said, my good friend, you are too close to the light. Let's see, I am selling some very odd items right now and I should make a handsome profit so that may help me buy you a proper wedding gift."

"Marshall, you are impossible." Hoping to change the topic, Benedict asked Marshall what he was selling that was so odd.

"We are selling sinkable shackles. They are a type of shackle to be used for prisoners on ships. If the ship sinks, these shackles will force the prisoners to drown. They are a combination of shackles for the wrists, waist, and ankles all connected with a heavier chain. The metal on the shackles is double the weight on the common shackle. They are used to prevent the worst prisoner on board to survive should the ship wreck or the prisoner needs to be thrown overboard for some reason. Even floating on driftwood will not keep them from drowning."

"How barbaric," replied Benedict. "But why not just stay with a ball and chain? Those cannon balls are quite heavy."

"Maybe," answered Marshall. "But I don't know if you remember a couple of years ago, a ship of prisoners went against the rocks and the prisoners killed all the crew and stole another vessel."

"I think I did hear something about that," said Benedict.

"How do you think they killed the crew? They managed to use the cannon balls to smash one of the guard's head in. Then they got the key and were free."

"Who are your manufacturers?" asked Benedict.

Marshall shrugged his shoulders. "Why, the shippers. They pooled their money together and hired a smith to specially design the shackles. I am arranging the negotiations with local merchants along the coast. Others have shied away because they think that the practice is questionable at best, but you know me. I am always the last resort."

Six months later, Benedict and Margaret were married in a quiet ceremony. The marriage was discretely performed by a priest, and the only witness was Marshall. They purchased a piece of land farther away from London and lived a quiet life. Marshall managed Benedict's affairs as a mediator so that Benedict could remain at home and that both could avoid questions. While it was not illegal that they had married, they decided that eventually questions about Benedict and Margaret would arise. Shortly before their first year of marriage, Margaret was pregnant. For the first time since he had come across the writing tool, Benedict did not care about anything other than that he was to be a father. Then in the last month of her pregnancy, Margaret took ill with a fever. The baby died during childbirth. For two months, Margaret was in and out of consciousness while Benedict agonized over her condition. Finally, by the third month, she began to recover.

After the child died and Margaret was no longer bedridden, she sank into a deep depression. Benedict mechanically went through the motions of his business and did everything he could to help Margaret, but it became apparent after some months that something beyond the loss of her child bothered Margaret. Benedict would find her going for long walks in the woods and coming back not speaking for days. She had no desire to have another child. Finally, she confided to Benedict that she was going to join the monastery and become a nun.

"You can't be serious, Margaret," pleaded Benedict.

"Benedict, my dear, you are a good man and I will never love another, but I believe that this gift you have is not a gift but a curse. I thought I fell in love with you with my eyes opened, but I see now that I was blind. I have entertained an occurrence that I should have walked away from and the only way I can have peace is to separate myself from the only one I have ever loved. I have made a vow to God that I will not break. Please forgive me for hurting you."

With that, Margaret walked out of Benedict's life forever.

Marshall found Benedict days later back on the bridge, leaning against the stone wall facing the water. While it was a warm sunny day, Marshall did not notice the cloud that hovered over Benedict as he approached him from behind.

"My dear friend, what brings you to the place you used to haunt so frequently?"

Benedict did not respond. He stared sullenly at the bright horizon as if nothing else existed.

"What is the matter, Benedict?"

"She has left," Benedict softly answered.

"What? Where? What do you mean she has left? Did you and Margaret have a falling out?"

Benedict looked into Marshall's eyes. Marshall noticed a great weariness on Benedict's face. In spite of his young age, he seemed like an old man.

"She is going to be a nun, Marshall."

"Why, Benedict? I know that she has been upset since she lost the child, yet you two were so much in love. What has happened?"

"Someday, my friend, I may tell you, but for now, can you do me a couple of favors?"

"Of course, Benedict, just name them. Are you sure that there is no possibility of reconciliation?"

"No, Marshall, she has reconciled, just not to me. You deserve to know more, but for right now, I need you to do something. I am travelling east by ship and would like to take a pair of your shackles. I have an old contact in Antwerp that I would like to show them too. For now, getting away and burying myself in business will distract me from my sorrows. Also, in the meantime, I would like you to manage my property until I return. Would this be too much to ask of you, my friend?"

Marshall put his hand on Benedict's shoulder.

"Of course not, Benedict, but I think that there is more to this than you are telling me."

"There is, Marshall, but for now, that is what I am asking."

A week later, Benedict was on a ship sailing east. He had contacts in Antwerp; however, he had no intention of doing business there. Shortly after leaving London, he retrieved the box of shackles which he had stored on the ship near the stern. With no one around, Benedict slowly and quietly opened the box. He attached the shackles securely before rolling over the back of the ship into the water. His absence would not be noticed for another eight hours, and even if he had been seen, the moment he had dropped overboard, no one would have been able to rescue him.

Benedict sank to the bottom of the North Sea. Even though he was on the shallower end of the North Sea, the pressure on his lungs from the depth of the water killed him before he was halfway to the bottom of the sea. He revived briefly, only to die again almost immediately. Even his instincts for survival were too slow to try and intercede. The pressure was too great and acted too quickly. By the time he reached the floor, he had revived and died three times. As he lay on the bottom of the cold sea floor, he shivered, drowned, relived, shivered, drowned, and lived again. It was an endless loop of death. For the brief moment that Benedict revived, he barely had a moment of observation before death would claim him once more. While Benedict could not change immortality, he had found a way to punish it and himself.

For years, Benedict regenerated, died, and regenerated. While his conscious mind was only active for a few seconds before the pressure of the depths of the water crushed his lungs, he observed what he could around him, which was mostly darkness. At some point, he was aware of fish eating away at his flesh. Because his body was in a continual state of regeneration, the fish never stopped feeding on his flesh. There were times when he would briefly regain consciousness and felt himself engulfed in a frenzied feeding. He would instinctively shake himself before his lungs collapsed again and the fish would quickly scatter before coming back to resume eating.

While Benedict's conscious mind went through a never-ending loop of painful reconnection with living, his subconscious mind never ceased to be active. At first he was in a state of constant confusion. However, as the years wore on, the process reversed so that he was able to live with clarity in the subconscious part of his mind and had learned to endure the interruptive nature of what his body was going through. Living in his subconscious mind enabled Benedict to recall his every memory. He became painfully aware of the inner motivations of all the decisions he had ever made. Until then, he had been ignorant of how self-serving he had lived. All actions and thoughts, good and bad, seemed to have their source in not only preserving his life but promoting it as well. He had always known that he was very different from Francis, but until then, he had no idea just how different. He deserved the judgment of the writing tool. Thrashing around on the bottom of the ocean perpetually dying was a just punishment for a life lived for self.

It was then that he saw Jesus walking on the floor of the ocean.

Benedict did not know how he knew it to be Jesus. He just knew. Jesus was walking toward Benedict, and for some reason, Benedict was no longer being crushed by the weight of the water. The fish had scattered, and Benedict lay on his side as Jesus approached. Benedict was not having trouble breathing under water. He wasn't sure if he was breathing. He felt no different than a man lying on his side in a field of grass on a summer day. Jesus seemed to have no more difficulty walking on the bottom of the sea floor than Benedict had lying on its floor. The water gave Jesus a dreamlike quality as he walked, but it was clear to Benedict that this was no dream. When Jesus was a few feet from Benedict, he lifted one hand and said, "Arise." Benedict stood in obedience, and as he did, the shackles fell off.

"Return the writing tool to me," commanded Jesus.

Jesus made a sweeping gesture with his hand, and Benedict began rushing through the water while slowly rising to the surface. When he reached the surface, the momentum of his speed hurled him into the air. Benedict landed on the shore of England just feet away from the London Bridge. The year was 1491. Benedict had been on the floor of the North Sea for over a quarter of a century.

8

---◀●▶---

A Thousand Deaths and
a Thousand More

enedict sat naked and dazed in the moonlight on the bank of the river Thames. Just as earlier when he exited the ash-covered building, he was fortunate that it was the middle of the night and no one was about. He had no idea how long he had been underwater, so he decided to do what he had done many years before. He would seek out his estate. As he walked, discreetly dodging between trees and bushes and around corners of buildings, Benedict began to get an idea how long it had been as he noticed many more buildings and less trees and bushes. Once or twice he heard the voice of someone cry out, startled at the sight of a naked man running through the town in the dead of night. When he reached his estate, even though it was night, he could tell that the foliage was much taller and thicker than he remembered. He wondered how long it had been since he had last set foot in his own house.

Benedict went to the front door hoping that it might be unlocked. Oddly enough, it was, and Benedict entered the house quietly and tentatively. He wasn't quite sure what to expect as he fumbled about in the dark, though it appeared that his few pieces of furniture had not been rearranged. This did not stop him from stumbling into a desk as he was attempting to find his bedroom. His toe hit one of the legs of the desk, and Benedict instinctively shouted out in pain. As he did so, he heard some movement and saw a figure in the bedroom doorway.

"I have a sword and a knife and I am quite handy with either, so my advice is to turn and flee," said the voice from the doorway.

Benedict smiled at the familiar, though somewhat gravelly voice of his old friend.

"I once knew a kindhearted man from Ulster with as thick a Gaelic accent, only he wasn't so out of breath."

"Jesus, Mary, and Joseph and all the saints before me, that sounds just like my old friend Benedict. The only problem is that it sounds like the Benedict I knew and not the one it should be."

"Marshall, I am unclothed and I cannot remember the last time I slept in a bed. We have a lot to discuss but can it wait until morning? For now, I could do with some garments, a little bread and ale, and then I would like to sleep like the dead."

Marshall hurried as fast as he could in the dark and found everything Benedict needed. Benedict savored every bite of the stale bread and drop of the warm ale before falling into a deep sleep. He slept soundly until noon, and when he awoke, Marshall was sitting in a corner chair opposite the bed. He was thoroughly engrossed in a book he was reading. Next to him was a table that Marshall had stocked with cheese, bread, some fruit, cooked rabbit, and a bottle of French wine. Benedict sat up and leaned leisurely against the wall behind the bed. He looked at his friend across the room, now much older with a bushy gray-white beard and curly white hair that was thinning out. He had put on a few pounds but still had the same boyish Ulster look that Benedict remembered.

"Judging by the look of you, I'd say I had been gone almost forty years," said Benedict.

Marshall looked up from his book and set his spectacles on the table.

"Not that long, my friend. How old do I look? It's only been shy of thirty years."

"If you weren't in front of me now, Marshall, I would swear it had been an eternity. What are you reading?"

Marshall lifted the front cover toward Benedict.

"It's a printed book by a man named William Caxton called *Mirrour of the Worlde*. Look, it has pictures. They're called woodcuts."

Marshall sat the book down on his lap and tossed Benedict an apple. Benedict smiled and rubbed it on his garment, then took a bite, letting the juice run down his chin. He had forgotten how delicious an apple tasted.

"Margaret told me," said Marshall plainly.

"I was wondering why you didn't look surprised when you saw me," answered Benedict. "Is she still alive?" Benedict tried to sound casual, but it was clear he could not help his interest.

Marshall smiled. "She is. And still a nun, so don't you go getting any notions. Besides she's also older now."

Benedict sighed. The shutters were open and a warm breeze was coming into the room. Benedict looked outside to an England he did not know anymore.

"I don't have any notions. I don't have any ideas. I don't have any answers."

Marshall cocked his head slightly and pointed one of his fingers at Benedict.

"Did you use those foolish shackles to try and drown yourself?"

Benedict nodded his head and took another bite of his apple. He stood and walked over to the food and grabbed some cheese, bread, and the bottle of wine. He looked at the meat.

"That's not fish, is it?" he asked.

"Rabbit," answered Marshall.

"Too bad, I have a debt to settle with fish," replied Benedict as he picked up a piece of the rabbit and went back to the bed.

"Are you saying that you were at the bottom of the sea this entire time?" asked Marshall.

"I was, but why are you here in my home? Is business so bad that you decided to take my house?"

"I made you a promise, my friend, to manage your affairs," answered Marshall. "And when Margaret told me who or what you were, I thought a day may come when I would see you again. I spend the nights here sometimes, watching the place and keeping it ready in case you returned."

"Thank you, Marshall. You are only the second friend I have had in my life."

"Who was the other to be so honored?" asked Marshall while he took a bite of some of the cheese.

"A monk named Francis. I introduced him to the writing tool. He was an honorable man who used the instrument for the glory of God while I attempted to use it for my own purpose."

Marshall lifted an eyebrow. "Immortality," mused Marshall. "How does immortality work at the bottom of the ocean?"

Benedict drank some ale and stared at Marshall.

"Painfully," winced Benedict at the memory of his lungs collapsing every time his body regenerated. "But there is one question you haven't asked."

Marshall looked quizzically at Benedict.

"How?" answered Marshall. "How did you get free?"

Benedict stared at the cooked flesh of the rabbit and set it down.

"Did Margaret tell you that I was once a monk like Francis?"

"Aye, she told me everything that you told her."

"Do you know," said Benedict thoughtfully, "that I never really knew what a monk was even when I served as one. I never knew what it meant to be a man of the cloth or a man of God. It was just something one did because someone told them that was what they were going to do."

Benedict had finished the bulk of the apple and took the thin core and put it in his mouth and pulled on the stem. He chewed what was left of the apple and tossed the stem on the floor and then rubbed his hands together wiping off the remaining juice.

"I wasn't sure what would happen to me, Marshall, when I went overboard. I knew I couldn't die, but I just wanted it all to be over. Until Margaret came to me, I never loved anyone, not even myself I suppose. I would have gladly suffered a thousand deaths and a thousand more if it could erase the memory of my misery. Every day Margaret was alive and I couldn't be with her was unbearable, so I decided that the pain of those deaths would best be served far removed. I wanted to be in a place where I could not save myself."

"But you are here, my friend," cut in Marshall. "How did you free yourself?"

"I didn't," answered Benedict slowly. "The God whom I served but never knew, the one whom I cared little about and used for my own benefit freed me and told me to get the writing instrument back to him."

Marshall's eyes narrowed as he stared intently at Benedict.

"What? How?"

"I was lying on the floor of the ocean, dying and then coming back to life again only to feel the overwhelming pressure crush my lungs before dying again. And then I saw him. Jesus came walking, not on the water, but below the water, just as if he were walking on dry land. The shackles broke as easily as snapping a small twig. He commanded me to bring the writing tool back to him and then sent me rushing toward the shore and I was spit up on dry land as if I were Jonah being thrown out of the whale."

Marshall sat back dazed and took a bite of the rabbit.

"I don't think that rabbit's good," commented Benedict.

Marshall kept chewing. After a moment, he looked back at Benedict distracted.

"What?"

Benedict pointed at the rabbit.

"The rabbit. I think it's bad."

"Oh," said Marshall absentmindedly as he spit out the rabbit.

"So you had a vision?" continued Marshall.

"No, Marshall, not a vision. It was Jesus. He was as real as you are to me now. It would have been no different if he had walked up to me on the bridge and spoke to me. It was all strangely casual and yet…"

There was a long pause, and finally, Marshall broke in.

"Yet…?"

Benedict looked thoughtfully at Marshall trying to find the precise words he could use to sum up the feeling he had when Jesus had spoken.

"Kindly authoritative. Like doing business with someone with whom you are late in payment. They remind you cordially, yet firmly enough for you to know they mean business."

Marshall rubbed his chin and instinctively brought the rabbit back to his mouth.

"Rabbit," reminded Benedict.

"Oh," grunted Marshall.

"This is all very strange," said Marshall as he set the rabbit on the table. "What will you do?"

"I guess I'll do what I've been trying to do, which is to find the instrument. Only now I'll probably return it to Rome. Outside of storming the gates of heaven, I'm not sure what else I can do with it. I just don't understand."

"What?" asked Marshall.

"I mean," replied Benedict as he gestured with his arms, "he's the God of the universe, he knows everything, he has all authority, so why doesn't he just go and get it himself?"

Marshall continued to rub his bearded chin.

"Maybe it's a form of penance. Anyway, I know who you should ask."

"Who?"

Marshall took in a deep breath.

"Margaret."

Benedict frowned quizzically at Marshall.

"I thought you said I should leave her alone."

"Yeah, well, I did, but this is different. Look, Benedict, I never had any use for the church. They never did me any favors. I've always been superstitious, but this whole thing is beyond anything I can fathom, especially when it comes to advice. But Margaret might know something about this. You should see her."

To see a beloved friend after they had aged almost thirty years was one thing. Benedict and Marshall felt just as comfortable in their friendship after a long absence as they did when they conversed daily as younger men. However, it was something quite different for Benedict to reunite with the only woman he knew he would ever love. There would be nothing comfortable about the reminder of how they had parted and the heartache that had driven him to the sea.

Marshall rode ahead a day early and prepared Margaret for Benedict's arrival. When Benedict arrived, she was sitting on a stone bench in front of a small fountain surrounded by a garden filled with lavender flowers. He stood beside a pillar, silently watching her as she sat in meditation, her hands loosely holding her rosary. Butterflies, drawn to the lavender, flittered about her, respectfully keeping their distance while they seemed to enjoy her presence as much as the lavender.

In spite of the differences the years had brought them, everything about Margaret that Benedict loved had remained. She would always be the woman Benedict first saw on the bridge. Leaning against the pillar while he watched her brought back the sweetest of memories while also reminding him of how much he had lost. He may have torturously died more times than he wanted to remember while underwater, but to be so close to Margaret now and so far apart was more agonizing than anything the blackness of the sea had produced. As if sensing his presence, Margaret turned toward Benedict and smiled. He pulled himself away from the pillar and walked toward her.

He sat down next to Margaret, and neither spoke as they each felt the joy and sorrow at being reunited. Benedict had asked Marshall to prepare Margaret because he did not feel comfortable explaining what had happened. While he longed to be with Margaret, he was reluctant because it seemed that such a meeting could produce nothing but additional heartache.

"Benedict, why did you do something so foolish?" asked Margaret, her face peeking through her veil. That face, now softer and wiser, was even more beautiful to him than before. Everything about her was glorious, and at the same time, everything about her pierced his heart with a deep ache. Her eyes and gentle smile were like rays of sunshine and small daggers to the heart. The pain of her beauty got the best of him.

"I could ask you the same question," Benedict replied, unable to hide the bitterness. He quickly recovered himself.

"I'm sorry," Benedict continued. "I didn't want that to be the first thing I said to you in almost thirty years. I suppose, however, that the way I answered is the answer. There is a poison in my grief."

"I understand, Benedict. I have thought many years about you and often wondered if I had done the right thing."

Just outside the garden, the cheerful chirping of robins could be heard. Margaret looked down at her hands and the rosary she clasped between her fingers.

"I was in love too, you know."

There was a long awkward pause as the two sat uncomfortably in the garden. Eventually Benedict spoke.

"I'm sorry the way this has started. I suppose it was inevitable that these things should be said. I've made a strange life for myself, and it was unfair of me to inflict it upon anyone. For many years, I tried not to. I've brought sorrow into your life and yet I see in you great peace and contentment. Perhaps that's why my words were cruel. It's not you that I am at war with. I suppose it is with myself. I thought I wanted something with the writing tool, but I did not know that it would cost me everything."

Benedict looked at some of the butterflies near him and envied the simplicity of their lives. He could feel the sympathy and kindness emanating from Margaret. He decided to change the subject.

"Marshall said that you might be able to help me. I'm not sure how but I could not resist the opportunity to see you one last time whether you were any help or not regarding my dilemma."

Margaret put her hand on Benedict's, and Benedict savored the moment, knowing it would be the last time he would feel her touch. She slowly pulled her hand away, and then her eyes lit up with wonder.

"Did you really see the Savior?" she asked.

Benedict nodded his head, but he lacked the same enthusiasm that Margaret felt. He sighed.

"I don't think that he is too happy with me. I am to find the writing tool and return it to him. Nothing has turned out the way I thought I wanted. It has all become a great weariness. When Bishop Speso used the tool for his own purposes, he imploded into a ball of ash. I think I might have preferred that to what my life has become. I have become an errand boy once again."

What little of Margaret's face could be seen quickly became quite animated.

"What are you talking about?" she scolded. "The King of Kings calls you to find something stolen from the heavens and you treat that like someone made you go the market and retrieve some potatoes. You have been given a great undertaking by the Lord of Glory."

"But, Margaret, that's just it. Why is he bothering with me? I have never really served him, never really known him. I am no different than the devil that stole the tool to begin with, if that is its true origin. Jesus knows where it is at this very moment and he has the ability to retrieve it himself. What does he want with a self-centered ex-monk?"

Margaret beheld Benedict and at that moment loved him. She loved him in a way she never had before. She loved him solely in the love of her Savior. She saw in Benedict what he could not see in himself.

"I have heard, Benedict, that some strange things have happened in Spain. There is a rumor that an entire village came back from the dead. These stories are often exaggerated fables, but I suggest you return to Rome and seek counsel. Whatever happens, Benedict, the Lord of Glory who visited you in the sea loves you more than you can imagine. I can see that, although I barely understand it. Go to Rome. Tell them what you know and ask for their help. If you are commissioned to return something to an Almighty God who does not actually need your help, then you have nothing to lose. That is my advice."

As Margaret finished, the garden seemed to have come to a halt. The sound of the birds had ceased, and the butterflies sat still on the lavender. Benedict, knowing there was nothing left to be said, gazed one last time upon the face of the only woman he would ever love and without a word stood and left. He found his way back to Rome, this time not as a priest but as a business man who was not dependent on the kindness of others or a letter of introduction. This was fortunate for Benedict for he soon discovered in the fall of 1491 that the current pope, Pope Innocent VIII, was corrupt and could, with some creativity, be bought.

9

The Order of the Calamus

B enedict was shocked with the decadence that permeated Rome. When he served under Bishop Speso, it was political, and there was a sense of doing what one could to achieve power, but under Pope Innocent VIII, there was no innocence. With a few placed coins, Benedict quickly secured a meeting with the pope. He found himself, almost seventy years later, sitting in the exact same room when he last saw Pope Martin V. The difference now was that Benedict was no longer afraid of the man before him, and this time, it was he who had a plan.

"I understand that you have wished for an audience with me," said the aged pope. "Your gift was most generous."

The pope motioned for Benedict to sit down next to him.

"How may I be of service to you?"

Benedict bowed his head slightly in acknowledgment of the pope's gratitude before speaking.

"I have heard a rumor from Spain that an entire village came back from the dead. I would like to know first if there is any truth to this rumor."

"You have paid a great price to talk of rumors," commented the pope.

"I have no desire to waste my time running up the ladder of intermediaries," replied Benedict leisurely.

The pope looked quizzically at Benedict.

"Have you ever been to Rome?" asked the pope.

"I have," answered Benedict. "Many years ago. I use to be under one of your predecessors."

"Is that so?" said Pope Innocent VIII as he arched his eyebrow. "With whom and in what capacity may I ask?"

"I was counsel to Bishop Speso under Pope Martin V," answered Benedict with a calm but firm look.

Pope Innocent VIII looked strangely at Benedict and then laughed derisively. Benedict sat patiently until the pope realized that Benedict was being serious.

"Come now, young man, you couldn't have possibly bought your way into my presence just to tell me some foolishness. Why are you here? We both know that you are much too young to know either of those two men. What you are saying is blasphemous."

Benedict stared hard at the pope without flinching.

"I am seeking the writing tool of Flavius Valerius Constantinus. Rome once possessed it but was never in possession of it. I have managed to use it and live, which, if you remember your history, is something that Bishop Speso was not able to do."

"You are a mad young fool and I believe it is time for you to leave! Your generous gift has purchased my presence, but we are done now."

Benedict stood slowly and pulled off his outer garment and set it neatly on the chair. He then quickly pulled out a dagger that had been held behind his belt. The pope froze in fear, assured that the dagger was meant for him, but Benedict quickly turned the knife upon himself, plunging it deep into his chest and then pulling it quickly out. The pope jumped up suddenly to call for a guard as Benedict fell to one knee. Benedict raised his hand to stay the pope.

"Please give me a moment," Benedict said in great pain.

The pope stood mystified as Benedict first appeared to be bleeding profusely, looking ready to faint, when suddenly the color began to come back into his face. He slowly stood up and smiled. He pulled back his shirt, and the pope was able to see the wound healing until it was barely visible. Benedict slid the knife back into its sheath beneath his robe and sat back down. The pope collapsed into his chair.

"I may have paid a large sum of money to obtain an audience with Your Excellency, but I just paid an even greater price to get your attention. I hope I have it now."

The pope sat in shock, his hands trembling. Benedict wiped the blade on his shirt and then lifted the shirt over his head. He used the bloodied undergarment to clean his chest before putting on the outer garment which was lying on the chair. Benedict sat down calmly and looked at the pope, whose face was pale.

"Are you well enough to continue, Your Excellency? Would you like some water?" asked Benedict. He was enjoying himself. This visit was a far cry from Benedict's previous encounter with Pope Martin V.

"What are you?" the pope asked.

"Immortal," replied Benedict.

"Impossible," stammered the pope.

"For someone who has a reputation of buying holy relics, I'm surprised to find that you don't believe in their power," replied Benedict.

The pope barely heard what Benedict had said much less the sarcasm in his voice.

"What do you want?" he asked weakly.

"I would like to return to my original question. Do you know of a rumor in Spain about an entire village resurrecting from the dead?"

The pope was beginning to regain his composure and sat up from his slumped over position.

"Yes, I suppose," said the pope. His voice cracked when he spoke and he swallowed. The pope glanced down at the Piscatory Ring on his right hand, the "Ring of the Fisherman," worn by each pope and used as a signet when signing official documents. Staring back was the image of Peter fishing in his boat, a reminder that all who held the office of pope were called first and foremost to be fishers of men. Pope Innocent VIII and Peter probably had little in common; however, the power of the ring and what it represented strengthened the pope and reminded him of his authority.

"We get these rumors constantly. Most we ignore. Common superstitious peasants. Most are handled locally by the nearest monastery. This particular rumor happens to come from the Friary of La

Rábida near Palos de la Frontera which gives it more weight. They do not know how the supposed miracles took place. No one has mentioned a sacred writing tool. I would have eventually sent someone out to investigate. What is your intention?"

"To be the one sent out," answered Benedict. "I could travel on my own, and as you have witnessed, I could manage. But I would prefer to go with the blessing of the church. Spain is very loyal, and your commission will open any necessary doors for me."

By now, the pope had completely regained his composure and was beginning to think of how this could benefit him. The cold steel look of power returned.

"And what is in this for me?"

"The relic," said Benedict plainly. The pope's eyes narrowed.

"You do not wish it for yourself?"

"No, I wish to return it to the church. That is where it belongs."

It was clear to the pope that Benedict was being sincere. However, since the pope had long since forsaken sincerity in himself, he found it surprising to see it in others.

"Very well, I will commission the Order of the Calamus."

"The Order of the Calamus?" responded Benedict.

"Yes," said the pope. "Calamus, from the Latin. Reed or quill. A borrowed word associated with Greek, Hebrew, and even Arabic. The "Order of the Calamus." It has an official sound to it, don't you think?"

"I would rather not have a title in any papers you give to me. I do not want to attract any unnecessary attention. If you could just give me a letter stating that I am investigating the miracles near Palos de la Frontera that would be sufficient. I only need them to know that I have your support."

"I will give you whatever you need. Bring the Calamus back to me, and you may have whatever you want," said the pope.

Benedict left the pope and headed for Palos de la Frontera in Spain. He enjoyed the same benefits he had received when he had left Rome nearly seventy years earlier for Bohemia. Wherever he showed the letter with the pope's seal, he was immediately treated with the best that could be afforded him. This time around though, Benedict was less than dazzled by the attention. He realized from his brief time back in Rome that the papacy and its hierarchy had become a bunch of corrupt men willing to sell each other for a small purse of gold. Benedict could see that the pope was not feeling well. He could not tell what was ailing him, but the pope's health did not look good. Benedict sensed that the pope was hoping that the calamus, as he called it, might give him what Benedict had—immortality.

Had Benedict never found a way to use the instrument, then he too would be facing the end of his years. How had those years been for him? Was everything he had gone through worth immortality? Now that he had tasted immortality, did it seem like a worthwhile endeavor to live forever in a world that was corrupt and where love was untenable? If the pope did manage to obtain the tool and use it for himself the way Benedict had, what kind of life was that for the pope? How would he use it?

As Benedict travelled, he mused on his life, immortality, Margaret, and meeting Jesus at the bottom of the sea. It was depressing. Benedict realized he had been nothing more than an immortal fool who now had the unenviable responsibility of finding the writing tool and returning it to an organization he never loved and now, in particular, did not respect. What was the point of it all? And after all these years, what would he even request of the writing tool if he could obtain it? There was a time when he had thought he would use it to become free from pain, but it was pain itself that held the memory of Margaret and their love together. To be free from pain and sorrow was to be free from the very things that produced those characteristics. If he felt no sorrow, then how could he love? How could he receive love?

Benedict realized that it wasn't so much that he didn't know how to use the writing instrument but that he had never fully considered the consequences. When he became immortal, it never occurred to him that immortality would have brought him so much grief. To live a normal life on earth meant experiencing a certain degree of sorrow and suffering. For some, it was more than others. But to live forever on earth meant that one would experience an everlasting ebb and flow of suffering. The agony of losing Margaret was so great that it drove him into the sea with the intent of tormenting himself forever. He never wanted to go through that again; however, the unpredictability of the tool's outcome meant that he had no confidence in using it to try and stop the ache of his broken heart. For example, if one wanted to never feel sorrow, would the use of the tool make them into a senseless laughing fool? The problem with the instrument was not its limitations but man's. Man lacked the depth of understanding to meddle with the divine. All Benedict wanted to do now was to rid himself of the instrument.

This made him think of his encounter with Jesus on the sea floor. In everything that Benedict had done in his life and with his opportunities, he had never really considered the reality of God in the writing tool. For the first time, Jesus had become someone real, someone who existed and controlled the universe. God was aware of Benedict. Standing on the sea floor just prior to sending him rushing to the shore, Benedict could see that though Jesus appeared serious and even stern regarding Benedict's misuse of the writing tool, he also loved Benedict. He cared about Benedict and wanted Benedict to know Him. To know His mind and His heart. In a way, Jesus seemed almost indifferent to the writing tool, almost as if it was a secondary issue in regard to Benedict. This somewhat answered Benedict's question to Marshall when Benedict asked him why didn't Jesus just go and get the tool Himself? What did he need Benedict for? At first, Benedict assumed, like Marshall, it was a sort of penance. He had misused the instrument; therefore, it was fitting for him to go to the trouble of returning it.

But Jesus seemed to be bigger than penance. Meeting him on the ocean floor, Jesus did not appear to need penance. In searching and finding the tool, Benedict was discovering a relationship with the creator of the tool. Bringing the tool to Rome was a way to display the conclusion of its return, but Benedict did not think that the same Jesus he met was interested in the Rome Benedict knew. There were those in Rome worse than Bishop Speso who would attempt by any means necessary to use the tool for their advantage. Jesus said to bring to tool back to him, but bringing it to Rome was the only way Benedict knew to accomplish that. Rome, even at its worst, was the church, and the church was the Body of Christ. Benedict could see no other way.

He reached the Friary of La Rábida in the spring of 1492. Though he had the means to travel more luxuriously, he had decided to comport himself as simple as possible. He travelled as a humble priest, though if he were examined closely, it would be discovered that he had enough gold coin to manage quite well should the need arise. He arrived at the friary riding a donkey on a hot Saturday afternoon. A small boy was sitting on the steps of the friary as Benedict rode near him and dismounted from the donkey.

"Hello, young man," said Benedict warmly. "Do you know where the friar is?"

The young boy stared confused at Benedict, and Benedict realized that he had forgotten to ask the question in Spanish. He repeated the question in Spanish, and the young boy's face lit up and he motioned for Benedict to follow him. He followed the boy through the front door and down a long hallway, and then through a doorway into a courtyard filled with flowers and a fountain in the center. The friar was sitting in a chair in the center of the courtyard with a large hat protecting his balding head from the sun. His head appeared to be bowed in prayer; however, as Benedict approached, he could hear the gentle sound of snoring. Benedict was about to clear his throat to wake the friar when just then the young boy excitedly spoke up.

"Friar, Friar, we have a visitor."

The friar jumped at the sound of the young boy and sat up quickly. For a moment, he seemed to wonder where he was. Then he rubbed his eyes before speaking to the boy.

"Matheo, what did I say about entering the courtyard?"

Matheo bowed his head in embarrassment.

"To enter respectfully and quietly and if you appear to be in prayer, to come back later."

"That is right. Now what did you say?"

Matheo's embarrassment quickly vanished as he excitedly pointed to Benedict.

"We have a visitor!"

The friar put his hand over his eyes to block the sun and looked at Benedict.

"I see, Matheo. I suppose we do. Could you please get our visitor some water to drink?"

"Yes, Friar," said Matheo as he raced away.

"Well, that ought to keep him busy for a while. I don't remember having that much energy. I suppose I did once. How do you do?" said the friar as he started to stand.

Benedict motioned for the friar to remain seated.

"Please sit. Would you mind if I sat with you? My name is Benedict, and I have travelled from Rome. It would be nice to sit on something other than an animal."

The friar's eyes lit with interest.

"Is that so?" said the friar. "I am Friar Paulo. I suppose if you are from Rome, then you are here regarding the miracles. How is Rome these days and how is the pope?"

"The pope is very interested in the miracles and has sent me to investigate. I have a letter from him if you care to read it."

Benedict pulled out the letter and handed it to Friar Paulo who read it with great interest before handing it back to Benedict.

"I noticed that you did not answer my question regarding the welfare of Rome and the pope. You are a wise man. Even as the pope has heard rumors of miracles here, I have heard rumors of Rome. Have you served Our Excellency for very long? You seem young enough."

"No," answered Benedict. "Just long enough to gain his trust. I assure you that Rome and the pope are strong in faith."

The friar let it rest. He had tested the waters.

"I am thankful to hear it," he answered. "Matheo, there you are."

Matheo came in with a tray and a pitcher of water with two glasses. He filled the glasses with water and handed them to the men. Benedict nodded his head to the young boy. The friar took a drink and cleared his throat.

"Matheo, could you please leave us so that we may discuss what this man has come to say?"

Matheo reluctantly left the courtyard but found a place close enough behind one of the pillars so that he could eavesdrop on the conversation.

"Friar Paulo, His Excellency is very interested to know whether you believe that miracles actually occurred and if so, what was the source of the miracles. There are a number of rumors, some suggesting that an entire village rose from the dead."

Friar Paulo stared hard at Benedict. There was something about Benedict that bothered the friar, but he couldn't quite put his finger on what it was. He seemed sincere enough, but the friar felt there was much more to the man than an errand boy trying to get information.

"May I ask if you have any personal involvement in this matter?" asked the friar.

"What do you mean?" replied Benedict.

"I'm not sure I know," answered the friar. "It's just that you have a way about you that seems odd to me. I have met men of the world and men of the cloth. Though you represent yourself as a priest from Rome and have the stamp to prove it, there seems more to you than meets the eye and I'm not sure what that is."

Benedict did not say anything. After a few moments of awkward silence, the friar cleared his throat.

"Well, then, I will tell you that a woman who appeared to be dying suddenly recovered. It was instantaneous, and when she rose and left her small house, the front of her house was covered in yellow flowers. The woman, who is the mother of the boy Matheo, who brought us our water, claimed that she was visited by Jesus who touched her head and said 'Arise.' Shortly after this, a boy who was lame was healed and a man who was blind from his youth was able to see. Other than a few of the older men and the one born blind, most of the men from the village were away fighting the Moors. There were a few other healings of people, but the most noticeable and dramatic were the three mentioned. I have known all of them and can verify that they indeed were in the condition they claim and that there is no other reason to testify for their healings other than a divine intervention from Almighty God."

Matheo listened intently as the friar spoke about his mother and the others. There was some silence as each took a drink of water. Benedict thought he heard some feet scuffling and looked at Friar Paulo. The friar lifted a finger to Benedict and gave a wink.

"Matheo, come out from hiding. I need you to guide our visitor to see your mother and the others in the village. I'm sure he has some questions for them."

There was a short pause, and then Matheo came sheepishly from around one of the pillars toward the two men with his head down. The friar did not seem upset with the young boy. He gave him a gentle scolding look and then motioned with his hand that Matheo was to leave with Benedict. Benedict stood and thanked the friar before leaving with Matheo. Benedict looked at the young boy. He was very interested in talking to him now that he understood that the boy's mother was the first to be healed.

As they followed the path toward Matheo's village, Matheo talked nonstop, asking Benedict many questions about himself and his travels, but asked nothing about why Benedict was visiting his village. When they reached the bend in the road where the instrument had been found, Matheo suddenly became very quiet. He could not help but turn his eyes toward the rocks where the writing tool had been kept hidden. Benedict noticed Matheo's sudden change and stopped walking and looked at the place where Matheo's eyes had fallen. It only took a moment for Benedict to put the pieces together. Matheo had used the writing tool and kept it hidden here. He did not know why Matheo had not given any of this information to either his mother or the friar. Benedict decided to be direct with Matheo.

"Matheo," said Benedict slowly as he looked at the rock wall. "Is this where you hid the instrument you found?"

Matheo could not control the surprise of learning that Benedict somehow knew of the stick Matheo had found. The stick had been clear in telling Matheo he was not to say anything about it. With all the excitement of what had transpired, it was difficult for Matheo to keep silent, but he had been faithful. However, suddenly all thoughts of secrecy seemed submitted to Benedict's knowledge about the stick. He could no longer control himself as his face lit up in wonder.

"How did you know about the stick?"

Benedict sat down with his back against the wall and motioned for Matheo to sit next to him. The sun was just behind the trees and sitting against the wall provided some cool shade. Benedict took in a deep breath and exhaled, his eyes closed while he enjoyed the shade.

"Matheo, the reason I know about the stick is because I used it once myself."

"Didn't the stick tell you not to tell anyone?" asked Matheo.

"No, Matheo, but the master of the stick was not pleased that I used it and requests that I return it to him."

A worried look came over Matheo.

"Is the master not pleased with me also?"

Benedict smiled warmly and looked at Matheo comfortingly.

"No, Matheo, you used the stick to help others. That is something that I'm sure the master was very pleased with. I used it for myself."

There was a brief silence between the two as Matheo absorbed this piece of information.

"Who is the master?" asked Matheo.

"Jesus Christ, the Son of God," answered Benedict.

"He told you to return the stick to Him?"

"Yes, Matheo. That is why I am here. I am very happy for your mother and friends. I know that you used the stick for their benefit. The Master was very happy to help you with the stick, but now I need to find it. I won't tell anyone that you used it if you don't want me to, but I need to know where the stick is."

Matheo stood up and pointed back to the monastery.

"Two men came and took it before I could use it to bring back my father."

At this, Matheo almost started to cry, and Benedict understood that Matheo had considered bringing his father back to life but the opportunity had eluded him.

"Matheo, if the Master had wanted your father back with you, then He would have allowed you to use it one last time. The stick is His and His will it will obey. Tell me about the men."

Matheo told Benedict everything he could remember. Benedict saw no need to go to the village to ask questions. Instead he returned to the monastery and questioned the friar about the two men. The friar remembered them and knew a little about their business. They were sailors who were planning on leaving in a month with Christopher Columbus on one of his three ships to India and China. Benedict determined that he must be on one of those ships.

10

Yalad and the Ceaseless Sleep

B enedict was prepared to pay whatever was necessary to be on any one of Columbus's three ships. It was difficult at first, because the crew for the three ships consisted of only eighty-seven men, most of which were from the Andalusia region of Spain. Benedict stood out like a sore thumb. His Spanish was broken, and his appearance was definitely Bohemian. Word got out that a foreigner was attempting to buy his way onto the voyage. Eventually, a man named Miguel agreed to sell his spot to Benedict for the amount he was to receive as an ordinary seaman for one year. His wife was ill, and with the money, he could stay behind and take care of her.

Benedict had been given a rough description of the two men by the friar. One, a man with an eye patch and long hair held back by a bandana, had been rumored to have killed a man; the other man was reportedly one of three friends who had helped him escape from prison. The Spanish Sovereigns had offered amnesty to convicts if they joined the crew, but only the man found guilty of murder and his three friends had taken up the offer. Benedict did not know which ship they would be on and he was hesitant to ask too many questions since he had already garnered enough attention as a foreigner by simply trying to procure a place on one of the ships.

Benedict ended up on the *Niña*. Life on the ship was back-breaking work. He had little experience and had it not been for Miguel's brother Antonio, who helped him learn the ropes, often literally, Benedict might have got himself tossed overboard for his lack of experience. Antonio was grateful for Benedict taking his brother's place, and while he couldn't fathom the reason why Benedict would pay to be on the ship, he did what he could to help Benedict. Benedict had never before performed physical labor to this extent, but he found he enjoyed it. At first, he spent most of his time pumping the bilge and cleaning the decks. He probably would have spent the entire voyage doing two of the most labor-intensive jobs on the ship, but Antonio taught him how to work the sails and check the ropes. While it was obvious to everyone that Benedict had no sailing experience, it was clear that he was more learned than most of them and also a quick study. His willingness to work, along with his uncomplaining attitude, in time, won over the others. Eventually he learned that the men whom he had hoped possessed the writing tool were on the *Pinta*.

On December fifth of 1492, Columbus's ship *Santa Maria* ran aground at Hispaniola. Columbus left thirty-nine of the crew behind in order to board the *Niña* and continued to sail along the coast. On January sixth, they met up with the *Pinta*. It was then that Antonio was able to point out to Benedict the two men on the *Pinta* that he was seeking. During the day, Benedict left the Niña and went ashore and while there, followed the two men. They had walked into the lush vegetation, cutting away the branches with a machete. With one hand they cut and with the other hand they shared the burden of carrying a box about four feet long with roped handles on each end. Benedict kept his distance and attempted to follow as quietly as possible. After about fifty yards, they came upon a clearing. There was a fire pit in the center filled with the remains of burnt branches and ash. When Benedict reached the clearing, there was no sign of the men, and the box was sitting in front of the fire pit. Benedict assumed they had felt comfortable enough to leave their burden while they foraged around, possibly for food or more branches for a fire. He stepped slowly into the clearing and headed toward the box.

The box had a simple padlock. Benedict would either need the key or find another way to break the lock. A stick or branch wedged in the loop of the shackle would probably not snap the shackle free.

Benedict looked around for a rock. He saw a group of round brown rocks at the base of one of the trees. He went over and grabbed one. He was surprised to find that it had a hairy surface and realized that it was not a rock but some type of hard fruit fallen from the tree. Benedict had never seen a coconut and wasn't sure if they were edible; however, after tapping one coconut with another, he realized they were just as hard as a rock, so he took one of the coconuts back to the box and knelt down in front, facing the padlock, ready to strike. While he was lifting the coconut in the air with his right hand, the man with the eye patch was doing the same thing right behind him. Just before Benedict was to strike the padlock, the one-eyed sailor brought a coconut down on Benedict's head and Benedict fell forward on top of the trunk.

He awoke about twenty minutes later, sitting slumped over the trunk with his hands tied securely behind him. His feet were fastened with shackles. Sitting fifteen feet in front of Benedict toward the other side of the clearing was a man in loose white clothes resting comfortably in a large bamboo chair. His skin was dark. Not like the Spanish men whom Benedict had come to know or even some of the darker natives on the island. Benedict had once met a man in Belgium who had come from Constantinople in Turkey. His skin looked as if it was like leather, brown and worn. The man in front of Benedict had the same skin color and his profile reminded him of the man from Constantinople, but this man's skin was smooth and relaxed. Next to the man in the chair was one of the men whom Benedict had followed. He was a short man with one leg slightly bent out, as if it had been broken and had never properly healed. His hair and beard were scraggly, and when he smiled, Benedict could count the remaining teeth on one hand. Benedict turned to his left and saw the man with the eye patch hovering over him. He noticed that the man had the machete in one hand and seemed more than eager to use it on Benedict.

"You appear to be European," said the man in the chair. The way he spoke reminded Benedict even more of the Turkish man. However, he spoke to Benedict in German.

"I'm asking because I can speak a number of languages, but you look Bohemian to me. Is German your preferred language or would you rather converse in Latin?"

Benedict wiggled his body a little, trying to adjust himself to a more comfortable position. He was sitting awkwardly on a board that ran across the cover of the trunk.

"Either is fine," answered Benedict shortly.

"Excellent," replied the man. "I think Latin then. I haven't had the opportunity in some time to speak it. You appear to be a lettered man. Before I ask you why you were trying to damage my lock, may I ask your profession? You clearly do not look like a sailor."

"I'm a businessman," replied Benedict.

The man quizzically eyed Benedict for some time, as if he were trying to solve a riddle.

"Yes," he said slowly. "I can see that. But there is something more. What were you before that?"

Benedict sat silent. For some reason, he had no desire to disclose that at one time he had been a priest. The man smiled as if he understood and was not bothered by Benedict's reticent reaction. He continued to stare at Benedict, and then a small smile came to his face.

"Diego, didn't you say that you knocked that man out with one of the fallen fruit?"

"Sí, I did. Hit pretty hard. Should I have killed him?" answered the man with the eye patch.

"No, Diego, as a matter of fact, I'm not sure that would have even been possible. The reason I ask, my dear one-eyed friend, is that I see no mark or blood on the man's head. I've seen men struck by one of those nasty fruits. They leave a pretty good bump if they don't kill you. Is there a mark on the man's head, Diego?"

Diego ran his hand slowly across Benedict's head, carefully feeling for any bumps. He found some dried blood at the base of his scalp where the coconut had hit Benedict's head, yet when he brushed the hair back, he could not see any bruising, bumps, or even a small gash.

"No, no, nothing," said Diego with a puzzled look. "All very strange. You want me to hit him again?"

"Thank you, Diego," answered the man in white calmly. "That will be all. You can leave the man with me. You do have the item in the chest, do you not?"

"Sí, in the box with a pile of rags. Buried deep so no one sees. Smart, sí?"

Diego gave a proud yellow-toothed grin. The man in white smiled warmly.

"Yes, Diego, very smart. Your brilliance is only outmatched by your charm and refined appearance. Could you please unlock the padlock, preferably with the key and not a coconut, and hand me the item. As agreed upon, assuming the item is the one I am looking for, you will receive the reward I promised. Of course, you will have to remove our guest from the top of the chest first. Gently please."

Diego was eager for his payment, so he pushed Benedict onto his knees, perhaps not as gently as the man in white wished. The key was around Diego's neck on a chain, and he quickly lifted it and inserted it in the padlock, unlocking the chest. The chest was indeed covered in rags, and once they were haphazardly strewn about the sand floor, all that could be seen was the writing instrument. Diego proudly pulled it out of the trunk. While it held a brief fascination to Diego, he quickly handed it to his toothless partner who had moved forward, who in turn brought it to the man in white. Benedict fixed his eyes upon the instrument for the first time in almost seventy years.

As the man in white held the writing tool in his hand, he heard Diego clear his throat. The man looked back up at the two thieves. The chest had been closed, and Diego was now sitting on top. The two men were resting their hands on their daggers calmly but certainly, their way of reminding the man in white that a payment was due.

"We've done our part," reminded Diego.

"So you have, Diego, and I have given you as much as you can possibly carry."

"You have given us nothing," growled Diego. "We have travelled a great distance to bring you this curse. Where is our reward?"

"You are sitting on it, dear friend. And in the future, do not even think of threatening me again."

Diego stood quickly and pulled out his knife.

"What are you talking about? We did not come all this way for a chest of rags. We want our money!"

The man in white serenely smiled while admiring the writing tool. "I will indulge you, Diego, one last time and then I never want to see either of you two again, or this curse…" The man in white nodded toward the writing tool. "This curse will be upon you. Now open the chest and be on your way."

Diego narrowed his eyes toward the man in white before slowly turning around to lift the lid of the chest. As the chest opened, the glow of a trunk filled with gold coins shown in his face.

"This is all for us?" Diego said to the man in white. The man in white nodded in return.

"As promised, I told you there would be a reward beyond your wildest dreams. I have to give you credit, Diego. Many a man would have just taken the object and tried to use it for themselves."

Diego looked at the man in white with a look of horror. Seeing the chest of rags suddenly filled with gold reminded him of the dangerous power of the man and the instrument.

"No, Padre Del Tiempo! I would never do such things."

"Well, Diego, we are done. Enjoy your wealth if you are able to. I would like to speak with our prisoner alone now, so if you two could take your earnings and depart."

The man in white made a gesture with his hand, and the two men quickly threw the clothes back on top of the gold, grabbed the handles, and hurried off.

Benedict sat cross-legged on the sand, his hands still tied behind his back and his ankles secured by the shackles. Both men were very conscious of each other's keen interest in the writing tool. The man in white spoke first.

"I assume this is what you were looking for. It's beautiful, isn't it? Those poor men with their pile of coins. They will probably be dead within a week. I'm surprised they made it this far."

"Padre del Tiempo," said Benedict. "Father of Time. They know of you and of the writing instrument?"

The man in white laughed easily.

"No, they really know very little of the calamus. That is the ancient word, is it not? There have been many names for this remarkable piece of creation, but I like calamus. All that the men know of me and the calamus are the legends and the little that they have seen of me over the years. I have known them since they were children. They were ignorant street thieves when I first met them. That is why they call me 'Padre del Tiempo.' The simple people on these islands call me the same name. For the sake of natives, I attribute my agelessness to a mysterious fictional fountain of youth called Aqua de Vida. It answers their questions and gives them something to look for. I have used this myth many times over the years in different places to explain why I haven't aged.

When the two men were young boys, I had lost the calamus. I should say that it has a way of losing itself. I have been in possession of it off and on for a very long time. One day while walking down a side street, I found the two boys playing with the calamus. They, of course, had no idea what it was. I gave them some coins for it for which they were very grateful. Sometime later, the calamus found its way out of my possession. I told the boys that if they ever found it, they were to bring it to me and I would give them even more coins. They found it a few years ago and then lost it briefly before bringing it to me."

"But how did they know you were here?" asked Benedict in bewilderment.

"Because I went back to Spain and told them where I was. I told them that a time would come when someone would sail west in hope of finding India, and that if they had the calamus, they were to bring it to me."

Benedict was puzzled.

"I don't understand. How did you travel to Spain from here, and how did you come to know that a vessel would come here?"

The man in white twirled the calamus in his fingers and smiled at Benedict.

"We have both used this instrument. We both know it has unlimited powers but that they are difficult to unlock. I have accumulated unconventional ways to travel and unconventional ways to find information. Most that have used the calamus have died trying. With caution and experience, I have used the calamus to obtain many invaluable abilities. Since you are still alive, I assume that you have seen some of its benefits and its dangers. I have only known two others in all my years who have survived more than a hundred years. If you do not mind my asking, how long have you known of the calamus?"

"I first saw its use in 1419," replied Benedict as he squirmed uncomfortably on the sand. "Would you mind unchaining me? I promise that I will make no attempt at taking the calamus from you."

The man in white looked at Benedict, nonchalantly twirling the calamus in his fingers.

"Not just yet. I'm sorry for your discomfort, but for now you will have to remain bound. I have been alive for a very long time because I trust no one. I will admit that you seem different than some of the others I have come across over the years, yet not enough I'm afraid for me to let you go."

Benedict furrowed his eyes.

"So…exactly who are you and just how long have you been around?" Benedict asked.

The man in white stood for a moment and stretched his legs. He slowly paced back and forth in front of Benedict as he spoke.

"I have been known by many names and I have used many names, but my birth name is Yalad and I am one of many sons of Nimrod."

Benedict's eyebrows raised in surprise.

"You are thousands of years old?"

"I am," replied Yalad. "Nimrod had many children from many women. So many in fact that most were simply called Yalad, which you may or may not know was another word for 'child.' As I grew, I envied others who were closer to my father and I longed for his approval. One day as a small child, I came across the calamus and drew a picture of Nimrod as a powerful man standing over many others. He was a well-known man and quite capable, but it was after I drew a picture of him that he became a legend. I knew somehow the calamus had produced the change in him and perhaps it could be used for other purposes. I was on the verge of trying things with the calamus which others would later attempt only to find it bring about their own destruction. But a cousin, in whom I had confided, stole the calamus and attempted to use it against another with the purpose of harming him. He confessed this to me just before the very thing he attempted came back on him. It was then that I realized the calamus, though brilliant in beauty and powerful beyond our knowledge, could be disastrous if used incorrectly. Over time, I have learned many uses which have benefited me without harm. I'm sure you have discovered some. One for certain is immortality. I could see it in you before you even told me you had encountered the instrument."

"What is your intention with the calamus now?" asked Benedict.

"I might ask you the same question," replied Yalad.

There was an awkward pause for Benedict as Yalad watched him, a slow smile spreading across his face.

"So you wish to return it to its owner," said Yalad with a grin. Benedict could not contain his surprise mixed with curiosity that his intentions had been revealed so easily.

"I told you," said Yalad, "that I learned how to use the instrument in many ways. Who do you think it belongs to exactly? God? Which god? The church…"

Once Yalad mentioned the church, he realized that it was indeed Benedict's intention and it made Yalad laugh out loud. There was no bitterness in his laugh. It was the laugh an adult might have for a child who has said or done something too silly for the child to grasp.

"I don't even know where to begin with that notion. It is absolutely ludicrous. You cannot possibly be serious? With the corruption that exists in the church…oh, and believe me, I know how deep the fowl stench goes. Do you think that they would do anything with the calamus other than destroy each other through their ignorance and stupidity?"

Benedict had nothing to say. He had thought of the wisdom of returning it to the church. Bishop Speso was proof how easily it could be misused. Pope Innocent VIII clearly wanted it for his own interest. But Benedict had nothing else. The church was Christ's representative, and Christ had told Benedict to return it to Him. Unless Jesus Christ himself appeared to Benedict, Benedict could think of no other way to fulfill his obligation; although, there was one question which troubled him, and Yalad seemed to sense it.

"Maybe the instrument does not want to be returned to the church," said Yalad as he peered at Benedict's face. He could see that Benedict had considered the same conclusion.

"You still haven't answered my question," said Benedict coldly. "What intention do you have with the tool now?"

"I suppose it will not hurt to tell you, seeing how you will be unable to stop me. My father deserted me in Babel, along with his many other children, while he wandered off building cities and establishing his empire. The Tower of Babel was built with the intention of having a structure high enough so that if God were to destroy the world again, those on the tower would live. We feared not only death but the judgment that follows. I have managed to avoid death but that is not enough. I want to avoid judgment. I want righteousness and power on my terms."

"But how will you do that?" asked Benedict.

"I am still working on that one. But enough about my future. Let's discuss yours."

With that, Yalad gave a sharp whistle and two natives came into the clearing. Yalad said something to the two men in a language Benedict had never heard. The two men quickly ran off, and after a few minutes, they returned with a large wooden wall which had hinges in the center so that it could fold out and stand on the ground. At Yalad's direction, they placed the wall as a barrier in front of Benedict. The two men left as quickly as they arrived. Benedict was surprised to see Yalad look down behind the wall and speak to someone in the unknown language. Even without seeing who was behind the wall, Benedict suspected that it must be a child. Yalad handed the person the calamus and said a few more words before turning back to Benedict.

"As you know, it would be foolish of me to try and bring about your destruction. However, I have learned over time that I can incapacitate your movement. Shortly, you will fall asleep, and you will not wake. You will live forever on some isolated island in an endless sleep. I would not say it is a sleep of death for I could never seek your demise, but it is just as useful. It has been a pleasure meeting you, Benedict."

Benedict felt his eyes getting heavy, and soon, he passed out.

11

Unless a Seed Fall into
the Ground and Die

At Yalad's direction, a young boy had drawn Benedict sleeping on a faraway deserted island. The moment he did so, Benedict was gone. Physically, Benedict had been transported to the sands of a small remote island where he slept night and day through rain and burning heat. Mentally, however, in his spirit, Benedict was everywhere. It was a strange sensation and certainly one which Yalad had not anticipated. Neither dream nor vision, Benedict, though asleep, felt more conscious of what was happening around him and had more freedom of movement and understanding than he ever could if awake. A verse from his days in priestly training came back to him. It was the words of St. Paul in the book of 2 Corinthians: "I knew a man in Christ above fourteen years ago [whether in the body, I cannot tell; or whether out of the body, I cannot tell: God knoweth]." This was the only way Benedict could perceive what was happening to him. There was a man sleeping on the shore of an island, and he recognized the man as himself. There was also the consciousness of his own being, abiding just a few yards away, viewing his physical body lying on the shore.

The Benedict who knew not whether he was in the body or not began moving around the island. The island itself was uneventful. It was deserted not only by man but by beasts of any size. All that he could see were lush vegetation and some insects. Once he had made the short trip around the island, he went back to the image of himself sleeping on the sand. Benedict sat down next to himself, gazing at the sea. As he sat, he witnessed the tides coming in and out thousands of times, the sun setting and rising, and the stars and moon appearing and disappearing as the cycle of time repeated itself over and over. He looked at himself sleeping on the sand, the sun burning his skin and then his body regenerating just as it did when he spent those years on the ocean floor. Rain poured over him as storms came and went. Years passed without any sensation of duration. As he sat on the shore, another verse came to his mind, almost as if a voice was speaking from somewhere. *"And the Spirit of God moved upon the face of the waters."*

After taking one more look at the sleeping Benedict, he walked to the shoreline and then began to move upon the face of the waters. It didn't really feel like flying or walking. It was simply moving, almost passively as if he were being driven in a carriage. He did not feel as if he was directing himself but more like being guided by another. There was no consciousness of time as Benedict floated above the water never seeing land. Eventually the light around him became darkness, and Benedict continued to move over the water. He sensed the presence of God everywhere around him. He was also keenly aware that there was no evil. It wasn't that the presence of God overwhelmed evil, but that evil did not exist. Then a voice spoke, and Benedict heard the command "Let there be light," and immediately there was light. There was a pureness to the light that was distinct from any light that Benedict had ever known, which made him wonder how light could have pureness outside of its contrast to darkness, but it was unmistakable. Then the night came and it was a pure darkness, and Benedict had the same sensation that he had about the day. Still he moved upon the face of the waters in the presence of God.

As he moved, the waters suddenly parted as land pushed its way out from the darkness of the deep, forming land masses and mountains. Benedict felt no fear as he floated. He began to move toward a large flat area of land and seemed to be directed to a region of lush vegetation. He stopped in an open field of grass surrounded by enormous trees. There was a conviction that what was before him was being viewed for the first time. A man was standing naked in front of Benedict. The man could not see Benedict. Benedict perceived the man to be Adam and that he was witnessing his first day on Earth. Adam slept and God made Eve. Benedict was being allowed to witness the creation of the earth and humanity. There was a creature, and Benedict saw the temptation of Eve and the fall of mankind. He longed to intervene to stop the action, but he was suddenly whisked away by the Spirit and placed in front of a man murdering another man. Benedict discerned it was the murder of Abel and the departing of men from the knowledge of God. As the days sped by, Benedict saw the way of man fall further and further from the knowledge of God and demonic forces dominating the world to a point where the world once so pure was now saturated with evil. And it grieved Benedict.

Then he beheld Noah like a faint beacon in a dark night and the animals entered the ark, and once again, Benedict moved over the face of the waters. The world populated again and evil resurfaced. Benedict was brought before Nimrod and beheld his ways. He saw Yalad and the calamus. He could see Yalad enter Nimrod's chamber and try to convince his father of the power of the calamus and Nimrod impatiently indulging Yalad before demanding one of the servants take the boy away. Nimrod became great because of the writing tool; however, he was too arrogant and blind to give credit to anyone other than himself. Benedict saw what Yalad had seen. His father would never appreciate him even if he recognized that Yalad had been the one to exalt his position and ability.

The Spirit showed him Yalad's inner most thoughts and intentions. He saw the longing of Yalad to please Nimrod and the deep sadness he felt upon his father's callous indifference toward him. The seed in Yalad was beginning to grow, which would involve Yalad learning how to use the instrument over many years as a tool to escape the need for salvation. Yalad had lived in Babel when the tower was built, and like many others, he saw it not only as a culmination of the glorious self-will of man but as a means of escape should another judgment come upon the earth. When the scattering at Babel occurred through the confusion of languages, Yalad realized his only way of escape was through the calamus. As he grew, the rejection of his father and the judgment on Babel became seeds of bitterness that would grow into a powerful tree but, however, over time pruned by the discretion of the instrument's abilities. Yalad yearned for the power he saw in his father, yeah, even greater power. He wanted to excel Nimrod. He wanted to excel all others. He wanted to excel God. He was looking for his own way of escape from judgment. He was not interested in salvation. He was drawn to prominence and domination. Benedict could see that Yalad's purpose was to change the plan of God by changing the will of the calamus. It was then that Benedict understood that the calamus must not only be returned to its creator. It must be removed from Yalad forever.

But Yalad could not retain the calamus. As Francis had told Jan Žižka, the tool seemed to take care of itself. In spite of Yalad's best efforts, the tool managed to find its way into the hands of others. Benedict watched through time as the calamus fell into the hands of evil men, ignorant men, and foolish men—who all found to their surprise and demise that it had its own will. There were others though, some simple and a few even great, who unwittingly used the calamus, such as Žižka's granddaughter to change events, and some who used it knowingly to bring about good for others.

Through the ages, Yalad managed to find his way back to the calamus. Yalad was always seeking the tool, even as Benedict had followed the rumor of the healings in the small town in Spain. But it also seemed to Benedict that the calamus had a way of finding its way back to Yalad, almost as if on purpose. The two seemed drawn to each other. Benedict could see the pride of Yalad's heart. He considered himself wise in his ability to seek and learn the writing tool's ways, but to Benedict, it almost appeared as if the calamus was purposefully, for reasons unknown to Benedict, allowing itself be used.

Yalad had learned, like Benedict, some of the characteristics of the calamus. A child, before the age of accountability, could use the writing tool for themselves unwittingly or wittingly, providing they were not harming others. They could also use it for someone else at their prompting, providing they were ignorant of its purpose. As

Benedict watched Yalad grow in his ability to extract as much as he could from the calamus through the manipulation of others, not just children but the simple and ignorant, Benedict felt ashamed. He realized while watching Yalad exploit others that Benedict had been no different. If not for his encounter with the Lord at the bottom of the sea, Benedict would have continued like Yalad to find a way to acquire as much power as he could from the calamus. Benedict realized that it was more than just a desire to control the calamus, it was a lust for power to control everything. If one could control the calamus, one could control God.

It was then that Benedict found himself at the foot of the cross. The sun had darkened as Jesus and the two thieves hung in silence. Benedict could see the fear in the faces of Rome's centurions as they grappled with a phenomenon greater than the power of Rome. Benedict looked up and could barely see the bloody, disfigured face of Jesus. One eye was slightly opened, and Benedict felt it was staring at him, examining him, unsurprised that one should fly through time as an apparition and land at his feet. It was the same face of the one in the sea, the same seriousness, the same joy, but now with an expression Benedict could never have imagined to see. It was a pained look of sorrow and a loss that suddenly revealed itself as Jesus cried out *"Eloi, Eloi, lema sabachthani?"*

A bluish light appeared at Benedict's feet leaning against the base of the cross. It was the calamus. He reached down and picked it up. Why was it here at this point in history, and how was it that he could pick it up? Benedict looked around. He was unnoticed by those around him, and he could not understand how he could have possession of something tangible while he was disembodied yet the possibility of its use became immediately apparent to him. He could change everything. He could erase the cross. He could bring Jesus down. Give him his life back. He could wipe away his pain. Perhaps the world could be saved without the cross.

Jesus had said to Benedict in the sea that he should bring the tool back to him. Benedict had thought that Jesus had meant to bring it back to the church, which was Benedict's intention when he sought it in Spain and then in the New World of Columbus. But here was

Jesus now and how could Benedict give it to him as he hung there on the cross? Was he to use the calamus and bring Jesus down to hand it to him? That seemed unlikely. Was the calamus more important than what Christ was doing now for mankind?

He leaned his back against the cross. Time seemed as immaterial as was his presence. All Benedict knew was that he knew nothing other than his own ignorance. He took the tool and placed it against the cross and said out loud, though his voice was unheard.

"Here is the tool. Thy will be done."

Just after he spoke, Benedict could hear the voice of the Lord say "Into thy hands I commit my spirit." Benedict slumped over and wept. He sat as they pierced the Lord's side and then brought him down from the cross. The days passed, and Benedict did not move. He had seen what he had been taught but never really believed. Now he understood. What had been a formality in his life became a living reality.

The physical distance of the events did not seem to impede his ability to witness the Lord's resurrection, ascension, and the birth of the church in the upper room. The church grew and spread beyond Jerusalem. Then, as he continued to sit at the foot of where the cross had been, he watched as Jerusalem was besieged by Rome and then leveled. It seemed to happen in a moment, and though the work of the Lord was glorious as the church grew and spread, Benedict could only wonder what any of this had to do with him. He was a man who in time had lived as a selfish religious man, with no appreciation for what he had seen and heard. He had become something he regretted and was trying to do the right thing by returning the instrument to the Lord, but all he could see in himself was an ungrateful, ignorant, inconsequential immortal.

After the fall of Jerusalem, the Spirit of God moved Benedict through the years as he watched the church grow in spite of Rome's persecution. Countless faithful saints persevered in the midst of Rome's attempt to annihilate them. Then after Constantine and the end of Rome's persecution factions arose and the Roman Church became more formalized. It evolved into an institution, sometimes united but often divided; sometimes spreading the Gospel and sometimes creating a barricade to those seeking truth. He watched as many became like he was when he lived—religious, superstitious, hungry, unsatisfied, ignorant, fearful, and self-serving.

But there were remnants: voices crying in the wilderness that the Word of God was the true authority and that Word should be available to all. For those in power, however, reformers such as Wycliffe and Hus were seen as heretics. When Benedict had been in Prague, he did not care about such things and only saw people like Hus, Žižka, and Francis as sincere people with whom he could not relate. Now the Spirit was opening his eyes. He witnessed Luther and the nailing of the ninety-five theses to the door of the castle church of Wittenberg. He saw a hunger for the Bible and an opposition to that hunger. He saw Tyndale and Zwingli, Calvin, and then the Moravians and the missionary movements. The Spirit of God was awakening and moving and new lands were opening to the living gospel. He saw the rise and fall of nations and the correlation of the Gospel in relation to history. Everyone was attempting to go into the uttermost parts of the earth, but not all with the same purpose.

Wars were fought around the world as they had been before, only now with advanced weaponry and larger conflicts. Technology advanced and travel changed. Benedict saw vehicles flying in the sky and enclosed ships going under water. He saw great leaders rise and fall, some by their lust for power and some by the hands of lesser men. He saw people starving and others prospering. Man was not changing but advancing.

Benedict had lost track of time watching the future as history unfolded. Occasionally, he would see Yalad and his use of the calamus through centuries past, long before Benedict had come across the instrument. A strange thing happened as Benedict witnessed the various times that Yalad had used the calamus. Benedict could feel the results of whatever Yalad achieved with the calamus transferred to him. It was as if the Lord was attributing the fruit of Yalad's attempts to Benedict, but Benedict had no understanding why. Benedict also saw fear in Yalad. There was something that Yalad was not prepared to do and that was to make the instrument his servant. Through all the centuries, he sought ways for others to take risks for his reward, but he dared not take the ultimate challenge of trying to control the calamus.

There was a world war and then another world war, and then Benedict saw the convergence of the calamus, Yalad, evil men, and himself. Benedict knew he would intervene though he was not sure how. Then the revelation of the Spirit ended.

12

Awake Thou That Sleepest

Benedict was back on the same beach where Yalad had dispatched him. He was standing at the water's edge facing a vast ocean, and he assumed he was still in the Spirit. He turned around expecting to see his body asleep on the sand, but it was gone. A child was sitting on the sand drawing with a stick. It was the calamus. The boy looked up at Benedict and waved. Benedict lifted a hand in return. The boy smiled and pointed to the sea. Benedict turned and suddenly there was a large ship offshore, like nothing he had ever seen in his life, yet similar to some he had witnessed in the Spirit. The ship had not been in the ocean when he had first come out of the Spirit. Benedict turned back to the boy who continued to draw. Perhaps, thought Benedict, the boy had awakened Benedict by drawing him standing by the sea. He wondered if the boy had also drawn the ship. He walked over to the child who was still drawing. The boy spoke in Japanese. Even though Benedict had never heard a word of Japanese in his life, he understood what was being said. He remembered Yalad's comment on his love of language. Knowing this boy's language must be something that Yalad had acquired from the calamus, and now Benedict possessed it as well.

"Did your ship sink like mine?" asked the boy as he continued to draw. "Is that why you are here?"

"Where did you find that stick?" asked Benedict.

The boy sat silent for a minute, not sure how much to tell the stranger.

"I found it just before we were attacked. I hung onto some wood and fell asleep. When I woke up, I was next to you. You look different. That's why I asked if you were on a ship also. Did your ship attack us?"

Benedict was not sure how to answer the questions. He looked down at the drawing in the sand and saw a man standing, which he was now certain must be himself. There was a large ship behind Benedict that the boy had drawn. Now the boy was drawing smaller ships that had beached and also other men on the sand. A moment later, these same men were just behind Benedict.

"Are you two the only one's stranded here?" a voice behind Benedict asked.

Benedict turned around and saw three Japanese sailors. Behind them were a couple of smaller ships pulled up to the shore with other soldiers. One of the soldiers picked up the boy and took him back to one of the small boats.

"As far as I know," replied Benedict in Japanese. He watched as one of the small boats with the boy in it sailed toward the main ship.

"You speak Japanese?" answered the man in surprise. He appeared to be the leader of the small party. "I cannot make out your accent. I can't tell whether it's German or English. It is one I am unfamiliar with. How is it you speak our language?"

"I'm not sure," answered Benedict. What he wasn't sure of was just how in the world he was going to explain himself without sounding crazy. He decided it was better to play ignorant.

"I don't remember anything. I woke up on the beach and saw you. I don't know how I got here or who I am. I must have learned Japanese at school, I suppose, but I don't remember."

The leader turned to one of his men, and Benedict overheard the words "maybe amnesia." The leader then told three of his men to search the beach to make sure that no one else was on the island. He lightly grabbed Benedict's arm and led him to one of the small boats. Benedict could see that the man felt bothered by something as they walked to the boat.

The men boarded the small boat and rowed back to the main vessel. Having heard Benedict speak Japanese, they kept their conversation at a minimum. He had been searched for weapons prior to entering the small craft as a precaution. No one knew what to make of him or their situation. Benedict could feel an unnatural stillness in the boat as they moved toward the ship. The men were in uniforms, and it was obvious that they were in a war readiness mode of operation. Just who, when, and where they were Benedict was not sure. He was trying to remember what he had seen when in the Spirit, but there was nothing specific that he could recall. He had seen many wars through his travel, and it was impossible to place this moment in any particular historical context. For now, it was obvious he was not trusted by the men, and it would be best if he maintained his ignorance and feigned amnesia. What else could he say of himself? The truth?

The ship was made entirely of some type of metal. It seemed mammoth to Benedict. As they approached, he observed long sleek cannon-type tubes with smaller ones on the side of the ship and bigger ones on the deck. On the deck in the middle of the ship were three tall cylindrical-shaped metal objects. Benedict guessed that they had something to do with the movement of the ship. Black smoke was coming out of the cylinders toward the bow of the ship. The smaller boats transporting everyone back to the ship sidled parallel to the stern where there were some stairs. The boy was nowhere to be found. He reasoned that he must have already boarded since he had left sooner than Benedict. As they readied themselves to board the ship, the man who had spoken to Benedict earlier turned to him and placed his arm firmly on Benedict's forearm, indicating that Benedict should wait. When the rest of the men had boarded, the man pulled out some rope and quickly tied Benedict's hands.

"For now you are a prisoner of war until I find out more about you. You will be treated civilly, but you will be kept locked in a cabin until I can resolve this mystery. I would advise that you not try anything foolish. Do you understand?"

Benedict nodded his head. The man continued.

"I have told those who overheard us speaking not to mention that you speak Japanese. However, if the others find out that you do and think that you have a German accent, there could be trouble. I think it would be best for you not to talk with anyone until you and I have a chance to speak alone."

Benedict gave an almost imperceptible nod in return. The man grabbed Benedict and helped lift him out of the boat and onto the stairs. Benedict was escorted with all eyes gazing curiously at him. He was taken below deck into a very small cabin. Just before entering, the man told one of the other men to untie Benedict's ropes. As Benedict entered the room, he had to lean his head slightly forward because of the low ceiling and some large, black pipes running overhead. He was not sure what the pipes were for, but he could on occasion hear a rushing sound running through the pipes. The room was empty of everything except a small bed barely large enough to lie on. The width of the room gave Benedict about two steps from the bed to the wall. The length was four steps from the door to the side. The door was shut behind him, and he heard the turn of the lock. There was nothing to do but wait. Benedict lay down on the thin mattress pulling his knees up. His long legs prevented him from completely stretching out. Lying onto his side was just as awkward. He wondered where the boy was and how close Benedict now was to the calamus.

After about an hour, Benedict heard the sound of heels clicking on the hard floor as they approached his door. The men stopped, and the key was placed into the lock and the door opened. Benedict anxiously stood up as the man who had escorted him onto the ship entered. The man dismissed his aides and had the door shut. The door locked, and Benedict assumed that a guard was remaining outside should he be needed. Since there was nowhere else to sit, the man motioned to Benedict for them to sit on the bed. Benedict nodded, and both men sat down.

"I don't believe that it is necessary, but I want to warn you that I have a very capable man outside the door who will be in here quite quickly if I call him. Can I have your assurances that it will not be necessary?"

"You have my assurances," answered Benedict. "I am not at war, I am not a spy, and I am also not a fool."

"You do not appear to me to be a fool," replied the man. "But I need to know who and what you are."

Benedict knew that trying to explain what had really happened was out of the question. He had to convince this man that he was not a threat and to find a way to get to the boy.

"My name is Benedict. I don't remember much else. Like I said, I woke up on the beach. I suppose I must have been shipwrecked. The only thing I can think of is that the boy might have some answers. I assume he is also on board? Perhaps if I could speak with him."

"Not just yet," said the man. "We are questioning him now."

Just then, a whoosh of sound came from the pipes above their heads. The man paused awkwardly, and Benedict asked what the pipes were used for. The man looked surprised at the question.

"Sewage, of course. Why?"

"Do you mind if I ask you a question?" said Benedict somewhat hesitantly.

"You may," replied the man, "but then, you must answer a question from me."

Benedict glanced at the pipe above him and back at the man.

"What year is this?"

The man cocked his head slightly and narrowed his eyes.

"It's 1914."

It was difficult for Benedict to not show some surprise as he absorbed the knowledge that he had been on the island for over four hundred years. Everyone he had ever known had been dead for centuries. Margaret and Marshall were gone forever. In spite of all the years Benedict had lived, he had known only three friends in his life—Francis, Marshall, and Margaret, and now they were not just dead but had been gone for centuries. It made him feel more alone than he ever thought possible. The man studied Benedict as he sat.

"Now I need you to answer a question," said the man seriously. "I think that you know the answer. Even though I have no proof, I do not believe that you are a spy. I am the captain of this vessel, and I am the only one who can keep you from becoming a prisoner of war.

Most of the other men believe you to be a German spy and the fact that you speak Japanese makes it even more suspicious, but I do not see that in you. I also do not believe that you have amnesia."

"You haven't asked me a question yet," said Benedict.

The man stood and faced Benedict. His face grew serious, and Benedict could detect that there was some confusion on the man's part which went beyond just trying to figure out whether Benedict was a spy.

"One hour ago, we were leaving Tsingtao in China after recapturing the city back from the Germans. Now, somehow, by our best guess, we are more than three thousand miles away! We find ourselves suddenly coming upon your small island. My men are fearful and perplexed to say the least. They also know that this must have to do with you. Now you need to stop pretending that you do not know anything! What is happening?"

The captain's voice ended with a pleading tone. Benedict could see the controlled anxiety in his face. In Benedict's day, when something strange at sea happened, it was possible that someone might be thrown overboard out of superstition. Benedict didn't want to be that man.

"I need to see the boy," answered Benedict. "I believe only he can fix this."

The captain stared at Benedict for some time, trying to decide what course to take. Finally, he opened the door and spoke quietly to the man outside who quickly raced down the corridor and came back in a couple of minutes. He came into the room and placed handcuffs on Benedict. Three men marched down the corridor and eventually came to another door which was guarded by one of the sailors. He saluted the captain, who nodded and instructed him to open the door. The sailor opened the door, and the captain and Benedict walked in. The boy's room was a little larger and appeared to be a type of conference room. There was a table in the center along with some chairs. On the table was a piece of paper. The boy was gone. So was the calamus.

The captain turned and with anger in his voice demanded of the guard the whereabouts of the boy. The sailor had been standing outside the door and had assumed the boy was still in the room. He raced into the room and looked around and under the table.

"I don't understand, Captain! The boy has not left the room. The only exit is the doorway and I have been here the entire time." There was fear in the man's voice as he realized not only was he in serious trouble but that the boy had somehow vanished into thin air. Benedict walked over to the table as the captain continued to question the sailor. On the table was a paper with a drawing on it. It was a picture of the boy holding the hands of what appeared to be his parents. He had a smile on his face. There was also a small dog in the picture.

"He is gone," Benedict said simply.

The captain came back into the room and stood next to Benedict. He looked down at the paper. It was common paper that was used for notes and dictation. The captain examined the boy's drawing.

"What does this mean?" he demanded of Benedict. "Where has the boy gone?"

"Home," answered Benedict almost in a hushed voice. He envied the boy and the simplicity of his life and desires. The idea of home seemed like a long-lost concept to Benedict.

The captain, however, was starting to unravel and wanted answers.

"And where is home?" he barked at Benedict.

"I don't know. The boy brought you here. I wish you could be brought back home, but only he had the power to make that happen."

The captain stormed out of the cabin and commanded that Benedict be kept handcuffed and brought back to his cabin with a two-man guard. Benedict walked back to the cabin with the men. The calamus was lost once again.

Benedict lay back down on the short bed. He wasn't anxious about what was going to happen to him. After being submerged underwater for years, dying repeatedly, he knew in the end that he would outlive everyone on the ship and whatever war was going on would one day pass and he would continue. What he did consider was how he was able to speak Japanese. He knew nothing about Japan, much less the language. He sensed the understanding of the language had to either be connected to the calamus or with his experience in the Spirit when he sensed that Yalad's powers were transferred to him. It seemed less likely that the boy could have brought about Benedict's ability to speak Japanese by using the calamus. He would have had to know that Benedict could not speak Japanese prior to even awakening him. In all likelihood, the boy might also never have made the connection that the writing tool had the power to bring about any change.

As Benedict thought on these things, he heard the keys rattle and his door suddenly opened. The captain came through the doorway and studied Benedict, his skin pale white and his hands slightly trembling. The captain had come alone. Benedict stood slowly, not sure what to expect. The captain took one of the keys off his chain and motioned for Benedict to push his shackled hands out in front of him. Benedict lifted his hands, and the captain unlocked the chains.

Benedict gave the captain a puzzled look. "Is there a problem captain?" he asked tentatively.

The captain tried to keep his voice even and calm. However, it was clear he was far more disturbed by something else, something more than being suddenly three thousand miles from his previous location.

"We just docked at Yokosuka."

Benedict looked puzzled. "I don't know what that means," he answered. "What and where is Yokosuka?"

There was a small round window across the room. The captain walked toward it and stood, facing the window. Other than allowing a little light into the cabin, the glass was too thick and smudged to view the outside. It did not seem to matter to the captain.

"It is my home."

The captain slowly turned and faced Benedict.

"After I spoke with you, I went to the deck to assess our position and determine the best course back. When I reached the deck, the crew was excited to inform me that we were home."

The captain suddenly ran his hands over his face and then through his hair before calling out in exasperation, "We are back in Japan! Please tell me how you did this and what this means."

Benedict sat on the bed and rubbed his wrists. He had a strong suspicion how they were suddenly back, but the captain would have to remain in the dark.

"I wish I knew," was all he could say.

13

Generations

After Benedict's disappearance, Yalad contemplated what he would do next with the calamus. It had been hundreds of years since he had last possessed it, and he knew that his sole possession of it was not something he had yet learned to control. He was fearful that any attempt to permanently have possession of the calamus could result in the opposite action taking place. However, he was tired of waiting for its appearance only to lose it shortly after. He turned to the boy who had been at his side behind the partition to ask for the calamus back, yet when he looked down, the boy was gone and so was the calamus.

"Where has the boy gone?" called out Yalad angrily.

The two men who had set up the partition came scurrying back to Yalad, bowing respectfully before him. They stared in doubt at Yalad. One of them spoke.

"He is not with you?" the man asked.

"Do you see him?" growled Yalad.

"No, I do not. We would have noticed. He hasn't passed our way."

For a moment, Yalad sat contemplating the meaning of the disappearance of the boy and the calamus. He had patiently waited many lifetimes for its return. Better than anyone, he understood its intricacies and uncontrollable nature. It had become like a wild lion which only he had come close to taming. Now this interloping fool named Benedict had ruined everything by his interference.

Yalad had gained the ability from the calamus to understand certain things about men and events before they happened. Strangely, the sudden appearance of Benedict had eluded him. It occurred to Yalad that perhaps the preference of the calamus was toward Benedict. The thought of losing the calamus to another infuriated him. His face grew redder in anger until his voice thundered out an inarticulate yell which shook the ground and could be heard across the islands. The men fled in fear as Yalad easily grabbed the partition with one hand and flung it into the air where it flew out of sight.

Over seven thousand miles away on a sandy white beach in Japan, a young boy named Nestor sat cross-legged in a dazed state with the writing tool dangling from his fingers. He looked around to see where the man in white was who had asked him to make a drawing, but all he saw were some unfamiliar trees and miles of white sand. He looked down at his feet where he had just been drawing, and instead of seeing the picture of a man sleeping, all he saw were three words written. He had no knowledge of letters and words, but somehow he understood them and their meaning.

safe
guard
friend

The boy knew in his heart what each word meant as if someone had instantly taught him their meaning. *Safe* meant that Nestor was safe from the man who had made him draw. Nestor had heard about the man in white but had never met him. It was said by some that he was a god and others that he was a demon. Those in his village called him the Ageless One or the Father of Time. Nestor did not know what the man was. He only knew that when the men of his tribe told him to follow them because the man in white wanted him that Nestor felt weak in his knees. He was surprised when the man in white smiled at him and had asked him to draw something on the ground. Nestor liked to draw. He was always sketching images on the sand with sticks. Suddenly finding himself on unrecognizable beach away from his native island, Nestor felt no fear, for he knew he was now safe from the man in white.

The word *guard* impressed upon Nestor a seriousness greater than he had ever felt in his short life. The moment he saw the word in the sand, the stick in his hand glowed a fierce dark blue, and Nestor could feel its strength and he also felt that it yielded itself willingly to Nestor for safekeeping. It was then that Nestor understood that in some way, the stick had freed him from the man in white and brought him protection. He also felt that the stick held a power that others wanted for their own purpose and that purpose could be evil. For the rest of Nestor's life, the depth and seriousness of this impression never left him, and he vowed that he would guard the stick.

When Nestor saw the word *friend*, something unusual happened. He sensed the presence of God. He had never thought about God, and he was not certain what others meant when they had referred to the man in white as a god. He had lived among superstitious people and had assumed that their superstitions were correct. They would always sit in the boat in a certain order. They would cast their nets a certain way. If a dead fish was washed ashore in the morning, they would not fish that day, feeling it was a warning from the sea to stay away. This was the extent of young Nestor's religious understanding.

This presence was something different to Nestor. He did not know the name of the presence, but he could tell that it was a person and yet greater than a person. The stick was not the presence, but the stick showed Nestor that there was a presence. That same presence was the one who had impressed upon Nestor the seriousness of the word *guard*. Nestor did not know what holiness was, but the presence was right and true, and there was a greater fear that the presence produced than any fear the man in white exuded. Nestor could not define it. He only knew that one was good and one was bad. The good one was a friend, and Nestor knew that this presence would always be with him and help him.

"What are those markings?" spoke a voice behind Nestor.

Startled, Nestor turned quickly to see a man in simple clothes standing with a long spear in his hand. Nestor did not understand the words the man was saying and simply stared back. The man spoke again, repeating the words and pointing to the markings on the ground. Nestor shrugged his shoulders. The man stared intently at Nestor and could see that Nestor did not look like anyone the man had seen before. The man could see that the boy was confused and frightened and unable to understand the man's words. The man pointed to his mouth and motioned that he was putting food in his mouth. Then the man pretended to chew. After that, he rubbed his stomach and smiled. It was clear enough to Nestor that the man was asking him if he was hungry. Nestor smiled and the man beckoned him to follow. Nestor stood and followed the man away from the shore and into the brush.

The man was named Kaito, and he was the leader of his village. Kaito's wife Nara had never been able to have children. They adopted Nestor into their home and the family loved him as one of their own. Nestor grew into manhood and adopted the ways of his new family, their village, and their nation. He grew his hair long and he kept it atop his head tightly in a bun, held together by the stick he had brought with him. He learned to fish with his father and his life was blessed. Nestor married a girl named Taura and they had many children. He lived a long and happy life and worshipped and honored the God whose name he never knew. When he was dying he passed on the stick to his oldest son and admonished him to care and protect it. The son did so and the tradition was passed on from generation to generation. The family and the village were blessed because of the calamus. However, they were never aware of its power or importance. It had become a sacred family heirloom treated with respect and honor for the heritage it was associated with in their family.

For four hundred years, the tradition continued, the calamus protecting itself within the family who maintained its honor without knowing its nature. In 1909, a new boy was born into the family. His name was Jiro, which meant "second son." There was an older brother who had died two years after his birth and one year before

Jiro was born. When Jiro was five, he went fishing with his father. He had been in the boat with his father many times watching him, but today was the first day helping his father. When they launched out early in the morning, the weather was warm without a cloud in sight; however, soon after, storm clouds quickly approached. Before the father was able to right the ship and get back to shore, they found themselves being uncontrollably tossed about by the waves. Jiro was frightened while his father tried to remain calm. Suddenly in the midst of the storm, they sighted a ship in the distance. Moments later, there was a loud boom and they realized that the ship was firing. With the sea tossing and turning and blasts coming from the vessel, Jiro never knew as their small ship broke apart, if it was hit by one of the ships cannons or by one of the waves.

Within seconds, the small vessel was smashed to pieces. Jiro called out to his father who was clinging unconsciously to some wood. Jiro reached out to hold on to his father. He tried to grasp his father's hand, but the sea suddenly lifted and Jiro clutched his father's hair instead as he closed his fist. As Jiro cried out, another wave quickly arose, separating Jiro and his father. All that Jiro had was a few strands of his father's hair and the stick that had held his hair together. The two drifted apart with Jiro's father straddling some broken planks from their boat. Jiro reached out for a piece of wood and clung to it with one hand while the other held on to the calamus.

Jiro fearfully clung to the wood, gradually drifting farther and farther away from his father until Jiro was just a small dot in the ocean floating up and down with each wave. One moment, it was as if he were on top of an enormous mountain and could see miles of water in every direction, and the next moment, he seemed to be in a deep valley surrounded by menacing towers of waves. He cried out in fear, desperately clinging to the small board and the stick—the only reminder he had of his father. His legs began to get numb from the cold water, and he longed to be on dry warm land once again. Eventually he passed out, and when he awoke, he was on the shore of an island a few feet away from a sleeping man.

Jiro sat up and looked around. The island reminded him of home, and at first, Jiro thought that maybe he had landed back on his island, just not near his home. He decided to look for his house. He walked around the island, discovering that it was actually quite small and soon realized that he was not at his home. He tried to wake the man up, but the man seemed to be either dead or in a very deep sleep. The man did not look like Jiro. His skin was very pale which made Jiro think that maybe the man was dead.

Jiro took the stick and began to draw despondently in the sand. His stomach growled, reminding him how hungry he was and he instinctively drew a plum. The moment he did a plum appeared next to the drawing. Jiro laughed and picked up the plum. He brushed off the sand and took a bite. As the juice rolled down his chin, Jiro thought that it was the most delicious plum he had ever tasted. He ate the plum and drew another. When he was done, he lay exhausted on the sand and quickly fell asleep, his body aching from his ordeal. He slept for a few hours and awoke refreshed. The man was still there. Jiro sat up and looked at the stick, wondering for the first time how the plums had appeared. He was too young to consider the why of something but he had a wonderful thought. What if he could draw the man being awake? Would it happen just as it had with the plum? Jiro started to draw in the sand a picture of the man who was next to him. He drew him standing at the water's edge facing the ocean. When Jiro looked up, he couldn't believe what he saw. It was just as he had drawn. After a few moments, the man turned and looked at Jiro. It was then that Jiro wondered if the man had been on one of the ships that had fired the cannons. He decided to draw in the sand the image of rescue ships coming to help him. As the man from the shore drew near, Jiro looked up and saw ships just offshore with small boats approaching.

Jiro was taken to the large ship by one of the smaller ones. The men on the ship seemed very friendly as they directed him into a room and gave him some food. He was afraid that they would take his stick, but instead, one of the men pointed to some paper on a table in the room and told him that he could draw on that with his pen. It was the first time that Jiro had ever considered that the stick was in fact a pen. The men left him alone in the room. By now Jiro knew exactly what to do. He drew a picture of his mother and father in their home with him holding their hand. The last thing he drew was the pen back in his father's hair. When he was done drawing, he laid his head on the table and closed his eyes. When he opened his eyes, he was home with his mother and father.

Jiro didn't tell his parents about the pen. When he asked his father how he was rescued from the sea, his father looked at him strangely and asked what he meant. Jiro did not pursue the matter. It seemed from his family's point of view, the event had never happened. Jiro did not care. He was home with his family. Maybe it was all a dream. He slept deeply that night, and when he awoke the next day, life was back to normal, except that Jiro couldn't stop thinking about the pen that was holding his father's hair. Maybe it had not been a dream. Maybe the pen was magical, and now Jiro had the desire to use it again.

The idea occurred to him that he could make his father's boat the biggest and best boat in the town. Until then, Jiro had never envied anything that others had. He was very happy in his home, living the life of a fisherman's son. He did not understand riches or fame. But now, with the pen, he could have whatever he wanted, and in his small world, what he wanted was a boat so great that it would be the pride of the town. People would come from miles around just to see their boat. All the other boys in the town would look differently at Jiro. That had not mattered to him before, but now it was in Jiro's heart that he be seen as a great fisherman. The greatest in the world. Even better than his father.

Late one night, he snuck into his parents' room while they slept. The pen was on a table where his father left it while sleeping. Jiro walked quietly toward the desk with one eye on his father and mother. Gently he picked up the pen and walked back to his room where he drew the finest boat that he could imagine. He gave it three large sails. At the end of the ship, he drew a rope pulling a smaller ship. When he was done, he had one last moment of inspiration. He drew himself standing proudly on the ship and his name written in large letters along the side of the ship. Jiro sat admiring his design before suddenly remembering that he had to get the pen back into his parents' room. He took the drawing, folded it, and then placed it under his mattress. It took a while for Jiro to fall asleep; he was so excited to see what he would find in the morning.

He awoke the next day to the noise of people shouting. He looked outside his window and could see men running about frantically. Tree branches, nets, and broken boats seemed to be strewn about everywhere. Jiro saw his father running toward his boat, his long hair uncharacteristically flying about in the wind, untied and without the stick holding the bun. Jiro knew it was a shame for a man to be seen with his hair undone, and only an emergency would cause his father to appear in such a manner. Jiro jumped out of his bed and ran into the kitchen. His mother was standing anxiously at the window wringing her hands.

"Mama, what is happening?"

His mother turned to Jiro. She had forgotten that he was still asleep.

"How did you sleep through the storm?"

"There was a storm?" answered Jiro as he ran to the window and stood next to his mother peering out.

"About an hour ago," said his mother. "It tore through here so fast no one had time to prepare. It came as a complete surprise."

Jiro was nervous, for now he was beginning to wonder if somehow the stick had brought about the storm.

"Is that why father is not wearing his hair up?"

"No," said Jiro's mother. "He was in a hurry, and it must have been torn away by the wind. If he cannot find it and our boat is destroyed, I am not sure which will be more upsetting. What did we do wrong to deserve this?"

Jiro's mother sat down and wept. Jiro headed toward the door.

"Do not go out, my son. It is too dangerous."

"I have to go, Mama. I must try and find the stick."

Jiro ran out of the house. The wind was still fierce, but the worst of the storm had moved back out to sea. He ran down to the water to find his father and to see if there was any damage to the boat. The front was broken up from crashing into a tree, but the remainder was still intact. Jiro ran to his father's side and started to help him pull the boat away from the tree. His father looked at him, the wind whipping his hair about his face.

"Go back to the house, Jiro. It is still not safe out here," he cried out.

"But, Father, your stick is missing," yelled Jiro, but his father was not listening. He was trying to pull some boards away that had caused the boat to jam between two trees. The father looked back at Jiro and this time with some anger in his voice yelled at Jiro.

"Go!"

Jiro looked at his father with desperation before turning to flee. He ran back to the house, tears streaming down his face. He knew this was his fault. He had been deceptive with the stick. The stick had helped him, and now he had not only lost the stick but hurt his father. Jiro ran around the house fruitlessly searching for it. Finally, his mother came out and grabbed him, pulling him back into the house where Jiro ran to his room and cried.

The stick was never found. His father replaced it with another one, but there was a great sadness that a precious family heirloom passed down for hundreds of years was no longer theirs. The boat was repaired shortly. A family living off the fruits of the sea could not survive long without one. Everyone pitched in to help each other out. The sudden storm was talked about for many years and most believed that some type of curse or punishment had come on the small town, but no one was sure why. Life returned to normal for everyone except Jiro, whose guilt and shame silently clung to him as he grew older.

When Jiro was eighteen, his mother died of tuberculosis. After Jiro had been born, his mother was not able to have more children, leaving only Jiro and his father after her death. Jiro worked with his father on the fishing boat but also found work in the town cleaning at a local factory. Secretly he had vowed to help his father as long as his father lived, but he also wanted to be ready to leave when his father died. He had no desire to be a fisherman. He felt that he had dishonored his family with his greed, and if he could leave that world behind, then maybe the pain of his guilt would be eased. He never spoke of this to his parents for he knew they could never understand, and he didn't want to cause any further pain.

Six years after his mother's death, tuberculosis also took his father. Jiro was left alone with a small house and a boat. For generations, it was all his family had ever needed and now Jiro was going to leave it behind. He sold the house and boat and took his savings and headed toward the city of Nagoya where he heard that there were great opportunities for employment in manufacturing. The city was filled with people. Jiro hoped that the hustle and activity would help him fight off the feelings of constant guilt. He found a small room to rent and then began to look for work. Eventually he landed a job at an airplane manufacturing plant doing janitorial work. He didn't mind the manual labor. He loved the city and its fast pace. It took his eyes off his pain and kept him busy. On weekends, he would wander the city, walking for miles as he explored the many streets and shops. After he had earned some extra money, he bought himself a bicycle, allowing him to travel further away from his home.

One Saturday while peddling down a side street, he noticed a sign in front of a building. Jiro had never learned to read more than a few words; however, he did understand the words *Help wanted*. Even though he had a job, there was something about the building that intrigued him. He was not sure what the building was all about. There were no people around and in front of the building was a blue-and-white bus. Jiro decided to try the building's front door and see if it was unlocked. He rested his bike against a wall next to the cement steps and walked up to the front door. The door was open, and he walked into a large foyer. There was no one about. He wasn't sure why the building was so empty and still left open. He wondered if he should leave. Someone might take him for a robber. He turned around and headed toward the door. Just then, he heard a voice.

"Hello, can I help you with something?"

Jiro turned around and stared at the man. He was not Japanese. He was a westerner. His Japanese was understandable but not fluid. Jiro had seen westerners at the plant and sometimes overheard their language, yet this was the first time that he had heard a westerner speaking Japanese since the time he was a child and had met that strange man on the island. It never occurred to Jiro until now just how extraordinary it was that the stranger on the island had spoken such fluent Japanese. The man stepped closer to Jiro and pointed to the sign.

"Are you here to apply for the job?" he asked kindly.

For some reason, Jiro nodded his head yes. He was not really sure why he was there. Mostly out of curiosity, for he already had a good job and did not want another. Besides, this place was much too far to travel everyday if he were to have two jobs. Still, there was something about the man and the place that drew him. He wasn't sure what it was, so he followed the man who told him that they could talk in his office. As they walked, the man described what the job was about. He needed someone who could do a little of everything. Clean, fix things, and help the teachers in any way needed. It was only after Jiro heard the word *teachers* that he realized that the place was a school, which explained why no one was there on a Saturday.

"Normally, I'm not here on Saturdays," the man explained while they walked, "but today I had some matters to attend to. You are actually the first person to come and apply for the job. I just put the sign up about an hour ago. What is your name?" asked the man as they entered the office.

"Jiro."

"That means second son, doesn't it? Do you have an older brother?"

"No," answered Jiro. "He died when I was very young."

"I'm sorry to hear that." The man sat down in a chair behind his desk and motioned for Jiro to have a seat. Jiro sat down hesitantly, wondering just what he had suddenly got himself into. The man stared at Jiro with a slightly quizzical look on his face.

"Did you come here to apply for the job?" asked the man.

Jiro looked down at his hands. There was something about the man that Jiro could not put his finger on. There was a softness and kindness to him that made Jiro nervous.

"I'm not sure why I'm here," Jiro hesitantly replied. "I already have a job. I was riding my bicycle and saw your building. It interested me, and when I saw the sign, for some reason I decided to come in. I work at the airplane plant, and it is too far for me to travel every day. I would have to move to work here. I'm sorry to have bothered you."

The man smiled warmly and stood. "Nonsense. I'm glad you came. It kept me from having to do some dreaded bookkeeping. Since you came all this way, would you like a tour of the building and hear what we do here?"

Jiro instantly felt relieved. He nodded his head and the two stood. The man introduced himself as Father Joseph, and as the two walked the corridors, Father Joseph pointed out the different class-rooms and riddled off the teachers' names and subjects they taught. He then took him to a small cafeteria and kitchen area where every-one had their meals. As they walked, Father Joseph spoke a little about why he had come to Japan from America—to not only teach children but to tell them about Jesus and what He had done for them. Jiro did not know who this Jesus was, but he assumed he must be the person who paid for the building. There was a simple gar-den in the back that Father Joseph showed Jiro and told him that whoever did take the job would also be responsible for the garden. They entered back into the building through a side door, and Father Joseph pointed out the offices for the staff. One door was opened, and Father Joseph motioned for Jiro to come into the office.

"This is the office of the man who started all of this."

Jiro assumed it must be the office of this Jesus person.

"His name was Father Merriman. Sadly, he went home to glory a short while ago. He was a dear friend, and I am sometimes afraid this burden is too great for me without his guiding hand. I haven't decided yet what to do about this office. It seems a shame to move anything."

Jiro looked around the office. He was confused when Father Joseph mentioned a man named Father Merriman. Was he Father Joseph's father? Why was everyone called Father and who was this Jesus he was referring to? Where was his office? Father Joseph sighed and started to escort Jiro out of Father Merriman's office when Jiro noticed a framed photograph on the wall. Jiro froze. Father Joseph put his hand on Jiro's shoulder to lead him out of the office when he saw that Jiro was staring at the picture. Jiro's face had turned pale.

"Is something wrong, my son?" asked Father Joseph with concern in his face.

Jiro walked up to the photograph and stared intently. It was a picture of a man in the same office they were in. He was sitting behind his desk looking earnestly into the camera with a serious look. Behind him was the same bookcase that Jiro could see against the wall. There were books and papers on the desk, and the man had his hands on the desk. At the man's fingertips was the stick that had belonged to Jiro's father. It was unmistakable. Even though it was a black-and-white photograph, it seemed that as if Jiro could see the vivid blue glow of the tool that his father had used to pin his hair every day.

"That is Father Merriman," said Father Joseph. "It was taken shortly after the property was donated to us. We were having a difficult time getting started, finding a suitable building that was affordable and trying to get organized. Then a woman whom we had never met offered this building to us free of charge, asking only that we use the building for the Lord's cause, which we were eager to do. Since then, the school has been blessed. The picture was taken shortly after Father Merriman had settled into his office. I came in and took the photograph and then had it framed as a memorial for the occasion."

Father Joseph paused as he looked concerned at the young man.

"You seem particularly attracted to it Jiro. Does it mean something to you?"

Tears rolled down Jiro's face.

"Do you know how he obtained it?" Jiro asked.

"Obtained what, my son?"

"The stick on the table."

"That is a good question." Father Joseph sighed. "It was probably the only secret between Father Merriman and myself. He would never tell me its significance, but I would often come into his office and find him holding it in his hand. He would be transfixed. It was an unusual tool to which he seemed quite attached."

Jiro wiped away the tears from his eyes.

"Do you know what has become of the stick?" he asked.

"No, I do not. Father Merriman went back to the states shortly after settling in here. He intended on returning. However, he sadly passed away while journeying. He must have taken it with him, for though I have searched diligently, I have not found it. If you don't mind me asking, why is it so important to you? You seemed strangely moved by it."

Jiro thought back to the time when he found himself stranded on the island with the stick, thinking he had lost his father forever. Then, with the use of the stick, the stranger on the beach awoke, help came, and he was reunited with his family. But because of his greed, the stick was lost, this time forever, and he was alone with his guilt and shame. No one had ever known. There was a piercing pain in his heart, and he was overwhelmed with sorrow. He felt that if he did not speak his heart would collapse.

"It was my father's and my father's father, going back for generations. Because of me, he lost it when I was a child. I have never been able to forgive myself for its disappearance."

Father Joseph walked toward Jiro and put one hand on his shoulder. Jiro could not control himself any longer and bowed his head and wept uncontrollably. Father Joseph turned Jiro toward him, and Jiro buried his face into the priest's shoulders and sobbed. For some time, Father Joseph stood still as a statue allowing Jiro to let out the years of guilt and hurt that had piled up. Eventually Jiro stopped crying and lifted his head. Father Joseph gave Jiro a handkerchief for Jiro to wipe his eyes and blow his nose.

"I am sorry to burden you so," said Jiro with his head down while he continued to wipe his eyes.

"It is a burden I am glad to bear," replied Father Joseph.

The two walked silently out of the office and back toward the entrance to the school. When they reached the door, Jiro offered the handkerchief back to Father Joseph, but Father Joseph motioned for Jiro to keep it. Jiro tucked the handkerchief into a pocket and looked out the door into the bright sunlight. He could see that if he hurried, he would be back to his apartment before dusk. He would return to his small room and sleep and start another day back at the airplane plant. That day would come and go and then another. Suddenly the idea of going back seemed very bleak and uninviting. He realized that he had come to the city to find a place to hide from his thoughts. Now it all seemed to be just a lot of noise. He knew he never would go back to his town and be a fisherman like his father and his father before him, but he also knew that there was no joy in the place of escape he had created for himself. He turned back to Father Joseph, who stood silently at his side.

"Father Joseph, if I did apply for the job here, do you think that there is an inexpensive room that I could rent nearby should you decide to hire me?"

Father Joseph walked around to the front of the school and grabbed the help wanted sign and walked back into the foyer. He smiled broadly at Jiro.

"Did I forget to mention that the position includes room and board?"

Jiro smiled.

"Why don't you start on Monday. You can bring what you need from your apartment. We have a spot near the garden where you can keep your bicycle. Come, let me show you your room."

The two walked down the corridor toward the stairs that would lead to the room where Jiro would spend the rest of his days, serving joyfully in various capacities until one day he would be the headmaster of the school. As they walked down the hallway, Jiro had to ask one question.

"Father Joseph, when will I meet this Jesus fellow that you mentioned?"

14

Power Lost

Yalad was correct when he told Benedict that he did not think the two men with the gold coins would last long. Within an hour of their reward, they were robbed by two other sailors who in turn were robbed by three sailors from one of the other ships. The three men on their journey back to Spain got into an argument with four other men, and in the scuffle, the chest was thrown overboard. Much of it was found many years later by treasure hunters only to discover, much to their disappointment, that the gold had come with a curse. Misfortune befell any who managed to lay their hands on it.

Little of this mattered to Yalad who now found himself back to square one with the calamus. He knew eventually the calamus would find its way back to him. He had learned that from experience. It always did. However, something was different this time. Over the years, he had disposed of competitors in similar fashion, but he had never lost the child or the calamus in the process. This fool Benedict had somehow managed to inadvertently and temporarily rob Yalad. For that, he would spend the remainder of time in a blissful sleep. Yalad had waited for hundreds of years at a time, and he would wait again. Where the boy went was of little concern except it made Yalad realize that he had miscalculated Benedict's connection with the calamus. And that bothered Yalad.

Over the years, Yalad had come to define his desire to use the tool as a means to rob God's omnipotence, omniscience, and omnipresence. He had gained partial access to these attributes, yet he knew that he had only skimmed the surface. Through the calamus, he had gained the ability to mentally travel across space and time, and although he could never seem to directly find the calamus, he was able to get a sense of who may come into contact with the tool. This ability to anticipate had brought Yalad to the islands. He had no idea that a man named Columbus would one day travel, but he did know that there were islands to be found and that in time the calamus would reach those islands. Like Benedict, he had been able to tap into some of the ways of God's omnipotence. He too was immortal, but he had taken it much further than Benedict. Pain did not touch him, and unlike Benedict, Yalad was not affected by the ocean and its mysterious depths. One of the many skills he had obtained from the calamus was the ability to live and move under water. Unlike Benedict, who had died repeatedly from the pressure of the oceans depths, Yalad had managed many years earlier to overcome that difficulty.

After Yalad's attempt to obtain the calamus failed, he left the islands and moved to the main coast. Staying on the islands only reminded him of what he had lost and he always found that isolation seemed to help him focus. The locals were glad to be rid of him, for though most believed him to be some type of god, they had grown weary of his demands. His absence allowed them to revert back to superstition, and in time, Yalad had become the type of god who was associated with good and bad fortune. If life went well, it was because Yalad was not angry. If a child was misbehaving, they would be told to change their behavior or Yalad may bring evil upon them. Within a century, he had joined a long line of volatile deities whom the locals tried not to offend.

So, while Benedict slept on a remote island, Yalad walked. This experience with Benedict caused him to reevaluate his use of the calamus. Clearly, the calamus was connected to Benedict in a way that it had not been connected to others in the past. Yalad would have to be extra cautious when he next came upon the calamus. In the meantime, while he waited, he wandered, for that was his nature. Through the centuries, he had wandered through Europe, Asia, and Africa, but he had yet to walk upon this new land north of the islands. He walked north and south and east to west. He covered what would later become known as the Americas. He travelled through dense forests and over mountains. His hair and beard grew so long that he looked almost like an animal to the few Indians he would come across.

Yalad was unimpressed by the Indians. He saw them as simple in their ways and small in their ambition. The world was big to Yalad and was meant to be mastered. To Yalad, the Indians seemed content. Yalad could not understand contentment without control. He appreciated the fierceness they possessed but detested the almost religious fanaticism directed toward their identity. They would choose death over servitude and that was what made them useless to Yalad. He foresaw that the fruit of their autonomous nature would one day result in a conflict greater than their local squabbles. Knowing the power and advancement of European war and weaponry, it was clear that the Indian people were doomed. For this reason, their stubbornness and their passivity, he despised them. They were not worthy to be subdued. In his few encounters with the Indians, they would leave each other alone. Once however, he was walking, unbeknownst to him, toward a local tribe's burial ground. His head had been bowed as he walked when he suddenly heard the sound of a horse's step. He looked up to see eleven Indians on horseback blocking his way. All had their bows ready at their sides except an older man in the middle who sat calmly on his horse.

"You must turn back. You cannot pass through here," said the chief.

Yalad had gained from the calamus the ability to understand and speak languages. Normally, he enjoyed picking up a new language, but his distaste for the Indians left him uninterested. He continued to walk toward the burial site.

Immediately, each of the men on horseback raised their bows and pulled back their arrows. They waited for the old man's order. He lifted his hand slightly and spoke.

"I do not know if you understand my words, but if you continue, your dead body will be food for the crows."

Yalad sneered at the old man and spit on the ground. At his next step, ten arrows flew toward his chest. Eight of them were caught by his two hands. Two of the arrows found their way to his heart. Yalad slowly and deliberately put all the arrows he had caught into his right hand, and with his left hand, casually pulled the two arrows out of his chest. He smiled at the chief of the Indians, who now looked much paler.

"I understand your words. Now, understand what I am saying. I will show mercy only because you are not worthy of my sovereignty. But if you anger me again, I will order the birds to feast on your flesh until you are dead."

Yalad suddenly placed all ten arrows in his right hand and hurled them toward the leader's horse. All found their way immediately to the heart of the horse, which promptly collapsed. The old man rolled off the horse. Yalad calmly walked past the men and through their burial ground.

Word quickly spread. There walked a man who was not a man but something different, and the Indians steered clear of the strange man covered in hair. Yalad continued north until all that could be seen was a sea of ice. Along the way, he met groups of people living in strange ice houses. They marveled that Yalad did not seem to be bothered by the freezing snow. Yalad, who tended to see people as either being mastered or discarded, found these frozen nomads unique. Their isolation and daily fight for survival, not against man but against the elements made them appear almost as a different species. His dealings with them were the closest he would ever come to pity. On occasion, he would be invited to stay in one of their ice houses and help them hunt for food and fight off predators.

In time, Yalad moved south along the long western coast. The further south he went the more the weather reminded him of the islands. Along the way, he came across some Indians who had heard tales of a great spirit who walked the land as a man. Their chief made peace with Yalad and gave him their best horse as a gift. It was pure white without a mark. Yalad named the horse Salvaje. He rode the horse further south and then east until he came to the Yucatan coast where he met up with the Mayans. He reached the Mayans in Yucatan in 1520. They had experienced three attacks by Spanish forces in the last two years. At first, the Mayans were suspicious of Yalad and tried to kill him, assuming he was part of the Spanish army. Once they realized that Yalad could not die, like many cultures before him, they revered him as a god.

As the Spanish came in and slowly began to wipe out the Incas, the Mayans, and the Aztecs, Yalad began to realize that the world was bigger than he had ever imagined. It was clear that east was meeting west and that territory would be fought over. From all that he had seen in his travels, the Europeans would eventually extend themselves throughout the land.

Yalad had longed to live forever and be accountable to no one but himself. He had wanted the calamus, so he would not only have control over his own destiny, but like his father Nimrod, he wanted to rule over all mankind. Now he realized that it would be some time before the connection of cultures and lands would come together. He could rule locally, but that had only interested him for a short while. He now understood that all great world empires of the past were not literally world empires but simply empires that had commanded large portions of the earth. Yalad wanted more. He wanted to rule the world, and he could not do that until travel and communication converged.

Yalad was greatly impressed with the Mayan's level of education. That, combined with the advancement in travel, convinced him that a day was coming when communication, travel, and knowledge would meet. There would always be wars and superstition. Yalad wanted to be at the center of it. When the time came, he would need the calamus and he believed that it would come to him. He would wait. He decided to again move north to the coast that had reminded him of the islands. He could see that the new land would one day be populated like the ancient cities in the east. He would use this new land to ready himself for that day in which he could control all.

Yalad watched and waited. As the years rolled on, he watched as Europeans began to settle in on the east coast. They brought their religion and attempted to establish the rule of the land based on their beliefs. Yalad always preferred superstition over conviction. A man in fear could be brought to subjection, but a man of conviction was useless to Yalad. Still, he waited and watched. Along the way as the land was settled and migration moved westward, he began to build up a small fortune, while attempting to remain as unnoticed as possible. While some attempted to promote their religion among the Indians, Yalad witnessed what he had assumed would happen. The Indians were slowly being eradicated.

The steamrolling power of the European's marching across America was bringing the changes that Yalad needed. He would invest his money in whatever actions promoted the two ideas of transportation and communication. By the mid-1800s, he began to see his vision coming true with the Transcontinental Railroad, the invention of Morse code, and later the telephone. For Yalad, it was like watching a child taking its first steps. He did not know how it would eventually end, but he knew that once the two had matured enough, the calamus would present itself and he would be ready. Then in 1914, a strange and unexpected thing happened to Yalad. The powers he had obtained from the calamus were gone.

15

Power Gained

In 1914, on the other side of the world, Benedict realized that somehow he had brought the captain's ship back over three thousand miles to dock at Yokosuka. The benefits which once belonged to Yalad had been transferred to him just prior to being awakened. He wasn't sure how much Yalad had accumulated over the years, but the moment Benedict had returned the calamus to Christ at the cross, he had released his obsession to it. Now he possessed what he had willing given away. There had been a time when Benedict longed for many of the same things Yalad did, but after the cross, Benedict felt gladly submitted to whatever he possessed or did not possess. He thought of the verse from St. Paul, *I have learned in whatsoever state I am, therewith to be content.* Benedict, like Yalad, had sought others to bring about their will through a form of deception. Now Benedict was submitted to the will of the calamus. If he possessed some of its power, it would be at the behest of the calamus. However, he did not forget the last thing he had seen in the Spirit. Yalad must be stopped. A great evil was coming, and Benedict had seen Yalad's hand attempting to manipulate it through the use of the calamus.

The captain kept Benedict locked in his room for another day. Benedict felt no compulsion to leave, though he knew if he chose to, he could find a way. Besides, he wanted to keep the captain from getting into any trouble and he wanted to honor the captain for how he had been treated. Benedict had a great peace about what to do and what not to do. For the first time in his life, he sensed that he was being led instead of being driven, and if it was the Father's will for him to sit in a small room for an indefinite period of time, then he would do so with great joy and contentment.

When the captain returned, he came with some documents in his hand and two escorts. He asked the men to remain in the hallway while he spoke with Benedict.

"I apologize for keeping you detained for so long," said the captain as he sat in one of the chairs. He set the papers on a table and rubbed his hands through his hair.

"Is everything all right?" asked Benedict.

"Yes…yes, and I suppose also no," answered the captain. "I still don't know what happened, but I think you do and I also think that you will not tell me."

Benedict sat still as the captain examined his face, hoping that he might be wrong.

"Yes…well, we have discussed what to do with you. Some wanted to send you to America. However, we decided that it would be best for you to go to England. In England, you might have a better opportunity to remember who and what you are. You are going to be sent to England on the HMS *Triumph*. I have your papers here. I remember that you had told me your first name was Benedict, but I need your last name for the documents which will allow you to return."

Benedict had never heard of America and wanted to question the captain about the place but knew that it would only produce more questions from the captain, so Benedict nodded his head as if he understood. He was, however, not sure how to answer the captain regarding his last name. He had come from a town called Lubań and whenever he needed to refer to himself in any official capacity it was simply Benedict of Lubań.

"Luban," replied Benedict. "Benedict Luban."

The captain filled in the last name and handed Benedict the documents.

"These will ensure safe passage to England. I have vouchsafed for you, Benedict Luban. Many wanted you to remain here during the duration of the conflict, suspicious that you were a spy, but given the circumstances and our sudden safe return, I cannot in good conscience keep you here. Also, I think that your presence here produces unanswerable questions regarding what has happened and your absence may help us to move on to the tasks we have at hand. I don't know who or what you are, but I trust you. I am relying on your honor not to betray that trust. I have convinced our allies in Britain to trust you also."

As he handed Benedict his papers, an image of the captain at home with his family came into Benedict's mind. The sense of his experience was similar to when he was on the beach and the Spirit had taken him across the waters. The scene was so vivid it was as if Benedict had been transported to the room. He saw a woman, sightless with dark-shaded glasses, holding a cane in one hand. He felt an overwhelming sense of compassion on the woman as he stared at her. The woman removed her glasses and looked at him, and Benedict could see that she could recognize him and the others in the room. She stood, awkwardly at first, before feeling secure enough to walk confidently toward Benedict without her cane. Then the image suddenly vanished, and Benedict was back in the cabin room with the captain.

"You have a wife who is blind and uses a cane." It was not a question. The captain was startled by the statement.

"Yes, she was injured in a factory explosion. How do you know?"

"When you return home, you will find that she can now see your smiling face as she runs to you without her cane. You can trust me captain without knowing who or what I am. The one true God known by the name of Jesus has healed her. You are an honorable man. May God bless you for your kindness toward me."

Benedict walked out of the room as the stunned captain stood to his feet. One of the two men asked the captain if they were to escort Benedict to the British ship, and the captain, his back to the men, nodded his head slightly. He dared not turn around until the men had left lest they see the tears running down his face.

Benedict returned to London. It had been over four hundred years since he last touched his foot to English soil. As he walked the streets covered in some solid grey substance it seemed everywhere there were buildings. All of London seemed to be one building jammed next to another. Metal horseless carriages sped past him emitting black smoke. There was a time when Benedict enjoyed the bustle of the business crowd on the bridge, but he could always retreat to the country. Here it seemed that all of London was like living on the Old London Bridge. To Benedict the pace was breathless.

Men in uniform were everywhere. It was clear that Benedict had returned at a time in human history when war seemed to be in many places simultaneously. He wondered if this was the end of the world. In the Spirit, he had seen wars, but he could not be certain if he had seen the last war or if there even was a final war that would end all wars. A plane flew overhead as he walked, and he looked up at it in wonder. He had seen a few since Japan, but the sight never ceased to bring him to marvel.

"That sure is something," said a man in uniform standing next to Benedict.

"I don't think I will ever get used to it," answered Benedict.

"It is a most terrific sensation."

Benedict stared at him. "You have been in one?"

"Yes, many times. If you have not signed up yet and you are interested, you should certainly consider it. My name is Francis. What's yours?"

The man put out his hand and Benedict shook it numbly.

"What's wrong, my friend?"

"I'm sorry," answered Benedict. "It's just that a good friend of mine was named Francis. You reminded me of him."

"Was?" asked Francis.

"Yes, he died many years ago. I had not heard the name mentioned in many years."

Francis frowned. "Seems strange for such a common name."

"Yes, I suppose it is," said Benedict slowly as a thought began to form.

"Excuse me, Francis," said Benedict. "Do you know if men of the cloth are allowed to assist in any way in the war effort?"

"Do you mean chaplains?" answered Francis. "Of course. I'm sorry. I didn't realize that you were a chaplain. Anglican, I hope. But I suppose that's your business. The only reason I say Anglican is that you do not strike me as Catholic."

"Yes, Anglican," replied Benedict after pausing a moment to consider. "Do you know where I might sign up to help?"

"Two streets up, on the left," answered Francis sharply.

"Thank you very much," said Benedict as he started to walk down the street.

"Say, I didn't get your name," yelled Francis.

"Benedict. Benedict Luban."

"I would appreciate your prayers, Mr. Luban. I leave tomorrow."

"Will do," answered Benedict.

The moment the man had given his name as Francis, Benedict knew immediately that he wanted to serve as his friend Francis had served with the Hussites. Back then, Benedict served reluctantly at best, but now more than anything in the world, he wanted to make up for what he failed to do earlier. Memories of Francis ministering to the needs of the poor and the wounded flooded his mind and the disdain he had felt was now replaced with an urgent need to emulate his first and best friend. He opened the door to the building marked "Enlist Now" and stood in a line of about eight men. When he reached the front of the line, he was escorted to a small back office and asked to sit down. A man was sitting calmly at a table writing down some information in a large ledger. He had a tall thin frame and wire spectacles. When he was finished, he looked up at Benedict and gave a perfunctory smile. He pulled out a form and picked up a pen.

"Name," said the man as he began to put his pen to a form.

"Um, Benedict Luban."

"Which service do you wish to apply to?"

"Chaplain," answered Benedict.

"Denomination?"

Benedict paused and the man looked up. Benedict was not sure what the man was asking. He understood the word denomination, but he wasn't sure in what context the man was referring. He remembered the word Francis had spoken earlier.

"Anglican," replied Benedict hesitantly.

This satisfied the man at the desk, and he went back to his form.

"Papers please," he said.

"I'm sorry?" answered Benedict.

"Papers," repeated the man. "Ordination papers. Identification papers. What do you have to show for who and what you are?"

Benedict stared doubtfully at the man. Then it occurred to Benedict to give him the papers that the captain had given to Benedict. They were folded in the inner pocket of a suit that the captain had provided for Benedict before he boarded the British vessel. He pulled them out and handed them to the man at the desk. The man stared at them for some time before looking up.

"What are these?"

"I was travelling by ship when there was an accident. I was marooned on an island, and it was the captain mentioned in the documents who found me. I was taken back to Japan where I was eventually released. All I owned was lost at sea. He gave me these papers when he sent me back by ship."

"What vessel?"

"The HMS *Triumph*," answered Benedict.

"Do you have any family members who can confirm your identity?"

"No, they are all dead," answered Benedict.

"Where were you serving?"

"My first duty and so far only one was on the ship just before she went down."

The man looked suspiciously at Benedict.

"What ship?"

"The SS *Volturno*," said Benedict quietly, as if he were remembering the very moment it sank. The truth was he had never heard of the SS *Volturno* until he was returning from Japan and he overheard one of the sailors talking about the recent tragedy that killed over five hundred passengers.

The man leaned back and put his pen down.

"I'm sorry. I heard about that. Terrible disaster that was. Terrible."

The man leaned forward and wrote on his form. He stamped it and handed it back to Benedict.

"We are in great need. Otherwise, I would require you to find a way to secure more official documentation. You are officially Benedict Luban CF4. You will report to the address shown on the paper tomorrow at 6:00 AM for your orientation and assignment. You will be trained for combat. However, your primary function will be that of serving the men in the capacity and manner of chaplain. The details of that will be explained to you tomorrow. Thank you for your commitment to your country."

The man handed a document to Benedict.

"CF4?" questioned Benedict.

"Chaplain to the Forces, Fourth Class," answered the man. He looked up at Benedict. "It is the lowest of the ranks among chaplains. We are glad to have you serve. However, given your lack of documentation, that is the best that I can do."

"I understand," replied Benedict. "Thank you."

With that, the man stood and saluted Benedict. Benedict had seen the men on ship salute and returned a similar salute to the man behind the desk. He left the building and searched for the address he was given so that he would know where to go the next morning. He had been given some money by the Japanese captain, and when the men on the HMS *Triumph* heard that he was returning with nothing but a few pounds, they took up a collection for him. That night, he found a room to lodge, and early the next morning, he was officially a chaplain in the English Army.

Benedict did not feel a need to "redeem himself" by serving the way he had seen Francis with the Hussites so many years ago. He just wanted to experience the joy he had seen in Francis when he watched him serve. It had always been a mystery to him whenever he observed Francis. He could appreciate the heart of Francis, but if he were honest with himself, Benedict knew that he just did not care about others. But something had happened. He now had an intense desire to help and assist others. He had wanted for so long to obtain power from the calamus, but now that its properties had been transferred to him, Benedict had no desire to utilize them unless the Spirit propelled him to do so, as was the case with the Japanese captain and his wife. Benedict did not want the calamus to be a cure all for humanity. He did not feel it was what the Spirit was leading him to do. His joy in serving was not determined by the use of the calamus. Benedict felt that he could slog around the mud helping the soldiers with or without the power of the instrument. He was free from it and yet commander over it.

The spirits of the prophets are subject to the prophet, he mused.

After a short period of orientation and training, Benedict was sent to the front lines in Belgium, which the German forces had been attacking since the beginning of the war. The expectations and training for the chaplains had been general and unspecific. They were there to minister to the spiritual needs of the soldiers. The army was focusing on the training of soldiers to fight while the chaplains were being brought in under the assumption that they had been previously prepared as chaplains. For Benedict, it was an ideal situation since he was free to minister in any way that was needed. When soldiers were injured, he assisted the doctors. When there was no doctor, he did what he could to relieve the pain and help stop any bleeding. His joy was often infectious in an environment filled with tension and suffering. Benedict would comfort, counsel, and pray with the soldiers. He was often asked to hold impromptu services and Bible teachings. It had been hundreds of years since Benedict had read or studied the Bible, and even then, it was done reluctantly. At first, he was certain that the men must have been somewhat skeptical of his grasp of scripture.

He carried a Bible with him, and whenever he had a free moment, he would read it voraciously. He remembered in his vision those who had broken away from the Catholic Church and put the emphasis on the Word of God, and he could see now what they had found. He read the book of Romans as if for the first time, and his eyes were opened to what the apostle Paul was teaching. His chapel services and small Bible teachings came alive, and many men were saved. Benedict would spend eight days on the front line and then be moved back to a reserve trench, and after that, four days would be spent in a rest camp where he would often hold his larger services. Whenever there was a need to spend more time on the front lines because of a shortage in manpower, Benedict would gladly volunteer. At first, he was offered a gun, but he refused to use it. This did not bode well with some of the other soldiers, and they questioned his nerve and loyalty.

One day, a man was left wounded out in "no man's land," the open area between the trenches. It was considered suicide to go there alone, especially during the day. The man was lying down as if dead, but the men could hear him calling for help. When Benedict heard his screams, he immediately climbed out of the trench and retrieved the man. Bullets whizzed around him, yet none managed to hit either him or the man he was carrying. When he returned to the trench, the man was laid onto a stretcher, and it quickly became apparent that the man was in a German uniform. Immediately, every soldier's gun was aimed at the man. The German haltingly lifted his hands in pain, grimacing from a wound to his shoulder. The man was crying out in German, but no one could understand his pleas for mercy. Benedict leaned down and in German asked the man his name.

"Klaus," answered the man, who showed a sudden relief that someone could understand him.

"Wait a second, Padre," interrupted one of the soldiers and turned toward Benedict suspiciously. His name was Thomas and he had been one of the more vociferous of those who were not happy that Benedict had refused to carry a gun.

"You speak German?" he said incredulously.

"Yes," answered Benedict. "My aunt was German. Her husband died and she lived with us while I was growing up."

This seemed to satisfy the soldier. He turned his gun on the German.

"Tell him to give us one reason why we shouldn't put a bullet in his brain right now. Ask him," commanded the soldier to Benedict.

Benedict leaned forward and explained to the German soldier that the men wanted to kill him and that he better have something to offer. Otherwise, he would not live much longer. The German quickly spoke, pointing back to where he came from, pleading with Benedict for the men to hold their fire.

Benedict looked up at Thomas.

"He says please don't kill him. He will trade information for his life."

Thomas put the gun up to the German's face.

"Talk," he yelled.

The German realized that he was not in a position to barter, and so he spoke rapidly. When he was done, everyone looked eagerly at Benedict. Benedict stood.

"He says that eighty meters up is a small trench with two British soldiers. They were captured a week ago and have been left to die. They have serious injuries. They would have been shot, but a shell hit the trench and took out the remaining German soldiers."

"It sounds like a trap," growled Thomas. "Ask him why he was in the middle of 'no man's land.'"

The German spoke for a minute, and Benedict translated.

"He said that he survived the shell but in his confusion went the wrong direction. He thought that he was retreating."

There was quiet for a few minutes while the men considered what had been said. Eventually Thomas spoke up.

"I don't believe him. I think it's a trap."

"What if it's true and two of our men are there?" said a man behind Thomas.

Thomas angrily turned to the man. "Then you go get them if you're so sure. We got fire coming at us at five hundred meters. You think you can dodge their bullets for three hundred and twenty meters, because if there are two of our men, then that's two one hundred and sixty round-trip meter runs for each man, assuming this Kraut ain't lying."

The other man stood silently as did everyone else.

"I'll go," said Benedict.

The men looked at Benedict, and one of them offered him their rifle. Benedict nodded his head no. He looked down at the German, who even though he did not understand Thomas's words could tell that the Brit did not believe him. The German looked pleadingly at Benedict.

"Are you sure?" said Benedict to the German, who nodded his head.

Benedict went to the ladder, taking one last look at Thomas.

"It's your funeral, Padre," was all Thomas said.

Benedict started running across the Belgium wasteland, praying that God would keep the buzzing bullets from striking him. He was not concerned about being shot, but he did not want to have to try and explain to others how he had survived. A few bullets pierced his coat before Benedict was able to slide into the trench. He quickly looked around and saw that it was indeed empty except for the two British soldiers. Benedict found some blankets nearby and covered the soldiers hoping that it might provide some relief should a bullet strike. He picked up one man and leaned him against the wall of the trench next to the ladder. With one hand, he held him up while grabbing the other man and pulling him up. Benedict could feel the unnatural strength that he had acquired from Yalad as he hoisted one soldier on each shoulder and climbed the stairs. Praying once more for God's protection, Benedict ran as fast as he could across the eighty-meter field. When he reached the trench, he quickly lowered the men down while still in harm's way of rifle fire. When he was done he rolled into the arms of his men who were cheering madly.

Thomas was the first to greet him.

"Not bad, Padre, and in one trip no less."

Benedict looked down at the German who was gratefully smiling back. Benedict turned to Thomas.

"This man does not deserve to die. Take him as a prisoner but don't shoot him."

Thomas rubbed his chin. "A deal's a deal. Besides he may have more to tell us. We'll take him back when our relief comes."

After this, no one questioned Benedict's loyalty or bravery. Before the end of the war, Benedict performed a number of rescues and the men realized that he possessed a strange and unusual fearlessness which left them in awe.

Benedict's desire while serving was to aid as much as possible without using the power that had been transferred to him from Yalad. The Spirit had impressed upon him that if there were times for Benedict to use those powers, it would let him know. It was usually when it was unnoticed by others. There were times when soldiers would be injured, and Benedict would pray for them. As he laid his hands upon them, he could sense that they were being healed. When Benedict was back at the rest camp, he would visit soldiers who, while not seriously injured enough to go home, clearly were suffering "shell shock." Benedict would often pray for them and place his hand upon their head, and he would sense the peace of God restoring them.

As the war ended, Benedict began to discern that the Spirit was leading him to pursue a medical career. He felt it had something to do with Yalad, the calamus, and the convergence of evil he had witnessed in his vision. After the war ended in 1918, he returned to England and enrolled at the University of Oxford to study medicine. There was a secret delight in knowing that the same Spirit that was in him to heal was now leading him to help others by natural means.

16

To Seek and to Save

Father Merriman had been given the name Xavier Leo Merriman by the orphanage to which he had been abandoned by his mother at his birth. She was young, unwed, and had become an embarrassment to her family. She lacked the maturity and means to care for the young boy and could think of no other solution for her inabilities. It was a Catholic institution run by caring nuns and overseen by a board of Fathers. Together, they combined the orphanage with the various functions of the church to meet the many needs of the local community while also sending missionaries abroad.

Like the other children in the orphanage, at a certain point, Xavier understood that he had been abandoned by his parents. This knowledge that the children ultimately acquired affected them in different ways. It was an understanding that only later in life would they be able to evaluate its effect on their thinking and their decisions. As children, they were simply children. Some would have been a handful of trouble whether or not they had been abandoned. Many, however, found that the kindness of the nuns and priests was enough to help them grow into well-adjusted adults in spite of the absence of a parent's presence.

Xavier fell into the latter category. As he grew, he developed into an intelligent student who had an avid curiosity about the world around him and his place in it. In one of the classrooms, there was a large map of the world. Xavier loved to stand in front of the map and examine the different countries and imagine what it would be like to travel to a faraway place. He would read books about different countries and cultures and found himself over time increasingly drawn to the country of Japan. The image he gathered from the few books he read was that of a people who were both somewhat wild yet modest. He loved to read adventurous stories of the Samurai and Xavier thought of them as gentlemen warriors.

Each child was required to learn a trade so that by the time they were of age they could lead independent lives. A few, such as Xavier, decided that they wanted to be priests. Xavier studied at the seminary, and after passing all of his courses, he set his sight on starting a work in Japan. The first missionary work by the Jesuits had been attempted in 1547 by a man named Francis Xavier. There had been some success, but cultural differences had made it often difficult to gain any headway. By the middle of the seventeenth century, Christian work in Japan had become virtually nonexistent. It was not to begin again until the middle of the nineteenth century. The doors were now opened, though there was not much encouragement to pursue such a work. Nevertheless, Xavier felt that it was time to attempt a work in Japan and he began to seek support. A fellow colleague at the seminary named Father Joseph Goodson had similar aspirations, and together, they eventually were able to obtain the necessary means and permission to travel. By 1938, they were in Japan scouting out the best location to begin their work.

Shortly after arriving, Father Xavier's life would change with the discovery of the calamus. Father Joseph and he had been in Japan about one month, living in an apartment and trying to find an affordable building for their base of operations. One day, Father Xavier was walking the streets of Nagoya when he came upon a small store. He went inside and began browsing, not really sure what he was looking for. As he walked through the store, he came across the calamus. It was sitting on a shelf among other similar sticks, but this one stood out with its unique blue color. Father Xavier picked it up and rolled it around his fingers. The shading seemed to change as he did so. He tried the same with the other sticks, but they did not have the same reaction. Father Xavier walked over to the counter and motioned to the owner with the stick. He did not know the words to say to ask about the purpose of the stick, so he just raised the stick in one hand with a shrug and a questioning look, hoping that the owner would understand. The owner looked puzzled for a moment and then smiled broadly, pointed to his hair and said "kanzashi." Father Xavier, who was just starting to learn the Japanese language, assumed that the stick might aid in holding hair up.

As impractical as it was for Father Xavier, he felt drawn to purchase the item. He decided to also buy a pen, along with a brown leather journal. As he walked back to the apartment, he felt a little foolish about buying the stick, wondering how he would justify the expense to Father Joseph. When he reached the apartment, he was grateful that Father Joseph was not in. Father Xavier sat at a small table that was in their kitchen area and took out the pen and journal. He set the stick on the table, debating on whether he should hide it from Father Joseph, all the while feeling more and more foolish for buying it.

Leaving the stick for the moment on his desk, he picked up the pen he had purchased, opened the journal, and began to write a list. Father Joseph and he had engaged in many conversations about what they would need and like to have in Japan. They had agreed that the best way to make inroads into Japan with the Gospel would be to provide a school where children could not only learn the Gospel but also the English language. In time, they would also like to begin to offer various trade trainings. Father Xavier began to make a list of all the things that they would need.

He put the pen to the paper and attempted to write, only to discover that the ink would not come out. He tapped the pen on the paper a couple of times and tried a second time with the same results. Looking at the tip of the pen closely, he then tried once again to write. Irritated that nothing was coming out he tossed the pen onto the table and sat back, running his hands through his hair. As he did, his eye caught the stick. Father Xavier picked up the stick and looked at it closely. It was then that he noticed for the first time that one end of the stick looked different from the other end. It occurred to him that maybe the stick was not a stick but some type of pen.

He decided to see if it would write and to his surprise found that it worked perfectly. He felt great relief about explaining his purchase to Father Joseph.

Father Xavier wrote out his wish list.

It was a very specific list of the type of building and property that both he and Father Joseph envisioned someday owning. And as a wish list it also included the types of amenities that went beyond the practical, such as a pool, garden, and an additional building just for meetings. When he was done writing, he set the pen down and leaned back in his small chair, closing his eyes in prayer. He put the list before the Lord and asked that for the benefit of Japan God would bless. He then thanked God for his faithfulness and rose to make some tea for himself. The kitchen was an extension of the one main room and contained a refrigerator and a small gas stove. Father Xavier heated up some water and found a fresh tea bag. He had a habit of unconsciously humming a tune until he realized what it was he was humming and then he would begin to sing the song. After some time of humming, while he stared absentmindedly at the tea kettle, he realized he was humming "Let All Mortal Flesh Keep Silence." As soon as he remembered the hymn, he began to sing with great gusto.

> *Let all mortal flesh keep silence,*
> *And with fear and trembling stand;*
> *Ponder nothing earthly-minded,*
> *For with blessing in his hand,*
> *Christ our God to earth descendeth,*
> *Our full homage to demand.*
> *King of kings, yet born of Mary,*
> *As of old on earth he stood,*
> *Lord of lords, in human vesture,*
> *In the body and the blood;*
> *He will give to all the faithful*
> *His own self for heavenly food.*
> *At his feet the six-winged seraph,*
> *Cherubim, with sleepless eye,*

Veil their faces to the presence,
As with ceaseless voice they cry:
Alleluia, Alleluia,
Alleluia, Lord Most High!

Just as Father Xavier was finishing his alleluias, the kettle began to whistle, and at the same time, he could hear Father Joseph pounding his feet up the rickety stairs outside the apartment. Father Xavier walked back to his chair, tea in hand, and sat down just as Father Joseph burst through the door, face flushed and out of breath.

"Goodness, Joseph," said Father Xavier as he set the cup down. "You're completely winded. Is anything the matter?"

Father Joseph paced the room excitedly.

"Dear brother, you will not believe what just happened. It is the most fantastical thing! I am overwhelmed."

"What?" exclaimed Father Xavier. "Tell me, what is wrong?"

"Nothing, Xavier," answered Father Joseph. "Everything is right. More right than we could ever dream."

"Then tell me, brother, while I drink my tea and please sit down."

"I can't, Xavier. I'm too excited."

So, while Father Xavier sipped his tea, Father Joseph stood in the center of the room and told his tale of how he was approached by an elderly Japanese woman who told him that God had spoken to her about giving him a piece of property that she owned. Her husband had been a naval captain who had retired and purchased the property with the intention to use it as a school. He had passed away about a year ago, and she did not feel that she could continue the work on her own. She had contemplated selling the property, but while praying in her garden, the Spirit of God spoke to her about donating the property. She would meet a man whom God had chosen. As soon as she saw Father Joseph, she knew he was that man. She took Father Joseph to the place and showed it to him. As Father Joseph began to reel off the features of the property, Father Xavier looked down at his wish list, and picking up the calamus, began to check off one by one the different features that Father Joseph had listed.

After Father Joseph finished, he stood still, breathing heavily, somewhat exhausted by the afternoon, his rush back to the apartment, and his enthusiasm over everything he had just listed off to Father Xavier. Xavier sat still, staring down at his paper in wonder. Every item from the most practical to the fanciful was checked off as if each was as important as the other. He slowly set the writing tool down.

"Father Xavier, did you hear what I just said?" exclaimed Father Joseph, who felt that Father Xavier's mind was somewhere else. He couldn't understand why Father Xavier was not as enthusiastic.

Father Xavier slid his paper across the table and motioned for Father Joseph to sit down. With a puzzled look, Father Joseph sat down and picked up the paper. In his earnest telling of his story, he could not recall if Father Xavier had been writing the description of what he was saying as he spoke.

"Did you just write this down?" he asked.

"Yes, but before you arrived," answered Father Xavier.

"But it's everything I said we were getting. How is that possible?"

"Do you know who I feel like right now?" said Father Xavier with a chagrined smile. "I feel like the men in Acts who do not believe the maid Rhoda when she says that Peter is not in prison but at the front door. Before you came back, I had written this list and was praying over it. It is not possible that we should get exactly what we are asking for, but God says all things are possible with Him. I think we just witnessed a miracle in answer to prayer."

So God provided, and his servants began the work. The donation was as ready-made as they could have imagined. Father Xavier set up his office, and the two began their first year with an eager enrollment. Staff and students came almost as quickly as the building itself. Just prior to the first day, Father Joseph had come into Father Xavier's office and taken a picture of him sitting at his desk. He later had it enlarged and framed as a gift. Father Xavier hung it on the wall of his office. In the picture could be seen the calamus. Once, Father Joseph had asked about the strange pen possessed by Father Xavier. Father Xavier told him the story of how it had been purchased and how he almost, out of embarrassment, did not tell Father Joseph about the purchase. But that was all he said. He did not tell Father Joseph that he was increasingly becoming convinced that somehow this strange pen had brought about the sudden success of the school. He kept the pen with him at all times, praying, waiting, and pondering its mystery.

One day shortly into the first semester of their second year, Father Xavier received a letter from his mother who had found his address through the orphanage. She said that she was dying, and if he could return to the states, she would like to see him once before she passed. In the letter, she mentioned that she had married and that her husband had passed some months back. He had left her with quite a large sum of money, and she had never had any other children. Her desire was to give everything to Xavier. In her letter was included money for travel. Father Xavier told Father Joseph that he would need to take a brief leave of absence and that he would return hopefully within two months. He did not mention the money. He did, however, bring the calamus with him.

Since his first and only use of the pen, Father Xavier had often considered whether it was a coincidence that the pen and the answer to his prayer happened at the same time. As he lounged on the deck chair of the ship, a thought kept coming back to him. Was it any less divinely providential that a pen and not a prayer had brought about the miracle of the donation? Perhaps God was in both the pen and the prayer. The pen certainly was unusual in its appearance, and Xavier had to admit that he was reluctant to let it out of his sight. He would like to know if the pen actually had any divine powers. He had thought of using the pen again, but two things kept him from doing so. The first was that up until that moment on the ship he could not think of anything he wanted. The work had started miraculously and seemed as if it would continue. This was all that he had wanted. This is what he had felt called to do, and God was doing it through him and Father Joseph. He was not interested in fortune, fame, or any other source of self-fulfillment, which brought him to the second reason not to use the pen. Xavier sensed that the pen might not want him to use it for his own purpose. It seemed silly to him to think of the pen as having a will and he didn't think that the pen had its own will, yet he wondered whether the pen might be used to produce the will of God.

He did however want something now. He wanted to meet his mother. He had grown and come to understand why she had left him at the orphanage. He carried no ill will toward her. As a matter of fact, he had always been grateful that she had chosen the particular orphanage she had, because if not, he could easily have found a different, more difficult and harmful path in life. He had great sympathy for his mother and had always wanted to meet her, but the orphanage had no records of her whereabouts. He assumed that he had been born out of wedlock since in her letter, his mother mentioned that she had married and not that she had remarried. If he could meet his mother before she passed he might also be able to learn more about his father.

This concern of his to meet his parents was what drove him to consider using the pen again. As he sat on the deck chair, he prayed that God would be in the words he wrote down. He pulled out his journal and put the pen to paper, simply writing the following, "I want to meet my parents."

Xavier turned the journal over on his lap, still open, and closed his eyes. Soon he was asleep. When he awoke, he felt unnaturally refreshed. While he had closed his eyes, an elderly woman had sat in the deck chair next to him and was serenely gazing toward the sea. She had a long white shawl wrapped around her. The wind was blowing gently on her weathered face, brushing the remaining wisps of her hair behind her. She appeared completely content. She turned toward Xavier and smiled. He smiled back and nodded his head.

"What is that book that you are reading?" she asked.

Xavier picked up his journal and showed it to the old woman.

"It is just a journal. I like to write down whatever odd things come to my mind."

"Odd things?" inquired the old woman.

"Well, perhaps random is a better word. Thoughts, ideas, or if I am to give a sermon, I might write some notes down. Sometimes very plain things, like reminders. Don't forget to pick up some eggs. That sort of thing."

"I noticed that you were writing before I sat down. What did you write if you don't mind me asking?"

Xavier held the book in his hands and looked at it. For some reason, he couldn't recall what he had last written in the book. He remembered that it had some importance, and it didn't make sense to him that he would forget.

"You know, it's strange," he said to the woman. "But I can't remember what I wrote."

The old woman smiled like a little girl and clasped her hands together.

"Let's look. I want to see," she said excitedly.

Xavier looked at the woman. She didn't seem as old as when she had first sat down. There was a playful way about her that was very endearing. He grinned boyishly, caught up in her enthusiasm.

"Okay…let's see," he said.

He opened the book, as curious now as the woman to see the last thing he had written.

"I want to meet my parents."

The memory of the words came back to him. Below those words was written "1 Corinthians 2:9."

"What a lovely sentiment," said the woman. "You have never met them?"

"No," answered Xavier, looking down at the journal and trying to remember if he had written the verse down. Strangely, he wasn't even sure what the verse was.

"*But as it is written, Eye hath not seen, nor ear heard, neither have entered into the heart of man, the things which God hath prepared for them that love him,*" quoted the woman.

"That's such a beautiful verse," said the woman. "And so appropriate don't you think?"

"I must confess," replied Xavier, "that not only did I not remember that verse but I don't even remember writing it down. You certainly know your Bible. I feel a little ashamed."

"There is no need for shame here, my son. Only joy and the meeting of those who are to remain strangers no longer."

173

Xavier sat up and looked at the woman, only now she was no longer old. There was definitely a maturity to her, but it wasn't age. It was something else he had never seen before. She smiled warmly at him.

"Xavier," she spoke lovingly.

The moment she said his name he knew it was his mother.

"Mother?"

"Yes, Xavier."

"Am I dreaming?"

Xavier's mother laughed. It was a different kind of laugh than Xavier had ever heard. It was as if she were savoring the very sound, like the feeling one has taking a bite of something delicious as it rolls around their mouth, enjoying its taste and texture.

"I don't know if people actually ask that question when they are dreaming," she answered. "But, no, you are not dreaming. We are on the ship. We are crossing to the other side. The pen has given you what you asked for."

"You know about the pen? So it is the pen of God?"

"Yes, Xavier, and you have kept it well. It is unique, and I know very little about it and what little I know is only because you have been chosen to be one of its carriers. You used it once unknowingly, but not for your own purpose and once knowingly yet for the sake of love. However, one thing I do know about the pen is that it has been on earth since time began and many have attempted to use it for their own gain, much to their unhappiness."

"I did not wish for your death, though," answered Xavier. "I had just hoped to see you before your passing. I always wanted to know you."

"I know Xavier," answered his mother. "But the only thing that can be written is the will of God, and that was His will. It is your time, just like it was my time shortly after I wrote to you. We are united again. Not necessarily the way we would have chosen, but our ways are not His ways just as our thoughts are not His thoughts."

"And my father?"

"That has yet to be decided. His name is Emmanuel. My goodness, I just realized that you have never known my earthly name. It was Maria Cortez. I barely knew Emmanuel. We were young. He was handsome and yet had a wandering spirit. I was foolish not to have seen it. He left shortly after he heard that I was to have a child. I was frightened and my parents said it was in your best interest if I put you in more mature hands. I never saw Emmanuel again, but once I got to know the Master myself, I prayed often for his salvation. I have been watching your father through what some on earth call the 'crystal sea,' but since he is not yet redeemed, there is little I am permitted to view. That is why I said that our thoughts are not His thoughts. Only He knows all things, but love hopes all things and believes all things."

Xavier arose and walked toward the railing. His mother followed, and they stood together watching the sea. The ship was empty now. It was not the same ship he had boarded. It was much smaller and needed no helmsman. There were boats following alongside with bright upright figures.

"Who are they?" he asked his mother.

"They are your escort, Xavier. They are angels."

"Is this how you entered heaven?"

"All things are new and unique, Xavier. I was allowed to be with you because the will of the Father honored the will of the pen which honored the will of the user. I am with you because you wanted me with you, and it pleased the Father."

As Xavier's boat docked and he entered heaven, back on the ship where his earthly body lay, a young boy was passing the deceased body of Father Xavier and saw a bluish pen on the ground next to a brown leather journal. The journal did not look as interesting as the pen, which captivated the boy's eye. His name was Heinrich, and he liked to take things. Looking around to see if anyone was watching, Heinrich picked up the pen and tucked it under his coat before walking quickly back to his room.

Heinrich Otto Degler was travelling with his mother Sofia. Her husband Hans Degler had been part of the German Embassy staff sent to Japan in 1935. Hans, like Xavier on the deck of the ship, had died suddenly of a massive heart attack while serving in Japan. Sofia and her son Heinrich no longer had a reason to continue to live in Japan and were moving back to Berlin. This was unfortunate for Hitler because Sofia, unknown even to her husband, had been a capable spy working on behalf of the Third Reich. This was fortunate for Sofia, because while she was returning to an uncertain future in a country that was on the precipice of an unholy attempt to change the shape, face, and mentality of the world, she was secretly in love with Adolf Hitler. And while she had dutifully served with her husband and respected him greatly, she longed to be with Adolf and share his dream to rule the world. And Heinrich, unknown to all, had the calamus.

Approximately six thousand miles away in New York City, Yalad, who had changed his name to William Mortell, was quietly living in his penthouse apartment in the city. While he had lost the powers of the calamus, he had continued to accumulate wealth, waiting for the opportunity when that wealth may help him regain the calamus. As he read the papers, the name of Adolf Hitler increasingly became a subject of interest to the world at large. There was something about the man that reminded Yalad of his father Nimrod. One day as Yalad was walking down Central Avenue, he passed a magazine stand and noticed on one of the gossip magazines a picture of Hitler with the heading "Hitler and the Occult." Yalad normally did not find the gossip magazines of interest, but he bought a copy of the magazine and read the article about Hitler's rumored fascination with the occult and ancient relics.

The article was mostly idle gossip, yet there was something in the story that began to solidify in Yalad's mind that Hitler and the calamus may be linked. Yalad had money around the country, most of which was hidden from prying eyes. He decided to travel to Germany. As in the past, he trusted that he would be led to the calamus. Perhaps he could use this Hitler to restore his own greatness. So while Hitler was beginning his assault on the world, Yalad began his next attempt at recovering the calamus.

As Hitler began to descend upon the world, Sofia, Heinrich, and Yalad began to descend upon Germany, their paths narrowing to a point that would produce their respective collisions. Hitler wanted to conquer the world, Sofia wanted to conquer Hitler, and Yalad wanted, as always to conquer the calamus. Heinrich, who was too young to know what he wanted to conquer, was for the time being satisfied with being conquered by his own selfishness and greed.

17

Out of Control

Adolf Hitler had been standing alone in the room for some time. He was deep in thought with his hands clasped behind his back as he stared out the window. It was the spring of 1941. Thoughts of attacking Russia, the smell of Eva's perfume, and whether his stomach could handle liver dumplings for lunch all competed for his undivided attention. Unbeknown to Hitler however, Rudolf Hess, Deputy Führer of the Nazi party, was about to take it upon himself to fly a plane to England in order to broker a deal, thus possibly ruining Hitler's plans for Russia. Hess was slowly being pushed out of Hitler's inner circle by his former assistant Martin Bormann and needed to make a splash. Unfortunately for Hess, he would only be making waves. Had Hitler known Hess's intentions he might have set aside the dumplings for the moment, which were increasingly dominating any thoughts of Russia, and even Eva. He was in such concentration that he did not hear the door open when Sofia was led into the room with her son Heinrich. The door shut and he quickly turned around. Upon seeing the pair, he hurriedly walked toward them.

"My dear Sofia, I am so sorry for the loss of your brave husband Hans. You have served your husband so faithfully, and both of you have served the German cause equally with honor. Is there anything that I can do to help during this difficult time of grieving?"

Sofia blushed and hoped that Adolf would notice. She had lived a loveless marriage and had survived knowing that she was serving not only her beloved Fatherland but also the hero of all Germany. She had once met Adolf briefly before leaving for Japan as a spy in the German employ. At a large function, he had taken her hand and softly kissed it. Before turning his attention to her husband to discuss the couple's upcoming trip to Japan, he had looked into her eyes, and for a moment, Sofia felt as if he were trying to communicate his love to her with his hypnotic blue eyes. While in Japan, she served fearlessly, dreaming and wondering how she could ever be by his side again. She knew she was dreaming the desire of countless German girls, yet hoped that somehow she would be different. Sofia had kept her affections for Adolf a secret. She knew that should she express her affections mistakenly, Adolf might completely remove her and her son Heinrich from Germany. She had witnessed more than rumors of such things happening. Sofia bowed her head submissively.

"You are very kind, Mein Führer. My greatest sorrow is that we have had to stop the work in Japan."

Hitler smiled warmly and took Sofia's hand in his left hand. His hand trembled slightly until he placed his right hand over both their hands.

"Please, we are friends. Call me Adolf." With that, he brought her hand to his lips and gently kissed her fingers. Sofia's heart leapt while she kept herself composed and simply smiled.

Hitler abruptly stood back after the exchange and looked down at Heinrich. His arms stretched out in admiration.

"And this must be our young soldier Heinrich." Hitler beamed at the young boy. Heinrich stood proudly and saluted Hitler.

"Heil Hitler!"

Hitler returned the salute seriously, and when he had put his hand down, Heinrich followed suit.

"He is a fine boy, Sofia, and it is good for him to be back in the Fatherland. Germany will need boys as heroic as young Heinrich." He leaned a little closer to Sofia. Her face flushed with the thought that he might kiss her. Hitler did not seem to notice as he rested one hand on her shoulder.

"But he needs a brother and you need a husband. Do not grieve too long. Germany needs strong Aryan men like our brave, young Heinrich. You have served your husband in a difficult and distant post. It is time to serve your country at home. All German women need to build up the purity of the race." Hitler smiled a little conspiratorially. For a moment, Sofia was unsure whether Adolf was implying he was interested or suggesting the opposite.

"We have many fine officers who I would be happy to introduce to you."

Hitler was suggesting the opposite. Sofia's heart sank as she maintained the proper expression of embarrassment.

"I didn't mean to embarrass you, my dear Sofia. You have served faithfully, and you shall be taken care of."

Sofia regained her composure. "Of course. Thank you again, Mein Führer."

Hitler put his finger up and pointed it at Sofia. He wagged it slightly as he spoke.

"Adolf," he admonished.

"Yes…Adolf," said Sofia.

Hitler smiled at the two and then tousled Heinrich's hair as he walked the pair to the door. Sofia turned her head one last time to gaze upon the face of the man she secretly loved. The door shut behind her as a soldier walked Heinrich and her to a car waiting outside, instructing her all the way about where they would stay and what her new duties would be. As Sofia and Heinrich drove off in the chauffeured car, Eva Braun was just pulling up behind her, also in a chauffeured car. Sofia would never have the love of the man she idolized. That would belong to Eva. And while Heinrich Otto Deglar would live a long and selfish life, Sofia would not only fail to win the love of her leader, she would also fail to outlive the life of his mistress.

As Sofia was pulling out and Eva was pulling in, Yalad was attempting to find one Baron von Guttenheim, the leading seller of the rare and the unusual. Yalad believed that the calamus had found its way to Germany and that the natural magnetism that existed between them over the centuries would resurface with a little help. He did not necessarily know or even think that Hitler had the calamus. There was just something about Hitler and the time that gave him a sense that it was all connected. He knew he could not approach Hitler as if he were a man on the street asking directions to the nearest bakery; however, he felt certain that the presence of Hitler would bring him to the presence of the calamus. Yalad found the small shop of Baron von Guttenheim and opened the door. A bell above the door jingled.

"Guten tag," a voice called out.

Behind the counter in the musty store a small man with large, thick glasses was smiling at Yalad.

"Guten tag," answered Yalad. The old man's face lit even brighter.

"You are American!"

"I am from America," corrected Yalad.

"Ah…but you are not American. And your German is natural, but you are not German. Interesting. Interesting stories from interesting people. That is how I have survived all these years. Please come in and let me help you, or at least hear your story. My name is Baron von Guttenheim. I am the curator of my own eccentricities."

Yalad walked in, observing the oddities on the shelves, some behind glass, other's mounted on walls, and the rarities hidden in rich mahogany cabinets behind lock and key.

"William Mortell," replied Yalad.

"Yes, of course you are. William then, if that is not too familiar."

Guttenheim pronounced Yalad's name Villyam. Yalad nodded his head slightly without contest. Scattered about were various amulets and pendants. There were bowls with writings on their surface in various ancient scripts. A number of books were scattered about that appeared also ancient and mysterious. Yalad had seen them all before. From his childhood, he had seen people cling to these artifacts believing that they possessed some mysterious power. After the church had been established, the same thing happened in Rome with bones and pieces of the cross.

Yalad disdained the church as fools. He had always assumed that Jesus was just another failed user of the calamus, only Jesus had made the mistake of not using it for immortality. Instead, he had assumed that by claiming to be the Christ, he could become the Christ and the calamus had him crucified. He was like all other failed fanatics with delusions of grandeur and Yalad despised his followers as hypocrites and dupes.

Everyone seemed to want some way to see or experience the fantastic. Yalad, having the experience of the calamus, knew that what he had discovered actually had a power connected with something other than the natural. So he scorned the relics and artifacts as mythical toys, some of which on occasion could produce the unexplainable, but with no consistency and therefore without the reliability of the calamus' expression of power. Yalad was more interested in what was behind the locked cabinet doors.

Guttenheim intently watched Yalad as he took in the room and his collection. Over his many years, Guttenheim had seen three types of artifact searcher. There was the novice who found everything believable and fascinating. They were the easiest to sell to but also the most annoying because the conversations were more like lectures and Guttenheim no longer had the patience or energy of a teacher. Then there was the collector. They were more interesting and pickier. Depending on their station in life, they tended to be very generous with their money or were browbeating hagglers. They formed a small but loose community where gossip and backstabbing could get ugly. Then there was the rare connoisseur, or maven as Guttenheim preferred. He liked the word *maven* because it spoke better to its original Hebrew meaning for "*one who understands.*" Collectors knew information but mavens understood. Guttenheim, who was beginning to feel that he was older than the relics in the room, sensed that he had come close to meeting a true maven at times, but there was something about Yalad that made him feel for the first time he was meeting a true master.

"I'm afraid, Villyam, that I will not be able to help you," said Guttenheim.

Yalad smiled at Guttenheim.

"Why is that, Mr. Guttenheim?"

"I see in your face," replied Guttenheim, "that you are not impressed. A man not impressed either knows nothing or has seen everything. You do not strike me as a man who knows nothing so I have to conclude that you have seen everything."

There was a small table between the two men with an open box of various jewelry items. Yalad picked up an amulet box and recognized it from his time in Rome almost two thousand years earlier, just after the fanatic Jesus had been crucified. Filled with sulfur, the small box which hung on a chain around the neck had been quite popular for warding off evil spirits. Yalad set the item down.

"I hear that the Führer is very interested in…"—Yalad paused and swept the room with one hand before continuing—"these types of things."

"I think," answered Guttenheim, "that he might be more interested in you. What is it that you want?"

"What I am looking for I do not believe you have, and if you did, you would not let me know that you have it."

"But you think that the Führer might have it?"

Yalad shook his head briefly. "No, but I think that he will lead me to it. I would like an audience with him if possible. Does he send anyone in here?"

"Yes, occasionally," replied Guttenheim. "I am also instructed to let him know should I come across anything unusual."

"And have you?" asked Yalad.

"Yes," said Guttenheim. "A rare book of incantations."

"And how do you handle the transaction?" asked Yalad.

"The Führer either sends someone or I deliver it myself. It depends on the item. This one I will bring to him. Sometimes he has questions."

"Let me bring it to him," said Yalad.

There was a momentary pause before Baron von Guttenheim walked slowly to the shop's front door. He flipped the open sign around and pulled the shade before locking the latch on the door. Guttenheim turned and faced Yalad before speaking.

"I am probably the best in the world when it comes to the knowledge of the unknown. A large part of that is simply because I've been around so long, but even in the beginning, I was very good. One either has an instinct for this or one does not. I have seen many so-called experts miss the importance of something simply because they could not see "it" even with all their knowledge. I have spoken with you for only a few minutes, yet I know that you are a human artifact."

Guttenheim looked at the relics displayed throughout his store, and for a moment, he felt a cold shutter run down his spine. It was something he had been experiencing more and more lately. The moment passed, and the German shopkeeper smiled at Yalad.

"You look at the items in my shop as if they were one time familiar objects to you. Not familiar in the sense that you have seen them and studied them, but familiar in the sense that you lived when they lived. I do not know how this is possible but I believe it to be true. Whatever you are, I will not let you see Hitler unless you tell me your story. I am more curious about you than any ancient curio. I have kept many secrets. I will keep yours, but those are the terms of the transaction."

There were a couple of chairs toward the back of the shop. Yalad motioned for the two to sit down. As they sat, Yalad spoke of the calamus. He told the story of who and what he was in as brief a time as a life lived for thousands of years could be told. It was a relief for Yalad to speak of those things to someone other than those who had used the calamus themselves. The old man listened intently, absorbing every detail. When he was done, Guttenheim walked behind his cash register and reached under the counter. A hidden door opened at the back wall exposing a darkened room. Guttenheim entered the room, and after rummaging around for a few minutes, he returned with the book. He handed it to Yalad. The book, not more than a few hundred years old, had a thick wooden cover surrounded by worn leather with a lock on the front and the key kept in a leather flap of the spine.

"I have never seen this writing tool you call the calamus," said Guttenheim. "Nor have I heard anyone else mention it, but it does explain some legends I have heard. Perhaps they are connected. I agree with you that Hitler probably does not possess it. Otherwise, I think events would be even stranger than they are now. I would advise you not to mention it to him directly, but I am sure you know that better than I."

"So the rumors are true about Hitler and the occult?" asked Yalad.

"Possibly," replied Guttenheim. "It is more complicated than that. As I'm sure you have seen, men come to power on the backs of others. Climbing over your comrade requires great dexterity lest those underneath sense they are being used and decide to pull out. There is a great dichotomy in the history of Hitler and his merry men when it comes to the occult. Do you know Rudolf Hess?"

"No," replied Yalad. "I have not followed politics."

"I will tell you a little. You should know what you are getting into. Hess and Hitler go back to the beginning of their power. There was a time, not too long ago, when Hess had the ear of Hitler."

"Was?" interjected Yalad.

"Yes, as I'm sure you've seen in your long life, power is like a magnet. Others have since managed to maneuver their way closer to Hitler while pushing Hess further away. Part of Hitler's power comes from his ability to have his underlings fighting each other instead of undermining him."

"It is an old and useful tactic," commented Yalad. "How does this come into play regarding Hitler and the occult?"

Guttenheim continued. "All powerful movements, whether they be religious in nature or not, begin with a singular moment of discovery, which by nature seeks out a commonality within a community of their peers. And in all movements, there are degrees that separate the devotees. Probably most of those devotees in Hitler's inner circle have no ties to the occult. Quite the contrary. They want to eradicate it. However, Hess is a true believer, as is Heinrich Himmler, a dangerous man, who so far I've had the pleasure of avoiding."

"And Hitler?" asked Yalad.

"I think he is a man intrigued and repulsed at the same time. That is just my opinion. The reason I have mentioned Hess is that he was the one interested in the book. Not Hitler."

"Hitler is interested in Hess," said Yalad.

"Precisely," smiled Guttenheim. "Hitler summoned me one day on the supposition that Hess was purchasing occult artifacts. Someone, probably Martin Bormann, who has been seeking to supplant Hess, put a bug in Hitler's ear about Hess's fascination with the occult. Hitler has known Hess many years and was not ignorant of Hess's fascination. However, in the battle for power, the occultists are outnumbered, and Bormann has been relentless in trying to bring down Hess, so I suspect he has chipped away at the idea that Hess's enthusiasm is a weakness. I have been instructed by Hitler to notify him of any questionable purchases by Hess and bring them to him first."

"You think, however, that Hitler has a secret interest in these items?" asked Yalad.

"I think there is a curiosity. I don't know. It's just from my observations. He is a man in power. Power is a drug stronger than all others. Addicts will do whatever it takes to feed it. At any rate, I will write you a letter of introduction. Hitler is suspicious by nature and habit. He will not be pleased that I have sent an underling. The book is in Arabic. I can manage, but my Arabic is rusty. How is yours?"

Yalad grinned. "Fluent."

"Good…that will be our key. I will write that I have not been feeling well. Digestive issues, etc….Hitler has similar ailments and we have commiserated before on this affliction. You are a trusted client who I have not seen in years. Your grasp of ancient languages makes you a perfect substitute. The rest is up to you."

"Thank you," said Yalad. "When is the book to be delivered?"

"I will ring the Führer this afternoon and tell him that it will be delivered tomorrow at ten, if that is acceptable to you. Hess told me that he is on an important mission and will not be back for a few days. Remember, Hitler will be suspicious that I am not bringing it personally. He likes to ask questions. Do you feel comfortable answering his inquiries?"

"Yes," replied Yalad. "I have seen these books before. I have even known some of the authors."

The next day at ten o'clock, Yalad appeared at the front entrance in which Germany's favorite son was holed up, plotting to take over the world. Yalad presented his letter of introduction and waited in a small office while his letter was taken to another room where it was presented to Hitler. After waiting for almost an hour, he was patted down by an officer who then opened a door and announced Yalad's arrival. Upon walking in, Yalad found himself face to face with a rather perturbed Adolf Hitler. His lips were pursed in irritation, making his half-sized mustache look even smaller, almost like two black caterpillars hanging from his nostrils. He stood sternly with his feet firmly planted and his arms crossed high, almost toward his shoulders. In spite of the letter in his hands explaining Yalad's presence, Hitler grilled Yalad.

"You are not Baron von Guttenheim. Where is he and why has he sent you?"

Yalad eyed Hitler for the first time. After spending thousands of years among all types of leaders and pretenders, Yalad had learned to assess people quickly. While Hitler possessed the ego of many of the great leaders Yalad had met over time, it was clear from his first look that Adolf Hitler was a madman destined for destruction. His suspicious yet somewhat glazed expression, his exaggerated posturing, and the cold fanaticism in his voice all betrayed him. Yalad had seen many people serve madmen, fear madmen, but often fail to recognize them as madmen. He knew that Hitler's days were numbered. His experience had taught him that egomaniacs usually do not possess longevity. They are their own worst enemies. It was only a matter of time before Hitler would be brought down.

"My name is William Mortell. I am here at the request of Baron von Guttenheim because he thought I might be more useful in answering any questions you might have. I also requested to meet you. I have a great affinity for those interested in the supernatural."

"You are an American?"

"I am from America, but I am not an American," answered Yalad.

Hitler leaned in and examined Yalad's face. "I cannot recognize your nationality."

"Whatever nationality I had is buried with its past."

Hitler was intrigued.

Yalad handed the Führer the book Guttenheim had given to him. Hitler took the book and looked at it, examining it as if he was an expert in such matters. Yalad suppressed a laugh, knowing full well that Hitler had no clue about the book. He was a child playing with matches in a paper factory.

"The writing is Hebrew," said Hitler with some disdain.

"Arabic," corrected Yalad softly.

"Yes, of course," replied Hitler. He forced a smile. "That is what I meant to say. What can you tell me about it that I don't already know?"

"Well, as you can tell from some of the diagrams, this work focuses on the art of astrology. It is called the Picatrix and the title translates roughly to the 'Aim of the Sage.' It contains many spells covering many different subjects, some very risqué. This is a reprint of the original, probably from the sixteenth century. The original dates back to the tenth century."

"Are you able to read Arabic?" asked Hitler.

"I am."

Hitler was about to ask Yalad to translate one of the spells for him when the door suddenly opened and the officer who escorted Yalad announced, "Please excuse the interruption, Mein Führer. Major Pintsch is here and he says he has an urgent communication regarding Rudolf Hess. Shall I escort him in?"

Hitler turned and casually slid the book into a desk drawer. He turned back to Yalad, trying to read his face to see if there was any recognition that Pintsch was Hess's adjutant and whether Guttenheim had said anything to Yalad regarding Hess.

"Yes, send him in."

Pintsch walked in briskly and eyed Yalad. He would have preferred a private audience with Hitler, but there was no turning back. Hitler thrust his hand out, and Pintsch handed him the letter. Hitler started to read. As he read, his face reddened and his hands began to shake. He tried to compose himself and turned to Yalad.

"I'm sorry. There is something that I must attend to. You will be contacted shortly when I have the opportunity to meet with you. One of my men will show you out. An envelope is on the table for

Herr Guttenheim. It should cover the cost of the book. I will of course compensate you for any time you can allow when I am able to meet with you."

Yalad was quickly ushered out. On the couch outside the room sat a woman. As Yalad was being escorted out, one of the aides was speaking to the woman.

"I am sorry, Fraulein Sofia, but the Führer cannot meet with you now. He will be in meetings all day."

"Bormann!" Hitler howled.

Suddenly Martin Bormann came out of a room at the other end of the hallway and rushed past the two and into Hitler's room, slamming the door. Hitler's voice could still be heard as Yalad and Sofia were walking down the hall.

"That traitor Hess has gone to the British to try and broker a deal. We must get Mussolini on the phone and convince him we are not caving. Then, when that fool Hess returns, I want him shot."

Yalad and Sofia found themselves hurriedly led out the front door. There was an awkward pause as the two stood in front of the building. Yalad bowed slightly to Sofia.

"I see, in the cause of national interest, we have both been summarily dismissed. My name is William."

"Sofia," she replied. "You are American?"

"I am from America, but I am not American."

Yalad had known many women over the centuries, none of which he had ever loved. They simply existed for his convenience and were as unmemorable as Nimrods many wives were to him. The only woman Yalad had ever loved was his mother Anatu, who died when he was only seven. Sofia was attractive enough, but there was something about her that Yalad found intriguing. There was a simplicity to her that reminded him of his mother. Perhaps for Yalad, it was also the vulnerability of having lost all his power gained from the calamus, save his immortality. Sofia seemed to possess a similar vulnerability. Perhaps she was hoping to see Hitler for reasons other than business.

"He doesn't deserve you," said Yalad.

Yalad leaned in a little and smiled.

"Besides, his eyes aren't even that blue."

Sofia was startled at Yalad's presumption, but she could not hide the fact that he was correct and that her infatuation with Adolf was clearly ignored. A series of retorts came to her mind ranging from indignation to scorn and hurt at being spurned by the one she secretly loved. In the end, she dismissed them all for a simple statement of fact.

"I'm hungry," said Sofia. "What about you?"

Yalad smiled, his white teeth glistening in the shadow of a German cloud.

For the next few days, Yalad ignored Hitler, ignored Baron von Guttenheim, and ignored the calamus. He spent his time with Sofia, and for the first time in his long life, Yalad lived the life of a young man falling in love. Unlike Benedict, Yalad had not avoided any romantic involvements over the centuries because of any concern over their temporary nature. Relationships were only tools. All people were only as good as their use to him. They were no different than an automobile was for transportation or a knife and fork for eating. In this sense, he was very much like his father Nimrod. However, as is the case in love, there was something different about Sofia which Yalad could not explain.

Sofia forgot all about her feelings for Adolf. Yalad was like no one she had ever met. There was a transcendental uniqueness to him. It was as if he was a young lover, a mature adult, and a wizened sage all rolled into one man. He seemed timeless, and when she was with him, time stood still. Sofia had fallen in love. She knew, however, that eventually she would have to tell him about her son. One day at lunch she let Yalad know about Heinrich. To her surprise and relief, Yalad was very excited about her son and wanted to meet him as soon as possible.

For Yalad, the mention of the son was a wake-up call. He had come to Germany with the purpose of finding the calamus. His feelings for Sofia had distracted him; however, he was certain the young boy had the calamus. After lunch, upon Yalad's insistence, Sophia took him to her home to meet young Heinrich.

Heinrich had noticed a change in his mother the last few days. He had been very excited to meet the Führer and like his mother secretly hoped that the Führer could be his new father. Her happiness around the house after her second visit to Hitler gave Heinrich hope. While she had not spoken to Heinrich about Yalad, it was clear from things she was saying that she was seeing someone. Heinrich assumed it was Hitler. When Yalad entered his room, there was instant disappointment and anger. His mother was seeing a man who clearly was not representative of the Aryan future.

"Heinrich, my sweet, this is Mr. Mortell. Why don't you two talk while I make some coffee and cake."

Sofia shut the door and headed into the kitchen. Yalad smiled at Heinrich. Heinrich sneered at Yalad.

"You're an American," said Heinrich.

"I'm not an American. I'm from America."

"I don't see a difference," said Heinrich.

Yalad looked around the young boy's room. To his surprise, the calamus was placed in the open on the boy's bureau. Yalad resisted the urge to grasp the tool and flee.

"There is a difference, Heinrich," replied Yalad. "Sometimes people move. I moved to America from somewhere else many years ago."

Heinrich walked angrily to the window and looked down at the street. He hated the fact that he was too young to join the Deutsches Jungvolk, an organization for German youngsters in the Hitler Youth program.

"Wherever you are from, it isn't Germany."

Yalad sighed and wondered what to do. He walked over to the bureau and picked up the calamus.

"What an interesting stick this is, Heinrich. It looks like a pen. It is quite handsome. Heinrich, if you could wish for something, what would it be?"

Heinrich turned around and curiously looked at Yalad.

"Why?"

"Well," said Yalad. "Let's play a game. You write down on a piece of paper what you want and then I'll tell you what I want and you write that down."

Heinrich walked over to his bureau and pulled out some paper. He sat down on his bed and put a book on his lap and put the paper on top. Yalad handed the calamus to Heinrich. Heinrich looked up at Yalad and smiled. Yalad had not felt the thrill of what was about to happen for many years. He remained composed as Heinrich wrote. When Heinrich was finished, he handed the paper to Yalad.

Yalad looked at the paper.

"I wish Mr. Mortell was dead!"

Heinrich smiled wickedly at Yalad. "Okay, you're turn."

Yalad's face went pale. "Oh, Heinrich, what have you done?"

Just then, there was a loud thud in the kitchen. Yalad ran into the kitchen calling out Sofia's name. He found her on the kitchen floor dead. Yalad fell down by her side and lifted her head up in his arms and wept. He had not wept since his mother had died. While he wept, Heinrich ran out the front door, frightened by what had just happened. He thought he had killed his mother and he didn't know how. He ran into the streets, crying "Mama, Mama." He ran until he fell down in a back alley. The pen was still in his hands. Heinrich screamed out and threw the pen as hard and far as he could. He lay on the alley floor calling out, begging his mother to forgive him.

"Mama, Mama, verzeih mir, verzeih mir."

Heinrich sobbed on the cobbled back alley for many hours. It would be the last time in his life that he would shed a tear. He was eventually found and taken in by his aunt. Later, Heinrich would try and run away to join Hitler's Youth, but since he was too young, he was sent back to his aunt, where he was a royal Hitler's Youth wannabe pain in the neck. Once grown, bitter that he had been rejected by the Hitler Youth and now living in a disgraced homeland, he moved to Moscow and became a communist. With his German background, Heinrich found a place in the KGB as an expert in obtaining information from German spies or those thought to be spies. His specialty and greatest pleasure was torture, especially former members of Hitler's Youth.

By the time Yalad composed himself from the second and last time he would ever shed tears, he realized that Heinrich had fled with the calamus. Yalad searched the streets in vain to find Heinrich. Feeling defeated once again, Yalad boarded a plane out of Germany and back to America. He realized that ever since he had met Benedict, his connection with the calamus had been cursed. Filled with bitterness and hate, he returned to America to accumulate more wealth and wait for the day that he might again obtain the power he had lost. Years later while living in New York, Yalad noticed something about himself that he had never experienced since he had first become immortal. He was beginning to slowly age.

Hitler never knew what had happened to Sofia and her son, and had he been told, his interest would have been more about the stranger who could have helped him decipher the book of incantations. It did not matter. No amount of spells and incantations could save him. Yalad was correct. Adolf Hitler was a madman who would never have survived the success of prominence.

Meanwhile, in a narrow back alley, a small hand reached out between two boards and snatched up the stick that young Heinrich had thrown in his grief and pain. She was a young Jewish girl named Esther who was in hiding from the German secret police.

As for Baron von Guttenheim, shortly after Yalad had picked up the ancient manuscript to take to Adolf Hitler, Baron von Guttenheim felt another chill, and then another. The room of ancient, useless relics began to spin, and Baron von Guttenheim collapsed dead on the floor. It was just as well. He had met the ultimate relic, and every rare artifact would forever pale in comparison.

18

Secret Letters

I n the fall of 1940, in spite of her youth, Esther Bresler knew
enough about the times to know that it was not safe to be Jewish
in Germany. At the age of eight, she had felt the tension and anxiety increase each day as her mother and father sat up late at night having discussions about what to do and where to go. They had cousins
in Switzerland who would be willing to help them, but unfortunately,
leaving was getting to the point of impossibility. Simply going to the
market was becoming increasingly difficult. They would have fled
Germany sooner had not Esther's mother nearly died in childbirth a
few months earlier. In the tragedy, Esther lost a sibling and nearly her
mother as well. Now, her mother was well enough to travel, and they
had packed what they could and were preparing to flee.

They attempted to take side streets to avoid the soldiers who
seemed to be everywhere. As they were walking around a corner,
Esther, who was holding her mother's hand lagged a step behind.
Suddenly her mother stopped, letting go of Esther's hand. Esther
started to speak then noticed her mother motion for her to keep
silent. About fifty yards ahead a small group of soldiers were crossing
the same street the mother and father had just entered. One of them
had spotted the couple and motioned for the rest of the men to stop.
It was a small group of six soldiers who turned to face the Bresler
couple. Esther was hidden behind a fence and could not be seen.

"Esther, my dear, you must hide," whispered Esther's mother.

"Mama, come with me," pleaded Esther.

"I cannot my love. Remember, we talked about this possibility. Quickly, they're coming toward us. You must run and hide. Now!"

It was Esther's obedience that saved her ignorance of what would happen should she be caught. She turned and started running as fast as she could. She had no idea where to go. She just ran and looked for a place to hide. The Bresler parents walked slowing toward the soldiers. They were taken to a concentration camp and processed.

Esther ran down one side street then another until she found a large bush between houses and ducked into the green layers of leaves. She was breathing heavily and trying her best not to cry. She could hear the commotion of men in the distance and wondered if they were the soldiers. What had happened to her mother and father, she wondered. Esther, paralyzed with fear, wanted to run out of the bush and back down the streets calling after them. She didn't know what to do or where to go. She began to hear the sound of jackboots on the cobble road coming closer. A dog was barking. She had seen a group of soldiers once with a shepherd. They seemed barely able to hold the growling dog back as it lurched at some people coming out of a market. Did the soldiers have a dog trying to find her? The boots were getting closer.

Suddenly, a hand grabbed Esther from behind and pulled her into the yard. A large man put his hand over her mouth and carried her into the house. She was too frightened to kick or scream. Esther looked up at the man's face while he put his finger to his lips, motioning for her not to make any noise. He was balding with wisps of blond hair on the sides and deep-blue eyes. They were kind eyes, and they had a calming effect on Esther as she looked into them. She could hear the soldiers with their dog marching down the street and then pass the house. Once they were gone, the man set her down and took his hand off her mouth.

The man's name was Gregor Schmidt. The house was not his. It belonged to a family named Becker. Gregor was a carpenter and was working on the house while Herr Becker was fighting somewhere in France. Frau Becker was on holiday visiting her sister in Cochem. Gregor sat down on a chair next to young Esther.

"You are a Jew, yes?"

Esther nodded her head.

"You were hiding from the soldiers, yes?"

Esther nodded her head a second time. Gregor starred at the young girl and scratched his ear.

"Where are your parents?"

Tears came to Esther's eyes as she shrugged her shoulders that she did not know. Gregor gave her a cloth that was sitting on the counter and Esther rubbed her eyes.

"The soldiers have taken your parents?"

The question was too much for Esther. She fainted and collapsed on the floor.

When she awoke, she was in a small bedroom, and it was night. There was no light except for a full moon partially lighting the room. Esther could see a woman in the moonlight sitting in a chair. Her name was Elsa. She was Gregor's wife.

"Please don't make noise," whispered the woman. "My name is Elsa. You are in our house. It is different than the one you were in before. That was a house my husband was repairing. I am going to speak plainly, and I hope that you understand. You are being sought by the German police. Your parents have been taken. We can hide you if you want. However, you must do what we say. Though it is a great danger for us to do so, we believe it is God's will. Otherwise we will have to give you over to the police."

Elsa leaned in and grasped one of Esther's hands.

"Do you want us to help you?"

Esther bit her lip in fear while nodding yes. Elsa knelt down beside her. Tears came to Esther's eyes, and Elsa put her arms around her.

"We will do everything we can to protect you. I promise."

Esther settled into the spare bedroom of the Schmidts' house. Gregor's skills as a carpenter enabled her to have a loft hidden behind the wall of the spare bedroom. There was a false panel that she could slide to go in and out. She had to stand on the dresser to reach it. If a soldier was to check the house, they might pound on the wall but usually not toward the ceiling. During the day, she stayed in the small crawl space above the dresser while at night she could sneak into the room and have some mobility.

Esther's new life, which was at first frightful, yet somewhat adventurous, soon dulled to a monotonous, lonely existence consisting of the day-to-day task of remaining unseen. She was expressly forbidden to come out during the day and did her best to follow instructions, but sometimes boredom got the best of her. Unable to resist, she would sneak into the room. She would leave the panel of escape open for a few minutes to ensure that no one was in the house, and then when she felt it was safe to do so, she would crawl out of the secret room, leaving the panel open in case a speedy retreat was necessary.

The spare room was on a ground floor, and there was a window that faced a small portion of grass about three feet wide on the side of the house. A wooden fence acted as a barrier between an alley and the house. Sometimes Esther would open the window a few inches to breath in the air from outside. One time she dared to poke her head out the window just enough to look up and see the sun. More than once, she had to scurry quietly back into her crawl space when she heard the front door open and one or both of the Schmidts would enter.

The Schmidts were kind people and did their best to make Esther's fearfully bleak existence as comfortable and normal as possible. They had to balance this with the constant fear that they would be found out and sent to prison or worse. They would bring her treats when they could, and Esther would sometimes hear the woman softly singing hymns.

One day when Esther had snuck into the room and was taking in deep draughts of fresh air from the crack in the window she heard a boy scream, followed by a painful wailing. She opened the window cautiously and stuck her head out. Just as she did, she heard an object land on the opposite side of the fence in front of her. She held her breath and lowered her head, enough to peek out the bottom corner of the window's opening. She expected to hear footsteps but none came, and so she decided to do something very rash. She opened the window slowly and crawled out. Tiptoeing across the three feet of grass, she peered between a gap in the fence and saw on the stones a small stick. It had a bluish bright color which glistened unevenly in the sun.

Esther looked both ways and listened carefully. No one seemed to be about, and the crying from the boy had stopped. She pushed on one of the boards, and she could feel the board give some. Slowly she slid her hand out, and touching one end of the stick, she began to pull on it until she was able to grab it with her forefinger and middle finger. She scooped it into the base of her palm and secured it with her thumb. Sliding her hand back slowly to avoid cutting herself on the board, she pulled the stick through the fence. Esther then clumsily scrambled back through the window, now moving as fast as she could, the fear of being caught suddenly rushing in upon her.

Esther made her way back into her hiding place, breathing heavily from the excitement. She left the panel slightly open so that she could examine the stick in the light. It was a strange metal stick which she had never seen before. One end appeared to have a dark tip on it, and she wondered if she could write with it. She scribbled on the wall and found that it was a pen. Esther closed the panel, and exhausted from her adventure, she quickly fell asleep, clutching the pen in her hand.

As the days wore on, Esther settled back into the boredom of her routine. She would scribble and draw pictures with the pen, but eventually she ran out of space in the small cramped room and she longed to do something different. One night while she was in the room, she found a piece of paper in a drawer. An idea came to Esther. She desperately missed her friends, so she decided that she would write a letter to an imaginary friend and pretend to mail it. She looked around the room and found a small box large enough to hold the pen and act as a pretend mailbox. She would write to her new best friend and pretend that she was receiving the letter. She would call her Rebecca.

Dear Rebecca,

Hello, it's me Esther. I hope that you are doing well. I wanted to write you. I am still hiding here in the house. I have not seen my parents for some time. I do not know where they are. A kind couple is helping me, but it is very hard and I am lonely. I cannot go outside. Please write when you can.

Your new friend, Esther

Esther read her letter and then folded it neatly as if she were going to put it into an envelope. The sun was beginning to come out, so Esther picked up the letter, pen, and box and scrambled onto the bureau. She pushed the three items into her small room and climbed up. Once she was in and the panel was closed, she placed the letter in the box with the pen and lay down on her pillow, pulling up the sheet to her chin and fell asleep. When she awoke in the late afternoon, she opened her panel just enough to let the light in and opened the box. She pretended that Rebecca had written her back and she was going to read her letter. Esther took the folded letter out and opened it. It was blank!

A number of thoughts came to Esther's mind. One was that maybe she had dreamed the whole thing, but she knew down inside that she had not. Another was that one of the Schmidts had secretly removed the paper while she was sleeping and returned a blank piece of paper. That seemed even more unlikely. In the end, the simplest solution was the most improbable and fantastic. Somehow the letter had been mailed. A thrill of excitement shot through Esther as she considered that someone may have actually received her letter. She reasoned that the blank paper was meant for her to write another letter. That night, Esther sat down and wrote another letter.

Dear Rebecca,

Hello, it's Esther again. I hope you received my letter and that you are well. I am very excited to be writing you. Not much has changed since my last letter since it was only one day ago, and I do not have a very busy life. Writing you has made me feel less lonely.

Your friend, Esther

Esther folded the letter as before and put it in the box. Again, the next day the page was blank. Esther did this for a number of days, each day telling Rebecca a little more about herself and the things she liked. She would lie in her small room and imagine what type of girl Rebecca was and what she liked to do. After the fourth day, she opened the small box and discovered that Rebecca had written back.

Rebecca Rose Richmond was vacationing in a small town called Hope in British Columbia, Canada. She was eight years old and was enjoying the summer in a lake house. Each day she would either go swimming or hiking. She had two older brothers named Matt and Nick who would let her tag along unless they were hiking too far away or swimming too far out into the lake. Most of the time, they tried to accommodate their little sister and include her in their activities. However, one day while hiking, Rebecca made the mistake of trying to climb a rock the brothers had just scaled and she fell and broke her leg. For the rest of the summer, she found herself housebound while the two boys continued to enjoy themselves. It turned into a very depressing time for Rebecca, not to mention uncomfortable. She had a full cast which caused constant itching. She kept mostly to the house and the front porch because even with the crutches it was just too awkward to move around. Her one constant was to retrieve the mail each day. That was how she saw Esther's first letter.

Rebecca read the letter and tried to remember if she knew anyone named Esther. There was no one back home in Vancouver. She knew no one in her family or at school with that name. There was no return address on the stamped envelope. The next day, she went down to the mailbox before the postman arrived to ask him about the letter.

"I just deliver the mail. It had your name and address and it had a stamp. I don't know why it doesn't have a return address, but it's not needed to mail a letter."

Rebecca thought it strange but didn't know what to do about it. For the next three days, similar letters arrived. Each one was addressed to Rebecca with a stamp. Rebecca did not know what to do, so she decided to write a return letter and put it in the mailbox just to see if anything would happen.

Dear Esther,

Hello, it's me Rebecca. Thank you for your letter. I am sorry that you are lonely. Are you a friend from school? I'm sorry, but I don't remember you.

Rebecca

That was the first letter that Esther received from Rebecca, and she was so excited she leaped up, banging her head on the ceiling of the hideout. For the next few weeks, Esther and Rebecca wrote back and forth to each other. At first, Rebecca was suspicious that her brothers were playing a trick on her. One day, she decided to put the letter into the mailbox and then hide and watch to see if they approached the mailbox. After a few hours of peering out the window between the curtains, she went back down to the mailbox to retrieve the letter she had written. To her surprise, when she opened the box, the letter was gone. After that, she would go down to the mailbox every day and wait for the postman to bring the mail.

In the course of writing, Rebecca learned that Esther was a Jew hiding from the Germans in the house of a Christian couple. It was a strange thing for Rebecca to hear because she was not familiar with what had happened to Jews in Germany during World War II. Rebecca didn't know much about what happened in World War II because that was history and Rebecca was only eight. They were not teaching World History yet at Rebecca's school to third graders going on to fourth grade. It was history for Rebecca, for while Esther was writing from the year 1941, Rebecca was receiving the letters in the year 1975.

Too young to understand this paradox, she simply thought that for some reason Germans did not like Jews and children in Germany had to hide from them with the help of friendly Christians. Because

Rebecca took Esther's troubles at face value, she didn't question what Esther had told her, and as a result, Esther and Rebecca continued to write and talk of other things. Rebecca told Esther about her summer house and her broken leg. Esther would write about the school she had gone to and the friends she no longer was able to see.

Elsa Schmidt was a simple woman who spent a good deal of her time worrying that her husband Gregor, and she would be caught by the Germans. Until then, her convictions as a Christian had kept her life orderly and trouble free with the trials and testings of her faith being relatively small. In her heart, Elsa knew she had been spared. She was not unobservant, nor untaught. Christians suffered. She hadn't. Elsa and Gregor had had their share of difficulties. She knew though, that she had never really been tried by fire; then again, there had never been a fire such as the one that was sweeping across her beloved homeland. Her tranquil life in her peaceful home with its years of warm memories could easily, in a moment, become a cold cell for all three of them. Or worse. Elsa was not afraid of death, only of dying and humiliation. There were stories that filtered their way into the homes of the good-hearted Germans, stories of torture and shame to those who dared defy the superiority of the supreme plan. They were designed as a warning to strike fear into any soul seeking to do the noble thing. And it worked.

While she had no doubts that she was doing the right thing and she loved Esther as if she were her own child, every day was a day that she knew might be her last. At night, she would often go into the upstairs room and meet with Esther and they would talk quietly of the day and the events that consumed them both. She had told Esther that she would do what she could to try and find out about her parents, but it was nearly impossible to do so without arousing suspicion. One night while they were talking Elsa opened one of the drawers on the bureau and underneath some clothes pulled out a picture of a young girl and proudly showed it to Esther.

"This is our daughter Greta."

Esther's face beamed with excitement. Greta seemed to be about ten years old in the picture. The questions came tumbling out.

"Is she here? Does she go to school? What grade is she in?"

Elsa smiled.

"No, this is when she was your age. She is much older now."

"Does she live in Germany?" asked Esther.

"No, she moved to America to study Mathematics. She was fortunate enough to get out before all this fighting started." Elsa wiped a tear from her eye.

"She is engaged to an American who works in New York. His name is Thomas Wilson."

"Will you go to the wedding?" asked Esther.

"I don't know," responded Elsa. "We hope so. These are such awful times. Who knows? Anyway, she would like you, Esther."

Esther asked if she could keep the picture in her room above the bureau and Elsa handed it her. That night after Elsa went to sleep, Esther wrote Rebecca and told her about Greta.

Dear Rebecca,

Hello, it's Esther. How is your leg? Today I had a talk with Fräulein Schmidt. She is a kind woman. I can tell she is afraid that she will be found out for hiding me. I hope that she doesn't because she has a daughter named Greta who lives in America and is going to marry a man name Thomas Wilson. She let me keep a picture of her.

Your friend, Esther

The next day when Rebecca read Esther's letter, she thought it strange because even though she called her grandparents Grammy and Bumpa, she knew enough about them to know that Greta was the name of her grandmother and Thomas was the name of her grandfather. She had not told anyone about the letters she was receiving from Esther because in one way, it all seemed to make perfect sense that someone could mail her and she could put a letter back into the mailbox and it would disappear. On the other hand, there was something so strange about it that she did not want to sound foolish telling someone what she was doing. Her summer had become tedious since breaking her leg, and she didn't want this exciting adventure of magical letters to come to an end. By telling someone about the letters, she feared the mystery would be explained away and then cease to become an adventure. The last letter, however, did make her curious about her own grandparents. She decided to ask her mother about them.

"Mommy, did Grammy and Bumpa always live in New York?"

"No, Becca. Your grandfather lived in California when he was your age, and then his family moved to New York where he later met Grammy. Grammy was born in Germany and then moved to New York to go to school. Why do you want to know?"

"Oh, I don't know," answered Rebecca. Then she remembered something about women when they get married. Their last name changes.

"Mommy, what was Grammy's name before she married Bumpa?"

Rebecca's mother frowned at her daughter. "You certainly have a lot of questions suddenly."

"I'm just curious," said Rebecca.

"Well," answered her mother, "Grammy's maiden name was Schmidt. Her family was from Germany."

"What were they like?"

Rebecca's mother walked into the kitchen trying to think how she should answer her daughter's question, wondering if she was old enough to know the truth about her grandparents. As a teenager, Rebecca's mother had asked a similar question about her grandparents. Now she was wondering if Rebecca was old enough to hear what was difficult for her to hear when she was a teenager. She decided to give her a piece of the story and hope that Rebecca would be satisfied.

"Oh, I don't know too much about them. I think they died in Germany. It was during the war. It's almost time to eat. Why don't you go out and see if your brothers are nearby? Don't wander off too far with that cast."

Her answered seemed to satisfy Rebecca for the moment.

"Okay, Mommy."

Up until then, Esther had only one scare from the German police. It was during the day and she was sleeping when she heard a loud knock on the door. The police were doing a door-to-door search for Jews. She could hear their voices downstairs as they talked with Fräulein Schmidt. The sound of their boots seemed to thunder on the wood floor as they walked around the rooms banging their fists on the walls. Then up the stairs they marched into her room. Esther held her breath. The closet and bureau drawers were flung open. The police peppered Fräulein Schmidt with questions as they poked around the room. Then they banged on her wall. Esther closed her eyes and prayed. Then there was a terrifying silence before the police eventually felt satisfied and left the house. It wasn't until late that night that Fräulein Schmidt came up to see if Esther was all right.

After that, things quieted down. Months went by and it seemed that the Schmidts and Esther were safe. Then late one night as Esther was writing to Rebecca, there was a bang on the door. Esther scrambled up on the bureau as quietly as she could and slid into her small room. The voices this time were loud enough for Esther to hear.

"We have a report that you are hiding Jews! Where are they?"

While the Schmidts denied they were hiding Jews, Esther took out a piece of paper and wrote down the best she could in the dark.

"The police are here. I'm afraid."

Esther folded the paper and put the pen and the picture of Fräulein Schmidt's daughter in the box. Seconds afterward, the panel suddenly opened up and one of the police grabbed her roughly, pulling her out of the hidden room. One of them saw the box and seized it. He opened it, demanding of Esther what was in it. There was nothing to see however because the letter, pen, and picture were gone. Esther was dragged downstairs and thrown into a van where she was met by another family of Jews and two guards. The Schmidts were nowhere to be seen. Unbeknownst to Esther, they had been taken in for interrogation. She would never see them again. In the midst of her fear, as she was being taken to one of the concentration camps, she could not help but wonder why all the contents of the box had disappeared.

The next day, Rebecca went down to the mailbox and found a large manila envelope with a stamp on it. When she opened it, she read Esther's letter. Along with the letter were the pen and the picture of Greta as a young girl.

Rebecca moved as quickly as she could up to the house and went into her room. She read and reread the letter. Tears were running down her face onto the paper, and she took the pen and wrote.

Dearest Esther,

What happened? Are you hurt? I'm frightened for you! I don't know what to do. Please be all right. I just want you happy and with your parents. Please let me know what happened.

Your friend always, Rebecca

Rebecca sealed the letter and hobbled as quickly as she could down to the mailbox. She placed the letter in the box, anxiously standing by the mailbox, hoping that Esther would answer it immediately and send her back a reply. She decided to open the mailbox just to make sure the letter had disappeared as it had in the past. When she opened the box, she saw the letter was still there. Maybe Esther had written back and there was no stamp this time. Rebecca opened the letter. Written in the letter were a date, a time, a location, and the word *picture*. There was a strong sense that what was written did not come from Esther's hand but from someone greater and that the information given was not a suggestion but a command. She was to bring the picture with her.

She never heard from Esther again. She tried to write, only to find her letter still in the mailbox or given back to her by the patient, plain-spoken postman, with the advice that she put the letter in an envelope, address it, and get a stamp if she wanted it mailed. She kept the directions she was sent and placed the picture in a locket which she always kept about her neck. She always assumed it was the paper that was the source of their communication. She never suspected the pen. Every time she tried to use the pen nothing would come out and she just assumed that the pen was something that Esther had used and that it had been sent with the picture. When they left the summer home, the pen got lost in the packing. Her leg healed and she returned to her home in Vancouver, where, in the fall, she went back to school and lived her life, waiting until that time. The years passed and the memory of her summer often lost its clarity. When that did and the whole thing seemed at its silliest, she would open up the locket and look at the girl in the photograph.

On June second of 1990 at 2:45 PM, Rebecca entered the lecture room. A sign was posted at the entrance with the picture of a woman.

"3 PM. Esther Bresler—One Survivor's Story"

Rebecca sat in the back fighting back the tears as she heard Esther tell her story of how she was hidden behind a wall by a kind Christian couple who had given their lives to protect her. When Rebecca was a teenager, her mother finally told her the story of Rebecca's great-grandmother Elsa and her husband Gregor who died in prison at the hands of the Germans for attempting to hide a young Jewish girl. Rebecca listened in awe as Esther filled in many details about Elsa and Gregor that Rebecca's mother never had the privilege of knowing and passing down to Rebecca. Esther also spoke about how her own parents managed to survive their time in the concentration camp and that miraculously they were able to meet up again after the war. After Esther was finished speaking, there was a question and answer period. A young woman around Rebecca's age stood and spoke.

"Miss Bresler, I'm sure you have been asked many times, but how did you survive the day-to-day monotony of being alone in the wall of a stranger's house?"

Esther smiled and told the story of how she had invented an imaginary friend her age named Rebecca who lived in Canada and how she wrote letters to her and then pretended that Rebecca responded. She told of the last letter she wrote, placing the picture of the daughter of Elsa Schmidt in the box before being taken away.

The lecture ended, and some of the attendees stood around Esther asking her more questions until gradually one by one they moved on. Rebecca hung in the back and waited. When there were finally no more questioners she approached Esther, who was gathering the notes from her lecture. Esther gave a warm smile, not knowing it was Rebecca.

"You forgot to mention that my leg was broken," said Rebecca.

The notes in Esther's hand dropped to the floor as she searched Rebecca's eyes.

"Rebecca? Is it really you?"

Rebecca opened the locket around her neck and pulled out the picture of Greta, Elsa Schmidt's daughter. She handed it to Esther with trembling fingers.

"This is my grandmother Greta Wilson, daughter of Elsa and Gregor. It's the photograph you sent to me in your last letter. I've been holding it ever since."

Rebecca reached out and took Esther's trembling hand. Esther could barely get the words out.

"Greta was your grandmother?"

With tears running down her cheeks, Rebecca nodded.

"Oh, Esther, I was so worried for you."

Esther Bresler and her friend Rebecca Rose Richmond held each other and wept. They would remain close friends for the next seven years until Esther died peacefully in her sleep. At the hospital, Rebecca had sat at her side, holding the hand of her friend until the end.

The calamus over time had found its way to the barn of one Gérard Lapointe in Saskatoon, Canada. He could not remember how it had come into his possession. He had over the years done a number of odd jobs including junk removal. Occasionally, various smaller items, easily lost in transition, came his way. He thought that it was an odd-looking pen but since he had no use for it, the calamus sat in his barn on an old table with his toolbox and other miscellaneous items.

19

The Salvation of King Grampy

"**A**re you enjoying the pastry, King Grampy?"

King Grampy was known to anyone unrelated and older than five as Eli Lapointe. He was doing his best to remain balanced, on what was for his sizeable frame, a ridiculously small plastic chair, situated unsteadily in front of a slightly larger plastic castle. His granddaughter Emily, more formally known as Princess Emily of Candyland, was dressed royally in her regal princess gown and sat comfortably across from King Grampy, who was trying his best to appear equally comfortable. It was high tea time. King Grampy took a pretend bite of the pastry, which was in fact hardened Play-Doh, and smiled warmly at his granddaughter while rubbing his stomach.

"Yes, Princess Emily. Your chef has done a magnificent job."

"Princess Emily of Candyland," corrected the granddaughter. She gave her Grampy a stern look of displeasure.

"A thousand apologies, Princess Emily of Candyland," answered Emily's grandfather with an emphasis on Candyland. He gave her a wink and Emily giggled.

"It's okay, Grampy. You're forgiven."

Now it was her grandfather's turn.

"Hey, King Grampy, if you don't mind."

Emily ran to her grandfather and threw her arms around his massive neck.

"I love you, King Grampy. I want to draw now. Can I get your art pens…please, please, please?"

Emily's grandfather laughed and stood slowly from the tiny wobbly chair. Pain shot out from his knees and lower back. He made a little groan.

"Grampy, are you hurt?" asked Emily.

Emily's grandfather patted her on her head and smiled.

"Oh, the king's just fine. A little stiff from riding my royal steed during the fox hunt, but I'll be okay. Listen, you get the pens from the back room and I'll meet you in the living room where we can color. I'm going to the little boy's room."

"You mean the bathroom," proudly declared Emily.

"Oh, you're too smart for me kiddo," waved Grampy as he walked away. "See you in a bit."

"Okay, Grampy," answered Emily as she ran to find the pens and some paper.

Eli was surprised that the plastic chair held him. At fifty-four years old, he stood six feet five inches and weighed 280 pounds. He knew he needed to lose some of the weight, but there was nothing he could do about the height. He had grown up on a small farm outside of Saskatoon, Canada. Up until the eighth grade, Eli was the size of the other boys he knew, but by the time high school ended, he was six feet five inches and would stay that height the rest of his life.

For most boys in Canada, one sport dominated all others, and that was hockey. Once you learned to walk, it wasn't long before you were skating. For Eli, like his friends, life revolved around hockey. Whether it was a shinny or pick-up game at a nearby lake or pond, or one of the many local rinks, every opportunity Eli had he would be skating. There were times when he would wake up before dawn, before anyone else would arrive, and just skate—pushing the puck around and breathing in the cold winter air. Later in life, when he looked back on his early years, those were the days he remembered the fondest. He loved it even more than playing a game. He loved it more than the competition, more than the attention and camaraderie, even more than winning. When he was skating alone in the dark with a sliver of sun breaking the horizon, he forgot his problems. The family's struggle to make ends meet and his parents' constant arguing faded away. The only thing that mattered was the sound of his skates on the ice, the feel of the stick in his hand, and the flow of the puck.

Like every boy in America, whether swinging a bat or dribbling a basketball, Eli, along with his friends, talked of playing professional hockey. When he was in the eighth grade and the same size of his classmates, he was a fleet-footed skater with a strong clapper or slap shot. Then he grew. Once he hit his teen years and started to rapidly sprout, he began to struggle with his skating. His legs felt so long and gangly that he often found himself getting tripped up, whether it was the work of an opposing player or his own newfound clumsiness. Even though his slap shot became more powerful as his arms and body weight grew, his skating skills deteriorated, keeping him from getting free enough to set up a slap shot. By the time, he was a senior in high school he had changed from a quick speed skater with a forceful slap shot to a grinder who could check players hard against the boards.

He became a physical player whom the team depended on to free up their finesse players to score. Eli could live with the change in his playing style as long as he was able to be on the ice. He didn't mind the physical part. That was hockey. He had his share of throw downs and missing chiclets. Losing a tooth was a rite of passage. With his size, he was often an easy target for a stick to the mouth. The physical contact of the game was something that any hockey player knew came with the territory. By the time, he was being considered for Tier II Junior A play in 1977 he had developed a good reputation of being a big guy who could be an asset to any team.

One Saturday night, he was about to take the ice against a strong city team that called themselves the Bandits. Eli's team had lost to them once in a humiliating drubbing. The Bandits had some extremely quick players, some of whom might soon be called up to the Canadian Hockey League. It would be a long night for Eli as he tried to slow them down.

As he walked through the tunnel to the arena, his coached pulled on Eli's sleeve and pulled him into a room.

"What is it, Coach?" asked Eli.

"Listen, Eli, we got at least three CHL scouts watching the Bandits out there tonight. I think an NHL scout might even make it. They're here to see the Bandits, but you can make an impression tonight. This is the last game of the season. Make it count. Play hard. Don't be afraid to put them down. This is your chance. Be aggressive!"

Eli couldn't believe what he had heard. He could feel his heart pounding as he took the ice. That night he played the best game of his life. No one could get past him, and on the boards he was fierce. His size was overwhelming for the Bandits, and with a little more than three minutes left, no one had scored. Eli had made it his mission that night to keep the Bandits leading scorer from getting either himself or the puck near the goal. As time was winding down, the Bandit forward had just received a pass near the neutral zone. Eli came at him hard and checked him against the boards. It was a clean check; however, the Bandit player had been turning when he was hit, and his face went directly into the glass wall. Eli heard a pop and knew instantly that the Bandits nose had probably been broken. But as the forward spun around Eli could see that he was also knocked out from the glass and was heading face forward onto the ice. Eli tried to reach out and grab his jersey but as he did so one of the Bandits had come from behind and lowered his shoulder into Eli, sending him away from the injured player. The player Eli had checked fell onto the ice and lay motionless.

Eli got up quickly and raced over to the forward. Medics came out and placed the Bandit player on a stretcher. Blood was all over the forward's face. His nose was a flattened mangled mess. The Bandit player who had hit Eli came over and started swinging at him. Eli just stood there, watching the injured player being carried off, while trying to block blows from the other Bandit player. Eli then skated to the exit. None of the referees had ejected him. He didn't care. He just wanted out of there. He walked numbly to the locker room, seeing only the image of the Bandits bloodied crushed face. While the game resumed, Eli dressed as quickly as he could without even showering. He just wanted out. He wanted to get away from the noise and the building as fast as possible. He made it outside before the game was over. He could still hear the crowd from inside, the sound filtering through the open doors. He ducked his head down, outside of view from the few people milling about outside.

"Just get to your car," he kept telling himself. "Just get to your car."

"Mr. Lapointe," a voice said.

Eli jumped. In front of him were four men. Had he killed the player? Was he being arrested?

Eli looked at each with a panicked expression.

"Yes?" he answered with a shaky voice.

They could sense Eli's anxiety. One of them put his hand on Eli's shoulder.

"Mr. Lapointe, we know that was hard for you. Those things happen in hockey. It was a clean hit. You didn't do anything wrong."

Eli's throat felt dry. "Is he dead?"

"No, no," one of them said. "They've taken him to emergency care, but he's not dead. It was a clean hit, Eli."

Eli numbly stared at the men. He didn't know who they were and he didn't care. He just wanted to get away. He started to walk.

"Mr. Lapointe," said one of the men who had an American accent. "I'm a scout with the NHL and these three are CHL scouts. We came to see some of the Bandit players, but we would like to leave our cards with you and talk with you about your future. We know that what happened was difficult for you and this probably isn't the best time, but after a few days when you feel like talking, give us a call. All of us were very impressed with your play tonight."

Eli took their cards and stared back expressionless. He could see fans leaving the building. The game must have ended.

"I have to go," was all he could say. He turned around and headed to his car.

The next few days, Eli hid in his house, not answering the phone that seemed to never stop ringing. Sometimes the pressure got so great he would retreat to the barn and hide between bales of hay. He had heard on the radio that the Bandit player was alive but in a coma. It didn't matter to Eli that even on the radio, they had said it was not a cheap shot but just a freak accident and one of the risks of playing hockey. Even the father of the player said that it could have happened to anybody on the ice, and he didn't feel that Eli should be held accountable. Nobody seemed to be blaming Eli except Eli.

Eli had skated since he could walk, and as long as he had played hockey, he knew that there was a physicality to the game that was simply accepted. He had lost his share of teeth. He had broken his nose once and two fingers. He had run players hard against the boards and then laughed with them later after the game. He had his share of fights. He had never blamed others for his injuries. It was part of the game. Hockey made his life uncomplicated. When he was on the ice, everything made sense as the outside world disappeared and the only thing that existed was skating. For Eli, it was perfection and the closest thing to heaven he could imagine.

He couldn't explain that with all that understanding why his world was falling apart. Even with the reassurances that the player would live, the very thought of hockey now frightened him in a way he never would have thought imaginable. The idea that he could kill a man while doing the thing he loved plagued his mind. A fear of what could happen gripped him like a vice and would not let go. He would wake up in the middle of the night, drenched in sweat, an image of the Bandit player's shattered face staring back at him. When he looked at the business cards of the scouts lying on his nightstand, it made him nauseous. There was an overwhelming guilt and pain inside that was consuming him and he had no answer.

On the fourth day after the game, Eli was sitting in the corner of the barn with a bottle of whiskey. He had never been much of a drinker. Even when he went out after a game, he usually had only a beer or two. He hadn't eaten for a couple of days, and the more he drank, the more depressed he became. It wasn't just the injury now that he could not seem to reconcile with; it was the fact that he could not face the possibility of what he might do in the future if he were to play. His passion had turned into a nightmare. As he drank, he became more and more morose. If he couldn't skate because of living in fear, then there was no reason to live. His father's shotgun was resting on his lap while he drank. He was trying to get up the courage to put the gun to his mouth. While he was sitting there, the door on the other side of the barn opened, and he could he see his father standing in the doorway silhouetted against the daylight.

"Eli, one of the CHL scouts is on the phone. Why don't you come up and talk to him?"

Eli set the bottle down by his side. He tried his best not to slur his words.

"Sure, Dad. I'll be up in a minute."

His father shut the door, and Eli shakily stood up. He picked up the shotgun and the whiskey bottle and started to walk toward the door. He stumbled and half fell onto a workbench. He leaned the shotgun against the table and took another drink from the bottle. When he set the bottle down, he noticed some tools on the table. Along with the tools was a strange blue pen he had never noticed before. Seeing the pen, it occurred to him that he should right some kind of note. There was a pad of paper sitting under a wrench. Eli, his eyes dizzy and blurry, reached clumsily for the pad, knocking the wrench to the floor. He grabbed the pen in his right hand and brought it toward his face. It was a strange-looking pen and he wasn't sure which end was used for writing. He scribbled on the paper with the pen, but nothing came out. He then turned the pen around and tried again. This time a dark-blue ink scribble appeared on the paper. He took another drink from the bottle and tried to focus on the paper. Sweat was pouring down his head and mingling with his tears. His heart was pounding and his hands trembled as he wrote out the words.

"I'm sorry. I'm so sorry. Please forgive me. I can't do this."

Eli reached for the shotgun and took one last gulp from the bottle. He slid the muzzle of the gun under his chin, and reaching down with his long arms, he wrapped his finger around the trigger. He started to weep as he pulled the trigger.

Click.

Nothing happened. Eli brought the gun close to his eyes and checked the chamber. Even drunk, he could clearly see that both cartridges were inside. He pulled the gun an arm's length away as if it were a different shotgun from the one he had known since his youth. Why hadn't it gone off? He stared at the gun, trying to concentrate while his body rocked back and forth unsteadily. Everything was wrong. Nothing made sense anymore. All the energy drained from him, and he set the gun down on the table and sobbed.

After a few minutes, Eli wiped his eyes and face. He didn't know what he was going to do, but the strength needed to kill himself was now gone. Maybe another time, he thought. He reached for the paper to tear it up so that his father wouldn't see it. As he did, he noticed that the writing had changed. His drunken scribble of an apology and explanation had changed to three neatly written short phrases.

skate again
skate away
come back

Eli fell to his knees. Somehow in a moment, his head was clear and he knew what each phrase meant. "Skate again" meant that the Bandit player would live and skate again. "Skate away" meant that Eli was never to skate again. "Come back" meant that Eli was to return to the Lord. When Eli was eight years old, a cousin had brought him to his church youth group. Eli was touched by the message, and afterward, he raised his hand to ask Christ into his heart. When he came back home, he was afraid to mention anything to his parents, and eventually, he forgot about it and spent most of his time focused on hockey. As the years went by, his cousin would occasionally call him and try to talk about Jesus, but Eli was self-conscious and embarrassed. He just wanted hockey. Now the memory of the night when he was eight years old came vividly back to him. While on his knees, he asked Jesus to help him. Suddenly his head felt completely clear as if he had not had anything to drink. The presence of God was in the barn and Eli knew he would be all right.

The next day, he heard on the radio that the Bandit player was awake from his coma. He would need reconstructive surgery and time to recover from his concussion, but doctors told him the one thing he wanted to know the most. Yes, he would be able to play hockey again. Shortly after his surgery, he asked to see Eli. He wanted

Eli to know that it wasn't Eli's fault. They met alone before a disappointed herd of reporters and photographers were able to get in on the action. Eli never called the scouts back and got a job at a local lumber mill. Working at the mill gave him the idea that it might be fun to design houses. He had never put much time into learning when he was in school, so he decided to go to night school and get a degree in architecture. He also found a church and started attending regularly. Eli was content. Sometimes he would drive by a lake or pond and see some of his old friends playing hockey. Occasionally, he would stop and talk, jawing over the old games they had played. He always refused the offer to play in a pick-up game, but one afternoon, he had the day off and was driving back from the hardwood store when he saw a game going on. He stopped to watch. One of his friends waved him over to put on some skates and play for a while.

Why not? thought Eli. *What could one game do?*

It would be fun to skate again with his friends. He put on the skates and played for a few hours, laughing and having fun just like the old days. He even thought he might play once a week just for the exercise.

The next day at work, Eli was walking past the log yard toward the sawmill. He stopped to allow a crane that was transporting logs toward the mill. As he waited, he opened a book he was reading for school, cradling it on one arm while he carried his lunch pail in his other hand. When he heard the crane engine stop, he started walking with his head still down, trying to finish the page he was reading. Suddenly there was a large boom, and Eli looked up to see that the crane had lost control of two logs. He had been so sidetracked by his book that he hadn't realized how close he was to the crane. He dropped everything and tried to turn and run. In doing so, he tripped and fell. The giant logs shook the ground as they bounced around like candlepins on a bowling lane. One of them partially caught his right ankle before being bumped away by the other log. He screamed out in pain and tried to crawl away while the logs rolled around the yard.

Eli knew he was lucky to be alive, even more not seriously injured. Most of the injury was to the talus bone of his ankle and the ligaments surrounding it. He was on crutches and switched to office work while he healed. His family urged him to sue the lumber mill, but Eli knew in his heart that no matter how negligent the lumber mill might have been it was his fault that he was hurt. He realized that by going back to skating he had gone against the words he was given that had helped save his life—"skate away." Eli healed and in time finished his schooling and got his degree. He started working with an architecture firm as an intern and eventually got his license. He had met a woman at church named Bethany and they had married while he was interning. Their one daughter named Heather would grow up to be the mother of Emily, who was currently looking for the pens so that she and King Grampy could draw together.

Eli never used the pen again. He had at times thought of ways he might try to benefit from it or even help others, but he wasn't sure if the pen could be controlled that way or if it was even the right thing to do. The decision to never use it was solidified in his mind one day when his daughter Heather, who was six years old at the time, brought their dead dog back to life.

The Lapointe family had a terrier named Rocket who was given the name due to his ability to race off at a moment's notice. The couple had bought a piece of property that allowed Rocket plenty of space to dart off chasing rabbits, which seemed to be his favorite pastime. One afternoon, Rocket attempted to catch a rabbit that had crossed the road just ahead of a speeding car. Rocket was hit by the car and died. Heather, the only child of Eli and Bethany, was heartbroken over the loss of the dog. Eli and Bethany offered to get their daughter another dog, but Heather kept saying that she just wanted her Rocket back. All they could do was patiently wait until she got over her loss. Then one day, Rocket was at the front door.

Eli and Bethany assumed someone who knew of their loss had bought a replacement dog and left him at the house. It seemed strange to everyone except Heather that whoever gave them the dog just left him at their door. Everyone who knew the Lapointe family denied that they were responsible for the gesture. In the end, they assumed that whoever gave them the dog didn't want any attention and preferred to remain anonymous. Heather insisted it was Rocket and that she had brought him back. The more she insisted, the more Eli became suspicious that the pen was involved. He went upstairs to Heather's room and asked her to show him how she had brought Rocket back and Heather showed him a picture she had drawn of Rocket sitting in front of the house with a smile on his face.

"That's a beautiful drawing of Rocket, Heather. What did you draw it with?"

Heather looked around her room. There were toys scattered on the floor and stuffed animals and clothes strewn about. She scratched her hair and turned around three or four times before her eyes lit up.

"Oh...I remember, Daddy."

Heather got down on her stomach and crawled under her bed and pulled out the pen. The hair on Eli's neck stood up. He had always wondered about the pen's capabilities, but he had felt a strong impulse that to use it without its permission was wrong or against some higher law.

"Where did you get the pen, sweetheart?" he asked.

Heather lowered her head and nervously twisted back and forth.

"From your study," she quietly answered.

"Didn't I tell you not to go in there unless I was there?"

Heather slowly nodded her head. Eli stood silent for a moment before speaking.

"Okay. Don't do it again. Do you understand?"

Heather nodded her head again, this time with more enthusiasm knowing that she was not going to get into any trouble.

Eli held on to the pen. "No go downstairs for dinner."

Heather, glad that she wasn't in trouble, forgot all about the pen and turned to leave.

"Okay, Daddy. Rocket, Rocket. Come here, Rocket," she called out as she ran down the stairs.

Eli took the pen and the picture of Rocket back to his study. Hopefully Heather would forget about the picture. She was only five, and if she repeated the story, anyone would think that it was just a lovely story by an imaginative little girl. Eli had never told his wife about the time he had used the pen. It wasn't that he wanted to keep a secret from his wife. He just didn't know what to make of it at the moment. It was so strange. His life had changed and that seemed to be the important thing. Eli locked the pen in his safe under his desk.

The next day Eli had to travel to an office building he had helped draft. The contractor had some questions that could not be answered on the phone and asked if Eli would come on site. It was a little under a hundred miles away, and it took Eli about an hour and a half before he arrived at the site.

Eli slid his large frame out of the pickup truck and walked toward the office foundation. When he got to the site, he could see the contractor leaning over the blueprints. When he saw Eli, he gave a wave and Eli walked over to him.

"How ya' doin', Eli? Sorry to drag you out here."

"No problem, Tom. It got me out of the office." Eli noticed a small girl sitting on the bed of Tom's truck. She seemed about the age of Heather. Eli nodded over toward Tom's truck.

"You're hiring awfully young, Tom," he joked. "I might have to report you."

Tom looked back at his daughter who was slowly swinging her legs. She did not look happy sitting in the middle of nowhere in her dad's pickup truck.

"Yeah, that's my Milly. I'm trying to get her away from the house. She's a little blue. Her terrier got run over a couple of days ago. She really loved that dog."

Tom turned toward the prints.

"Ah, she'll get over it," he continued. "It'll just take some time. Now about this section here on the print. I need you to look at what we're facing her and see what you think. Walk with me over to the far side, could you, Eli?"

Eli was staring at the little girl, the sadness on her face mirroring what he had seen on his own daughter a few days ago. Was this just a coincidence or did it have something to do with the pen? He wanted to believe it was coincidence, but in his heart, he knew it was the work of the pen. Whatever thoughts he might have entertained about ever using the pen again were put aside forever. It had saved his life, but there definitely was more to it than he would ever understand. Through the years as Heather grew, then married and gave birth to Emily, Eli kept the pen locked away in his safe, unsure of its purpose while certain of its unpredictable power.

By the time "King Grampy" came out of the bathroom, he could hear Emily at the front door talking to her mother. Eli looked at his watch, surprised that it was already four o'clock. Emily was tiring, but the day went fast when he was babysitting her. Eli walked to the front door and gave his daughter Heather a kiss on the cheek.

"How'd it go, Dad? She wore you out?"

Emily had grabbed her backpack and was racing to the car. Eli smiled at Emily before turning to his daughter.

"No, we had fun. I was King Grampy and she was Princess Emily of Candyland. Those castle chairs are a little small though."

"Oh, Dad, you didn't actually sit on one of them, did you? With your knees."

Eli smiled and shrugged his shoulders.

"Like I said, we had fun. Bye, princess," Eli called out to Emily as she climbed into the back seat of Heather's van.

"Bye, King Grampy. I love you."

"Love you too, princess," answered Eli.

"I gotta get going," said Heather. "I got steaks in the back seat."

"Love you, sweetheart. Give me a call if you want me to watch her."

Heather waved and got in the front seat. She reminded Emily to buckle her seatbelt and then pulled out of Eli's driveway and sped off. Just then, a horrible thought occurred to Eli. Had he forgotten to shut his safe?

20

The Consolation of Princess Emily

E mily adored her grandfather. He always made her feel that their worlds were one. At least that was the way she would explain it to others years later. At the time, she only knew that being with her "King Grampy" was always like going on vacation. It couldn't possible occur to her when she saw the pen in Grampy's little box in his den that she might be taking something which would alter the lives of those around her in an unimaginable way. She had yet no capacity regarding the pen. It was pretty, and she wanted to use it to draw with Grampy. When her mother called her to leave, in the manner of her age, she absentmindedly forgot all about drawing with Grampy and got her things together to leave, including the pen.

While Heather drove Emily homeward, Eli raced to his den. He had indeed left the safe door open. He had been looking for some insurance papers earlier in the day and was in the middle of reading one of them when the doorbell rang. It was Heather dropping Emily off for a few hours while she ran some errands. Eli, who was at that stage in life where forgetfulness was occasionally a fleeting visitor, left the papers on his desk and walked to the front door to greet his daughter and granddaughter, neglecting to shut and lock the safe.

Eli was frantic as he pulled everything out of the safe. There was no pen mixed in with the documents and miscellaneous family heirlooms. Emily must have passed the den on her way to get the pens she was planning on using and seen the safe open. Eli knew that it wasn't like Emily to snoop through a bunch of papers. When he was getting his insurance papers, the pen must have been pulled out enough to catch Emily's eye. She probably meant to ask him if she could use the pen but forgot about it once her mother came to the door. Somehow, without making a scene, I must get the pen back, he said to himself. He stood as quickly as his sore knees and lower back allowed. Grabbing the car keys off the hook near the kitchen door, he hurried to his truck.

Eli pulled out quickly and started driving toward Heather's house. Normally a very cautious driver to the point where it had become an inside family joke, he found himself weaving recklessly in and out of traffic as fears mounted about the pen. What if she was drawing in the car on her way home? Oh Lord, please don't let her draw anything crazy, he prayed. As he drove and worried, he suddenly remembered that he had his cell phone with him. Eli was not a big fan of cell phones. His wife Bethany, who had died suddenly in a car accident three years earlier, liked playing around with her cell phone, taking pictures and listening to music, but Eli never quite felt comfortable with cell phones, mostly because he had a hard time seeing the buttons without his reading glasses. But he had always kept his cell phone with him, "just in case," as his daughter Heather would remind him. Eli stopped at the red light when he came to an intersection that crossed the main highway. He leaned to one side and reached in his front pocket for his phone and then pulled his reading glasses out of his shirt pocket. He couldn't remember his own phone number, much less his daughter's number, and tried scrolling through his list of numbers. Finally, he found it just as the light turned green. Eli hit dial and started through the intersection. Just as he did, a large semi-truck, transporting eight new cars to Big Bob's Car Emporium, ran the red light.

The truck driver, a short, wiry man affectionately known to his friends as Blue because of his lifelong love of blues music, was not being negligent. About eighty yards from the intersection, Blue's heart gave out while listening to Muddy Waters. For his birthday, the day before, his son had given him a CD version of Muddy Waters' *At Newport 1960*, and Blue had just finished listening to "Baby Please

Don't Go" and was enjoying "Soon Forgotten" when he collapsed onto the steering wheel.

The position of his shoulders on the wheel kept the vehicle going straight. The shift in his weight forced his leg forward and his foot pressed harder on the accelerator. Blue had been driving conservatively on the highway at about fifty-five miles per hour, but by the time he crossed the intersection, the truck had picked up to almost seventy. The impact with Eli's vehicle was devastating. The truck pushed Eli's car across the intersection toward the median on the highway. The back tire of Eli's truck hit the median curb, causing his truck to flip repeatedly. The contact knocked Blue away from the steering wheel and pulled his foot from the accelerator. As Blue's upper body slid to the side, the front cab made a sharp right turn, causing the load of cars it was carrying to follow. The sudden turn was too much for the cargo and the trailer began to tip. Once the trailer fell on its side, the impact caused the tie down ratchets holding the cars to snap. The four vehicles on the bottom deck were kept in place for the most part by the cage like frame of the trailer, but the top four cars easily slid out and rolled into oncoming traffic before eventually coming to a stop just as Muddy Waters was starting "Tiger in Your Tank." The volume had managed to get cranked up during the melee of the crash and it was the only noise heard up and down the street as stunned passengers and pedestrians stared in horror.

Emily had been sitting in the back seat swinging her feet while she listened to a collection of Disney songs on a small DVD player attached to the back of the passenger seat in front of her. She was singing along with "A Whole New World" from the Aladdin movie when she heard her mother's cell phone ring. Heather had a phone holder in between the front seats, and Emily leaned forward toward the phone.

"I wanna see, I wanna see," she said as she excitedly grabbed the phone. Emily was at the age where she knew how to use the phone while her parents were in the process of training her about what she could and could not do with the phone. They had recently agreed that she could look at the phone and see who was calling but had to ask permission if she could answer the call.

"It's Grampy, Mommy. Can I answer it? Please, please, please!"

"Yes, dear," answered her mother.

Emily excitedly pressed the talk button.

"Hi, Grampy. It's Emily. How are you?" Emily was trying her best to follow the recently learned rules of phone etiquette by saying hello, introducing oneself, and asking how the other party was doing.

At that point, anything normal Emily had ever experienced in regard to phone conversations was forever changed. She heard a human voice make a startled sound that frightened her.

"Grampy?" she said with an unsure voice.

It was then that she heard the awful sound of metal grinding against metal. Then there was a loud screeching sound from one of the tires that had popped off and the axle scrapping against the ground.

"Is it Grampy?" asked Heather as she looked in the rearview mirror at her daughter.

An indistinct guttural noise came from Emily's grandfather followed by a cry of "ah" as the car started to flip. Emily could hear a banging sound each time the vehicle rolled onto another side. *Bang, bang, bang, bang, bang, bang*—almost like a cannon.

"Grampy?" Emily said with anxiety. The sounds she heard were indistinguishable and horrifying.

Heather reached her hand out. She had no idea what was happening, but there was a feeling that something was terribly wrong.

"Give me the phone, Emily," she commanded. Emily sat frozen with her hand clutching the phone. Heather saw a turnout on the side of the road and stopped the car. With her foot still on the brake, she half-turned and grabbed the phone from Emily.

"Dad, is that you?"

There was no answer on the phone. Heather put the car in park and looked at the phone. She could see that the call was from her father and that it was still connected.

"Dad," she repeated a number of times. Finally, she heard a slight noise that sounded like groaning.

"Dad? Are you okay?"

She waited for a few seconds.

"Dad, can you hear me?" her voice beginning to panic. "Dad, where are you?"

Heather looked in the rearview mirror at Emily. Tears were coming down Emily's cheeks. "A Dream Is a Wish Your Heart Makes" from Cinderella was playing on the DVD. Heather reached over and powered off the DVD player. She put the car back in drive, turned her head to the left to see if any cars were coming from behind her, and made a quick U-turn. She drove as fast as she could back to her father's house. By the time she reached the intersection, she could hear muffled voices through the cell phone but she couldn't make out what they were saying. There was no need. The moment she reached the intersection, her heart sank. It was a chaotic sight of cars and people. She knew somewhere in that mess was her daddy.

Eli had one of those brief visual moments, no more than a few milliseconds, of seeing a truck out of the corner of his eye just prior to contact. His initial thought was that he must be at fault and had entered the intersection too soon. Upon impact, Eli's head slammed into the side window causing the corner of his reading glasses to pierce into his left eye. He cried out in pain. After the initial impact while his car was being pushed toward the median, Eli's mind, now semiconscious from the blow, was playing catch up, still seeing the semi just a few feet away prior to hitting him. Even as thoughts, pain, metal, and glass wildly caromed in a chaotic orchestra of confusion, Eli was still worrying how he could get the pen back.

Then he hit the median, and the car flipped. Each time it rolled onto the driver's side, Eli's head smashed into gravel and glass. By the time the car had settled, the body of Eli was dead. What no one could see was Eli's spirit just beginning to be free. His spirit stood next to the mangled mash of metal. A hand, which was his and now no longer his, lay face down on the dashboard. The hand seemed strangely familiar to Eli. Probably he would soon recognize it and wonder why his hand was inside his truck, motionless and bloodied. There, on the dashboard, next to the hand that was his, was his cell phone.

"The pen!" he exclaimed. Without realizing how he was moving, Eli sped across the street. He wasn't quite running and he wasn't quite flying. It was simply moving without effort. It didn't seem strange to Eli. He had not yet put the pieces together that he was dead. It was like being in a dream where the conscious mind doesn't dispute the oddities meandering in the unconscious mind. He was not yet questioning the reality of what had happened. A hand touched Eli's shoulder with the slightest of effort and Eli stopped.

"Eli," said a voice and Eli turned around. Someone who was like Eli, though different to Eli in an unexplainable way, was standing next to him. It didn't matter. Whatever it was, Eli pled with it to help him.

"I must get the pen back from Emily before she uses it!"

The angel took Eli's hand. "Come," was all he said as they moved back to the car. As Eli looked at the car, understanding came to his mind and he realized that he was not in a dream and he was not seeing a vision. He was dead. There was no fear about his situation or of the being next to him. This time, without any anxiety, he asked the angel about the pen.

"Eli," answered the angel. "Greatly beloved of God. You have been a faithful guardian of an object that was never meant to be in man's possession yet allowed by God's wisdom. You are one of a few who has possessed it and not used it for your own purpose. Where the pen goes is the will of the Almighty. It is no longer your concern. Come," said the angel as he escorted Eli into heaven.

In spite of the collision and the massive moving debris caused by the accident, the injuries were minor to everyone involved and the only two who died were Blue and Eli. It was one of those accidents that the news later categorized as both tragic and fortunate—an apt description for those unaffected of how sorrow and gratitude were often born of the same source. For Heather, her husband Ben, and mostly for Emily the consideration of gratitude was lost on them while they suffered their loss and wrestled with their limitations.

At the memorial service, Eli's pastor told of Eli's love for the Lord and the soft-spoken manner of the gentle giant. As a word of encouragement and an opportunity to reveal the Gospel message, he recounted the story of Eli's conversion as a small boy and his later recommitment to the Lord. Few people knew or remembered that

Eli, once a promising hockey prospect for professional hockey teams, had almost accidently killed a man in a hockey match. Only the pastor, Eli's daughter and son-in-law knew how it had devastated Eli so much that he had nearly killed himself out of guilt. Guilt can kill a man, the pastor commented. It can also restore. The pastor recalled that Eli had shared with him that God in a very unique way had intervened and led him to rededicate his life to Christ. While Eli would never reveal what it was to the pastor that had saved him from such overwhelming guilt, he did give the pastor permission to tell everyone who may someday come to his memorial service that God was able to rescue anyone who felt they were drowning in a sea of guilt.

Heather had now lost both parents in a matter of just a few years to tragic car accidents. Her mother Bethany had been killed by a drunk driver when Emily was just two years old. While it was a great sorrow that Emily would never know, Heather had often thought if her mother had to unexpectedly die, it was better that it had happened before Emily was old enough to have to go through something so difficult. For Heather, when she lost her mother, she lost her best friend. After some rebellious teenage years when Heather was certain that her mother "just didn't get her," Heather matured and realized not only how much her mother loved her but also how much they had in common.

What Heather could not see as she grieved when her mother died was what her father was going through at the time. Eli was tormented. While everyone, including Heather, assumed Eli was having a difficult time believing that his wife was suddenly taken from him, what they didn't know was that every moment he was awake he was wrestling with the idea of attempting to bring her back with the pen. Each night he would sit at his desk with a blank sheet of paper and the pen in his hand while the battle between personal anguish and his commitment to never use the pen warred. In the end, he did what many grieving people do who are trying to make a difficult decision. He considered what Bethany would want. Eli realized that no matter how much Bethany might desire to be back with him she would not want him violating something which had been so sacred and important in his life. In the end, he put the pen back in the safe and purposed that he would never consider the idea again. It was only then that he was able to grieve for his loss. As Emily grew, she became a source of healing for Eli, and over time he came to see that even if he were able to bring his wife back, not only would she be displeased but he never would have had the same relationship with Emily that had developed over the last few years.

Heather and Emily's world crumbled when Eli died. The expression of their sorrow was worlds apart, but each was inconsolable. Heather's husband Ben did the best he could. He made meals when Heather could not come out of her room, and he read to Emily at night from her favorite books even though she barely heard a word he spoke. For Emily, it was more than the death of her Grampy that shattered her spirit; it was the haunting sounds from the phone call that she could not forget. Unnatural, jarring sounds. Many of the normal daily events took on the shape of a monstrous reminder of what she had heard on the phone. When a neighbor dragged his metal trashcan along his driveway, Emily heard the scrapping of the axil on the road. One day, her mother accidentally dropped a plate on the floor. In a moment, Emily was back in the car vividly remembering the rhythmic pounding of her grandfather's car repeatedly rolling, each contact with the ground like an orchestra of symbols crashing at once. Noises became a reminder of death. She was not only too young to think of death, she was too young to have her day plagued by ghastly sounds and her nights haunted by twisted visions of violence. Heather could not sleep and Emily did not want to. While he waited, Ben cooked, read stories, loved, and wrestled with the mercy of God.

One morning, Emily was sitting in her room staring out the window holding her favorite stuffed rabbit, Fluffy. Fluffy had lately spent a lot of time in Emily's arms without complaint. As she sat at the table, Emily turned her head at one point and noticed her backpack in the closet, the same backpack she had taken with her the last time she saw her grandfather. Until then, she had consciously avoided it as a reminder of that day. Now, as she stared at the bag, it was the times she spent with her Grampy that came back to her and not that horrible hour in the car. Too young to define or articulate her feelings, the bag connected Emily to her last moments when she had carried the things important to her to the person who was important to her. Emily sat down inside the closet and placed Fluffy at her side. Picking up the bag, she held it in her arms and then closed her eyes and rested her head on the bag. After a few minutes, she unzipped the bag and took out the toys she had brought with her that day. At the bottom of the bag sat the pen.

She couldn't quite remember how she had gotten the pen, only that she wanted to draw with her grandfather before her mother returned and brought her home. It was a strange-looking pen, not like the crayons, markers, and colored pencils that she was used to. She went to her table, opened the top drawer, and pulled out a piece of paper. She drew a picture of her grandfather smiling. As she drew, she remembered a conversation she had had shortly before her last visit with her grandfather. He was making her a grilled cheese sandwich while she sat at his kitchen table eating Goldfish Crackers and drinking milk.

"Grampy."

"Yes, Emily," answered Eli while flipping the sandwich over.

"Where's Grammy?"

Eli paused for a moment.

"She's in heaven with Jesus."

Emily put a cracker in her mouth.

"Do you miss her?"

Eli smiled at Emily.

"Every day, princess. But do you know what?"

"What?"

"I'm going to see her someday. She's waiting for me."

"Isn't she lonely?" asked Emily.

"Oh no, princess. She has the angels to keep her company. One thing your Grammy loved to do was sing. I think she is having lots of fun singing with the angels."

"What are angels?"

"They're God's helpers."

Emily's eyes lit up.

"Oh, like Santa's elves."

Then Grampy laughed that big laugh of his which was so infectious that it always made Emily want to laugh also.

As Emily sat at the desk thinking of her Grampy, she decided to add Grammy to the picture, holding Grampy's hand. She remembered the angels. The previous Christmas she had seen a picture of angels singing around the baby Jesus, so she tried her best to add angels singing with Grammy and Grampy, struggling to make the wings look like the picture she had seen. The pen rested comfortably in Emily's hand, and as she drew, she started to feel a little better. That night, to her father's surprise, Emily fell asleep shortly after he started reading her a story, her newly drawn picture next to her on the nightstand. She slept straight through the night without a single nightmare, and when she woke up the next day, she crawled into bed with her mother and held her. Later, after Ben had gone to work, Emily asked her mother if she would make her pancakes, and for the first time since Eli died, Heather and Emily found solace in each other.

As time went on, Emily would continue to use the pen, never knowing its power, only knowing that it was connected with her Grampy. When she had the pen in her hand, she found that she liked to draw things that made her happy. One day she drew a picture of her mother in the kitchen cooking while the angels stood around her singing. That night Heather told Ben that earlier in the day she had the most incredible experience in the kitchen. She couldn't tell where the noise was coming from, but she heard the most beautiful singing.

Eventually the summer ended, and Emily started her first year in school. Spending time laughing and playing with other children, and learning her letters and numbers helped take Emily's mind off the loss of her grandfather. Her joy was infectious and Heather would tell her husband after Emily was asleep how she never would have made it without Ben's kindness and Emily's joy. Heather had never really accepted the Savior her father had tried to tell her about. As a child, she went to Sunday school while her parents were in church, and then when she was older, she joined them at church but in her heart, she never embraced what she was hearing. When she went through some rebellious years as a teenager and into her early adult years, it was in many ways a rebellion against what she felt she had been forced to hear.

Heather and Ben did not marry until Heather was twenty-five years old. By then, while she still had no interest in church, she had grown up enough to realize that she had two wonderful parents who had always wanted the best for their little girl. She started reaching out to them more often and eventually Ben and she moved in order to be closer to them. Both of Ben's parents had died when he was young and he often told Heather that she was incredibly fortunate to have parents who loved her and wanted to be near her. The couple held off having children until Heather was almost thirty. Emily was born and Heather's heart was starting to soften.

Then her mother died. The God whom she was not interested in became the unfair God who made no sense. Before, she did not care. Now, she demanded answers. God was silent except in the example and life of her father. Eli had managed to express to Heather in his own quiet way the overwhelming sorrow he experienced along with the quietness and peace that is manifested by someone who truly knows God. Until then Heather had only seen her father as someone who believed in an idea. Now she saw someone who was as broken as she was but who drew strength from a person. As Emily spent time with her Grampy, Heather's heart became softer toward spiritual matters. She would even on occasion ask her father a question about God. Eli was always careful to answer, knowing that the steps Heather was taking were as tentative and unsure as a child takes when they first start walking.

Then her father died. Now, Emily and her husband were her rocks helping her get back on her feet. The events and things she had experienced made Heather realize that what she had heard all of her life needed to be something that she knew to be true for herself.

"Ben," said Heather one night as the two sat in bed reading.

"Hmm," answered Ben as he turned the page of his book.

"Will you take me to church tomorrow?"

Ben put his book on his lap.

"Sure. Which one?"

"Daddy's," replied Heather.

Ben looked at Heather's face. He had never been to church in his life. The closest he had come was his wedding and Eli's memorial service. He was a loving husband and father, but he just never thought much about religion. He loved Heather and she had often spoken about her feelings of growing up hearing about Jesus all the time. He had seen her anger against God when her mother died. Eli seemed to be about as honorable a man as Ben had ever met and he was genuinely impressed by his consistent Christian lifestyle. It was Eli's life that made Ben amenable.

"Okay," he said to Heather. "Do you know what time it starts?"

Ben, Heather, and Emily began attending church, and in time, all three gave their hearts to Christ. The same words that Heather had patiently listened to as a child but never received became like water to a thirsty soul. If the term "born again" had not already been in the Bible, Heather would have wondered why, because it so fittingly described what had happened to their family. Emily loved Sunday school, and Heather saw in her what she never saw in herself when she had gone so many years ago. Ben had always been a kind person but he had never been a passionate person when it came to a conviction. But now everything seemed so alive to him and he realized that had he never gotten to know the Lord he would have become duller and duller until he was completely soulless, unnoticeable, and undesirable.

Emily continued to occasionally draw with the pen. It became a part of her collection of writing tools that she would sometimes pull out and draw in a book that she kept in her closet. She never knew that what she drew came to life or had any consequences. Sometimes her parents would hear of something strange happening nearby but had no clue that it was the result of the pen and Emily's imagination. Emily unknowingly became a guardian of the pen and the pen, though subject to Emily's creativity, always expressed the will of its true owner.

One night, twenty-one hundred miles away in New York City, a bored Yalad, now looking like a distinguished well-off man in his late fifties, was on his third glass of Chateau Mouton Rothschild, 1945, and on his second pint of Ben & Jerry's Cherry Garcia. He seemed unconcerned that red stains were piling up on his bouclé and suede sectional sofa as he absentmindedly changed the channels on his remote. His eyes glazed over movies and television shows he felt he had seen a hundred times. He clicked ferociously, angry at the repetitiveness of insipid ideas and moronic jokes. He paused long enough to have another spoonful of Cherry Garcia and drained his glass of wine. While he poured himself another tall glass he heard the voice of one of the cable newscasters.

"So, Sandra, what is the deal with Saskatoon?"

Yalad picked up his ice cream and took a bite. The two newscasters were sitting at their desk, looking very happy talking about everything from a killer tornado to a local Shakespearean festival.

"Apparently, everything but the kitchen sink, Carson," answered Sandra with a perky frozen smile as she looked at Carson. Yalad fumbled for the remote. Sandra turned toward the camera.

"Over the last few days, some of the most unexplainable sights have come out of the Saskatoon, Canada area. Our neighbors to the north have reported incidents of circus animals wandering the streets, a day of rain that produced seven rainbows, and one street that suddenly grew palm trees."

As Sandra mentioned each incident, footage was shown. Yalad set his ice cream down, knocking over the bottle of rare wine in the process. As the wine spilled onto his white carpet, Yalad sat transfixed while the newscaster continued.

"And, Carson, those are just a few of some of the strange goings on in Saskatoon, the most recent one being the sudden appearance of a castle, complete with a mote and drawbridge, that seems to have been built overnight at a local park just outside of Saskatoon. Some are calling these events as unexplainable phenomenon while others believe that they are the result of elaborate hoaxes by a group of very creative pranksters."

"Very creative, indeed, Sandra. I'm not sure how they pulled off the rainbows, though."

Sandra laughed and the two continued to banter. Eventually they shifted over to the weather forecast, but by now, Yalad was on the phone making airline reservations for the soonest flight to Saskatoon.

21

Convergence and Conscription

Since Yalad had banished Benedict to a remote island, the two men's lives had drifted further and further apart until in practically every way possible, they had become polar opposites. One was content, free from the obsession of obtaining the calamus, yet knowing a time would come when he would be led to its earthly conclusion. The other, perpetually bored and now gradually aging, stripped of his powers and immortality, feeling irrevocably distanced from the calamus since his failure in Germany yet clinging to a faded hope that he was destined to control all of its potential. Benedict, now over five hundred years old, had since his awakening from his enforced sleep enjoyed a life fuller than he could ever imagine. By all outward appearances, he seemed to have the quiet average life of a local doctor helping his community. He seldom relied on the calamus' power. When he sensed the Spirit leading, he would not hesitate to draw upon its ability to help others, but with each day, he was increasingly strengthened in the conviction that the calamus was not meant for anyone other than its creator and a time must come when it should be returned to Him. Though Benedict had given it back to Christ at the cross, the physical presence of the calamus still abode on earth, in reach of mankind, good and bad—in particular, Yalad.

Benedict remembered the type of person Yalad was when he had his short conversation with him on the island. Yalad would not take the loss of his power lightly. He would continue to search for the calamus, even as Benedict had once done so, with the exception that Yalad's intent was power and ultimate control. For some reason, God had not yet taken the calamus back. Benedict rested in the thought that he was not responsible for orchestrating such an undertaking. Still, he sensed that at some point, there would be a final meeting with Yalad regarding the calamus.

A few years prior to the outbreak of World War II, Benedict was at the point where it was necessary to uproot again and assume a new identity. He decided to move to America and for a brief time lived just outside New York City, and unbeknown to him, about an hour's drive away from Yalad. Benedict established a medical practice in a small town. When war broke out, while Yalad was seeking the calamus in Germany, Benedict was not far away, once again serving his new country, only this time as a doctor on the battlefield.

After the war, Benedict went home to his practice in New York, and Yalad returned to the city, one contentedly serving and the other becoming increasingly bitter and driven. One thing they both saw was that the world was changing dramatically. Up until then, life had run at a comfortable pace. For Benedict, it had been hundreds of years without much changing. For Yalad, it had been thousands. There was a time in the two men's distant past when the world was thought to be flat. There was a time in their more recent past when mankind travelled either by foot or ship. There was a time for the two men when they lived in an unknown, much larger world. Now the world was discovered to be not only round, but more easily accessible and therefore increasingly smaller.

As the years went on, Benedict served people while Yalad accumulated wealth. Wars continued to come, and the world got smaller and smaller until at one point the world became so small that people began to look outward to other worlds. People were not only flying around the globe but they were starting to fly into space. A hundred years earlier, a letter might take months to travel halfway around the world. Now someone could reach into their pocket and pull out a phone and connect with someone on the other side of the planet in seconds.

Ideas travelled faster than the time needed to digest the details. Information became its own commodity, and truth was only relevant to those who possessed the power to manipulate and shape it for whatever purpose they wanted. Fortunes rose and fell in an hour. People bought and sold without needing money to change hands. Anything could be obtained, unless of course one was poor. "*For you have the poor always with you*," only now they were more painfully aware of not only how poor they were but how rich others lived. No one existed in a bubble and discontentment ruled regardless of their financial well-being. The rise in technology corresponded to the rise in discontentment. The more men had and the greater their inventions, the more they wanted. This coexisting fulfilling and lacking created an insatiable hunger for something spiritual. For a few, it led them to Christ as the answer, yet Benedict could see that while there was an increase in the desire for spiritual knowledge, there was an equal disinterest in the absolute spiritual knowledge that could save the soul. People had developed an insatiable hunger for spiritual garbage but an intense distaste for the manna from heaven.

Yalad appeared to others as middle-aged. For the first time in thousands of years, time became a limited resource. He had taken immortality for granted, assuming he would eventually conquer the calamus, thus dominating its originator. He believed in God and in judgment. The calamus was the evidence. However, the calamus had its own way, and Yalad was determined to have his. He had no interest in the person and designs of God or in the spiritual hunger of mankind. He could, however, see his vision of communication and travel coming to fruition. If he could retrieve the calamus, he could reverse the curse of aging on his body and then begin to find a way to rule the world and storm heaven's gates. He would succeed where his father had failed.

There came a time in the early 1990s when Benedict decided it was time once again to move on and assume a new identity. He moved to Canada and wandered around for a couple of decades. A great weariness began to settle in and he sensed that it had to do with the calamus. He still looked as young as the day he first felt the touch of immortality, but his soul felt old and tired. He often thought of the verse in Hebrews 9:27: "It is appointed unto men once to die but after this the judgment." He had come to believe every word in the Bible. He must die and so must Yalad. While Benedict knew that Yalad's powers with the calamus had been stripped from him, he was uncertain about Yalad's immortality. Either way, a time of conclusion was drawing near. Regardless of how their lives were lived, no man was meant to live on earth as an immortal. Benedict came to consider that the times he had died, particularly while at the bottom of the sea, were in fact, not full experiences of death but simply a process of physical destruction and then healing. Lazarus had died and was brought back to life. Perhaps the verse in Hebrews about dying once meant death in God's time, God's will, and God's way. Benedict, who at one time thought that immortality would bring him what he wanted, now knew that every second on earth was time away from eternity, which was something he increasingly longed to experience. Eventually he settled in Saskatoon, changed his name to Wilson Meadows, and renewed his practice in medicine.

Benedict opened a small general practice. His experience in medicine was much greater than those in Saskatoon were aware. Over the course of almost a century, he had done everything from the requirements of a general practitioner to complex surgeries. However, in spite of his youthful appearance, Benedict felt more like a retiring kindly old physician who saw a small handful of patients suffering from the common maladies of everyday life.

On Saturdays, Benedict loved to visit the nursing homes. He felt more at home with those who had lived full lives than those of his "own age." Benedict found great joy in not only helping them with their medical needs but by sitting with them and listening to them talk of their lives. Many were ready for death but were grateful for anyone who was willing to help them through to the other side. Some, like an elderly woman named Rose Sandra, were battling not only the physical discomforts of age but a mind that was slipping away.

"Good afternoon, Rose," said Benedict with a warm smile as he stood at Rose's doorway. Next to him was one of the staff members named Katie.

"Rose, Doctor Meadows is here to visit."

Rose had been sitting quietly in a chair in the corner of the room. A television was on, but the sound had been muted. Rose was looking out the window. Katie walked over to the television and turned it off. Rose had not moved when Benedict had been introduced. Her mind had been focused on something else and it was only when Katie came partially into her view that Rose became startled, realizing that someone was in the room. Katie placed one hand gently on Rose's shoulder and leaned in.

"I'm sorry, Rose, dear. I didn't mean to startle you. Doctor Meadows has come to visit. Would you mind if he sat down?"

Rose nodded her head absentmindedly and turned her head back toward the window, her vacant gaze lost somewhere in the past. Katie smiled at Benedict, who nodded that he would be fine alone with Rose. Katie left the room, and Benedict pulled a chair next to Rose, resting one hand on her forearm.

"Hello, Rose. It's good to see you today. How are you feeling?"

She wasn't sure if it was Benedict's voice or his hand on her arm, but immediately the fog of faded memories lifted and she could feel her mind focusing. She turned to look at Benedict.

"You're a handsome young man. How old are you?"

Benedict chuckled.

"Older than I look."

Rose looked back out the window and starred glassy-eyed at the garden on the other side. Benedict whispered a prayer that God would help him with Rose. He waited patiently until she turned her head back to Benedict. He wondered if she had remembered anything they had just said to each other.

"Well, you certainly age well. You're not family, are you?"

"No, I'm a doctor. I'm just visiting. How are you feeling today?"

For Rose, the more Benedict sat and talked, the clearer she could feel in her mind. She had seen this man before. Where was it, she wondered.

"Have we met before?"

"No," answered Benedict. "Do I look familiar to you?"

Rose stared at Benedict, and he could see that she was remembering something from her past. A distant smile crept across her face.

"I was dancing with my Danny. He was with the twenty-first in France during World War II. A man who looked just like you came over to us, and Danny gave him a big bear hug. The man was a medic. He had saved my Danny's life."

Benedict remembered Danny. He should have died, but God had led Benedict to restore the injuries that Danny would not have survived. A bomb had exploded, leaving Danny barely alive. He was unconscious, and while his limbs were intact, so much blood had left his body that Danny had less than a minute before his last breath. No one was nearby as Benedict laid his hands on Danny and restored the bones, muscle, and tears throughout his body. Benedict then picked Danny up, who was still unconscious and carried him past enemy fire and toward an ambulance. A few days later, Benedict met Rose at a canteen with Danny. She was a WASP, flying soldiers from factories to bases and transporting cargo. She had bright red hair, a fun sense of humor, and was greatly relieved that her Danny had survived an explosion with only a minor concussion.

"Perhaps it was a long-lost relative I don't know about," said Benedict. Rose was just about to speak when a woman and small girl came to the doorway.

"Excuse me, I'm trying to find Agnes Cutworth. Do you know what room she's in?"

One of the aides from the nursing home overheard and led the mother and daughter to the room, apologizing to Benedict for the interruption.

Heather and her daughter Emily followed the aide to the room of Miss Cutworth. Shortly after Heather had decided to go back to church, she got involved in the weekly visitations to the nursing home. She wondered how Emily would feel about going with her, but to her surprise, Emily loved visiting. Sometimes she would talk and entertain them with her simple childlike ways and other times she would just take out some paper and pen and draw a picture. Many of those they had visited had pictures drawn by Emily on their walls.

Agnes Cutworth was new to the nursing home. She often sat quietly staring out the window, her cane resting on her lap. She spoke very little to the staff or visitors. Her mind often seemed lost in some train of thought or maybe just lost without any thoughts left. Unbeknown to most, she had experienced great loss in her life and faced even greater personal struggles and sorrows. Her life had been one of abandonment. As a child, she was abandoned by her parents. As a wife, she had been abandoned by her husband. Two of her boys had died in a botched robbery and her only daughter, after two abortions and an attempted suicide, died alone in an abandoned warehouse from a drug overdose. All familial relations she had ever known had abandoned her. There was one brief period in her young life when she had been taken in by a loving Christian family. It was a wonderful time of joy and laughter, and then suddenly for a reason she never understood, she was moved to another foster home. That memory, later combined with the incidences in her life, convinced her that she had also been abandoned by God. Now, finally with her health abandoning her, she was past bitterness, past retribution, past vengeance, and past recouping her faith or even caring that faith mattered.

"Hello, Miss Cutworth," said Heather. "I'm Heather and this is my daughter Emily. Do you mind if we visit for a bit?"

The woman did not respond, so Heather came in and sat down in a chair next to Miss Cutworth. Emily pulled out her bag and the pen, which was the calamus, and started to draw. While Emily drew, Heather prayed silently, asking God if there was a way to communicate with the woman. Just as Heather was about to speak, a fire alarm went off. There was commotion as the aides guided the residents and visitors out the building. Some of the residents were extremely agitated while others calmly followed the aides and nurses outside. Agnes sat silently at the window without moving. Heather wondered if she had not heard the alarm or perhaps just didn't care. An aide came to the door.

"I'm sorry, but we have to evacuate the building. I'm sure it's just one of the residents a little confused or one of the guests playing around. Sometimes we get some of the younger boys who like to pull the alarm for fun. Could you please grab your bag and come with me?"

Heather and Emily left. An aide helped Miss Cutworth stand and the two exited the building. Later, it was discovered that there was a small fire in the kitchen, and it would be sometime before residents and guests would be allowed to reenter. Heather decided that it would be best if they just went home and come back the next week.

Eventually the residents were led back to their room. On the desk in Miss Cutworth's room was the beginning of Emily's drawing and the calamus, which Emily had left behind in her rush to leave. Once the aide left the room, Agnes noticed the picture that Emily had started. It was a picture of a woman, and even with Emily's limited skills, Agnes understood the picture to be her. Emily had drawn Agnes with a big smile, her long gray hair pulled back into a ponytail. She was standing with her cane in one hand, and Emily had placed a flower in her other hand. In Agnes's room, there was a small flower vase next to her bed put there by one of the aides which held some pink amaryllises. Emily's drawing of the flower looked like one of the amaryllises. That night while Agnes slept, she dreamt she was lying in an endless field of pink amaryllises. She could feel joy and hope flooding her soul, wiping away the bitter, tear stained slate of her life. Heaven was real and God was love. Jesus was standing next to her, and he reached his hand out. Just as she put her hand in his, she awoke. The moment she awoke, she thought to herself that she would never forget the feel of her hand in his. When she sat up in bed, she was holding one of the amaryllises flowers in her hand, and for the first time that she could remember, there was a smile on her face.

After lunch, energized by her dream, Agnes decided to take the pen and finish the picture the young girl had started. If the child returned, she would give it to her as a gift. In her youth, Agnes had minored in art at college. There was a time when one of her greatest pleasures was painting, but she had not picked up a brush since her daughter's suicide. Agnes took the pen Emily had left behind and added some of the things she thought the young girl would enjoy. So she drew rainbows, palm trees, animals, and even a castle. When she was finished, she asked one of the aides if she could have it framed and hung on the wall.

Yalad had not been the only one who witnessed the strange events on the news. Benedict, who was closer to home, realized that the calamus was nearby. Yalad saw its manifestation as a sign drawing him nearer to power while Benedict saw it as a sign drawing both him and the calamus to a conclusion.

Benedict did not know where the calamus was, only that it was close by. He also knew that he would find it, so he went about his normal routine and waited for it to come to him. The next Saturday, he visited the nursing home again. He made the rounds visiting the residents and listening to their ailments and their stories. His last stop was Miss Cutworth. When he walked into the room, there were two visitors. The woman and her daughter. They were the ones who the previous week had asked for directions to Miss Cutworth's room.

"I'm sorry. I didn't mean to interrupt," said Benedict.

"That's okay. We were just visiting Agnes. My name is Heather, and this is my daughter Emily."

Benedict smiled at Emily and noticed the calamus in her hand. He had not seen the calamus since he was on the island and the small boy had awakened him. He felt a sense of excitement, not at using the pen but in the work of the pen towards him. Emily was sitting next to Miss Cutworth and holding a framed picture in her lap. It was of Miss Cutworth. Surrounding her were drawn all the recent odd occurrences that Benedict and others had seen on the news. Heather saw Benedict looking at the picture, almost as if the picture and the recent events were not a surprise to him.

"Do you know anything about this? We thought that Agnes had drawn this after the events, but she told us that she had drawn them before."

Benedict smiled at Emily.

"Is that your pen, Emily?"

"Yes," she replied. "Actually, it's my Grampy's. I took it from his room before he went to heaven. I didn't mean to. It was an accident."

Heather frowned at Emily.

"I didn't know that, sweetheart."

"I'm sorry, Mommy. I didn't know what to do with it after…"

Emily's voice trailed off as she tried to stop a tear. It was still hard for her to talk about what had happened. Heather gently held her daughter's hand.

"Oh, it's okay, Emily. I just didn't know it was your grandfather's. I'm sure he would want you to have it."

Heather looked back at Benedict. He seemed calm and purposeful. She looked back at the picture.

"You know all these things in the picture just happened in the last few days?"

"Yes," replied Benedict. "I saw them on the news."

"Could there be a possible connection? It sounds so silly, but it's such an odd coincidence."

Benedict smiled warmly at Agnes.

"What do you think, Agnes?"

Without hesitation, she answered, "It's the finger of God."

There was a brief silence as everyone considered not only what Agnes said but how confidently and serenely it was said. Finally, Benedict spoke as he turned to Heather.

"She's not far from the truth. It is a unique pen. Timeless, as far as I know. It belongs on the Throne of God, and I have been sent to retrieve it. It has been on Earth since time began and has been used and misused. By God's providence, it has stayed, but I believe that the time has come for it to be returned to its creator. Emily, your grandfather guarded the pen while he was alive. I'm sure he is proud of the way that you have taken care of it. He is in heaven now, and I think that he would like it returned to the Lord of heaven also. May I take it back to him?"

For a moment, Emily wavered, and Benedict could see the same look he had seen on others when they realized what they possessed. But it passed quickly, and Emily handed the pen to Benedict.

"Do you have a piece of paper I could borrow, Emily?"

Emily, excited now to be a part of the adventure, quickly reached into her bag to get her notebook and tore out a page. Benedict sat the paper on the table and began to write.

"I submit myself to the will of the pen. If it is thy will, I wish the pen to be returned to the Lord of lords in heaven and that by His grace I might return with it. All praise be to the only true God."

Yalad had landed in Saskatoon earlier that day. He had no idea where to start looking, but when he saw a news station showing a report on the state of local nursing homes, he was surprised to see an interview with a woman, with a picture of the strange things that had happened hanging on the wall behind her. Yalad called the news station and found the location of the nursing home. Jumping into a taxi, he was surprised at the level of desperation he felt. He had always been confident that time and destiny was on his side. Now, there was a sense of fear, a premonition that he was too late, that the calamus had chosen another. He reached the nursing home and found the room of the old woman. When he entered the room, Benedict had just finished writing and turned along with everyone else to the man who was now standing in the doorway. Yalad looked at the paper realizing that Benedict had just used the pen. Horror and rage seized him. Horror in what he assumed Benedict had just done, and rage that he had been cheated once again.

"You didn't," sneered Yalad.

"It was never ours," answered Benedict.

"It was mine!" cried Yalad. "It was meant to be mine."

Suddenly the room was filled with a brilliant light. Benedict's voice rose, and it sounded like the voice of a multitude.

"*Now unto the King eternal, immortal, invisible, the only wise God, be honor and glory for ever and ever. Amen.*"

For everyone in the room except Yalad, it was if a large door had opened and the four—Benedict, Agnes, Heather, and Emily were standing in the doorway gazing into heaven. Each saw those familiar to them who had gone on beforehand. Benedict could see Francis, Jan Žižka, Andela, Marshall, Matheo and his family, Margaret, and others whom he had come to know. Heather and Emily could see Eli and Bethany standing next to Jesus. Agnes recognized the Christian family who had taken her in as a child and a woman standing next to them. At first she did not recognize the woman and then her eyes were opened and she realized it was her daughter. Agnes wept in amazement. Jesus stepped forward with his arms stretched out, welcoming Benedict and the pen into heaven. Emily watched in wonder as angels were round about singing praises, knowing this was a special gift just for her. The glory of the Lord spread throughout the nursing home. For some, there was a great sense of peace and joy. For others, it was confusion, and many cried out in fear, causing the aides to run to their rooms.

For a moment, Yalad saw a light, and salvation was offered. But it passed quickly as his heart hardened from the bitterness of what he felt was the theft of his right. In that brief moment, he chose to despise for the last time that which was holy and apart from him. He had lost all, yet it was not enough to cause him to relinquish all. The moment he cursed God in his heart, the room ceased to become light and turned to fire. To the others, the room was filled with light and God's glory. To Yalad, as he stood in the nursing room doorway, the walls, floor, and ceiling of the room appeared engulfed in flames and he could no longer see Benedict or the others. The heat from the flames rushed toward him. He fled from the room and ran to the entrance of the nursing home, collapsing on the floor in front of the door, the shoes on his feet burned off and his feet singed. He wept without tears in the gall of bitterness. After a few minutes, he stumbled out the front door of the nursing home and slumped down at the top step of the stairs leading from the porch. He buried his head in his hands.

For the first time in thousands of years, he felt old and tired. He had lost all and now he was slowly dying, forever mocked by a righteousness he could not overcome and would not freely receive. The calamus was gone. Since his father had first rejected him, Yalad had never felt so destitute. He had wanted to succeed where his father had failed, yet not because he sought his father's approval. He had quickly dissolved himself of that reality. He only sought his father's way. His desire was the desire of Cain—to have his own way not just be acceptable but to be the standard. Not to submit but to be submitted to. All lost souls since Cain, who reject mercy because they reject God, have unsuccessfully attempted their own way. With the calamus, Yalad knew he had a better chance than any before him.

The authority to have his own way and to make that the only way. He had been a burning flame. Now he was a miniscule candle slowing burning out. There was no more expecting, no more assuredness, no more confidence. He was a man who had ruled time, people, and the elements. Now he was no different than someone who leaves the world unnoticed and unremembered yet having to face a God who forgets nothing. He had wasted thousands of years only to be mocked by heaven. He looked down at his feet, realizing for the first time that the fire had scorched his shoes and socks, leaving his feet black with the soot from the flames. A car honked its horn, and Yalad looked up.

It was a long black limousine with darkly tinted windows. It certainly was the last thing Yalad expected to see on a sunny afternoon in front of a nursing home after losing the calamus forever and nearly being burned to death by the glory of God. He stared, like someone lost in the desert and uncertain whether they were viewing water or a mirage. As he stared, the front passenger window rolled down. A man dressed neatly in a dark suit and wearing sunglasses put one hand to his ear for a moment and with the other hand motioned for Yalad to wait. After a moment in which the man appeared to be in some type of communication with someone else, he opened his palm upward and with his fingers motioned for Yalad to come to the car. Yalad did not know what to make of the man or the car. He briefly turned around and looked to see if the man was motioning to someone else and when he turned back, the man emphatically pointed his finger at Yalad and motioned again with his hand, this time more forcefully. Yalad slowly stood and shuffled toward the car, unconcerned about his appearance.

When he reached the car, he approached the man and started to lean in.

"What do you want?" he asked the man who was now staring straight ahead.

The moment he asked the question, the window went back up and the back seat side passenger window came down. Yalad looked into a sea of blackness. There was no light and the leather seat and carpeting were dark black. He faintly saw the outline of a figure on the far side of the car.

"Please come in," said a voice. It was smooth, calm, and inviting. It was the effortless, pleasant voice of someone accustomed and comfortable with wielding power undisturbed. Yalad had met many in his life who possessed this same controlling voice. It was the honey soft voice of wealth and power which managed to convey authority without hysterics. Yalad looked down at his feet.

"Do not worry about your appearance," spoke the voice. "You've been through a great ordeal. Please join me. My name is Kaden."

"What do you want?" said Yalad, who had regained enough of his composure to not let the power of another mortal frighten him.

There was a quiet pause from the man in the dark before he spoke.

"We have much to talk about, Yalad. You think that you have lost all, but I am here to tell you that the power you have dreamed about will be yours."

Yalad scoffed as he opened the door. He would hear the man out. At the very least, he reasoned that he would be spared from walking on his tender feet.

"You have no idea what I just lost," replied Yalad as he sat in the seat and closed the door. "Whatever you think I might have or have access too is gone forever."

The man smiled and the white of his teeth seemed to light up his side of the seat.

"It is because of what you have lost that enables me to finally approach you, Yalad."

"How do you know my name? Have we met?" asked Yalad.

"I know your name and I know the tool which you call calamus. I know this and I know much more."

"Such as?" said Yalad.

"I knew your father Nimrod. I know that the name Yalad is nothing more than a reminder that you were of little worth to him, in spite of the fact that you made him a legend. I know how you have carefully used the calamus and how you have dreamt of what it could do for you. I know of the past, the present, and I know what we will do in the future."

"We?" said Yalad doubtfully. "If you know so much, then how are we to obtain the calamus? It is gone forever."

"Precisely," answered Kaden.

"Precisely?" replied Yalad incredulously.

"Please stop repeating my words with a question," said the man. "It's annoying. What you do not know about that tool, as powerful as it was, was that it was keeping you from what you wanted to achieve. As long as the writing tool has been available to man, it has been a hindrance. Our master learned in the beginning that it could never be controlled. However, in his infinite wisdom, he realized that it could be used to find the one who could wield an even greater power. He has watched you since you first used it on your father. He has watched as others attempted to use the tool to their own destruction. He has watched Benedict and others foolishly submit to it and its master. Only you were faithful to the purpose of its potential. You have longed for the same power that our master desires to give you. Your only mistake, and it is an understandable one, is you thought it was the only way available. However, we will take the kingdoms and you will lead us."

Yalad was tempted to ask who "we" was, but after his last rebuke, he simply asked how.

"In some cases by subtlety, in some cases out of necessity, and in some cases by force. Mostly by demand. Not ours, but theirs. We will be invited to control. You were right many years ago when you concluded that transportation and communication were the two requirements for control. But there is another. It is will.

It has taken thousands of years for it to happen. It has occurred in certain places at different times with various groups, but now the entire world has the will to be controlled, whether they understand that control or not, and you will be the one they demand. It is now our time and you are the man. The world is yours and you will rule. Nimrod could never conceive of the power and greatness that you will possess. Your father is no longer Nimrod. We are your father and we will be your calamus, and you will rule mankind. You will be their messenger, you will be their savior, and you will be their god. But we must change your name. You are no longer an unnoticed and unwanted child. You are the son of the Morning Star, and you will rise to rule all that your eye can see."

Yalad looked at the man and scoffed.

"Am I to understand that…?" Yalad laughed derisively. "Not that fairy tale."

Kaden smiled, and there was a look about him that Yalad had not seen before. There was a ferociousness and hunger to devour. Like a lion that seeks its prey, only his went beyond the desire to satisfy its natural appetite. This lion called Kaden took pleasure in the slaying of its prey and had no interest in devouring. It did not feed off the flesh, it feed off the kill. Some would call it evil, but Kaden would call it mastery. In seeing this in Kaden, Yalad recognized it in his own soul for the first time; always there but never acknowledged. More than a desire to control, more than a desire to avoid judgment; there was an intense longing to destroy for the sake of destroying.

"Not everything is a fairy tale," replied Kaden. "We are all princes of the darkness seeking to spoil and ravage the one who unjustly cast our master from the heavens. We have ruled the night and we will make the day ours, bringing to darkness the hypocrisy of the so-called light. You've been an Antichrist since you first decided to use the calamus to deny judgment. Anti is not even the right prefix. Proto would be truer. We are the protochrists. We are the true originals. We are the true messiahs."

"Whatever I gained from the calamus, I have lost," said Yalad.

"That is true," nodded Kaden.

"Then why me? All I have is money and I can see you don't need that."

"You of all people Yalad should understand the nature of power. We set up princes and kings as we choose and just as efficiently have them deposed if it is in our best interest. There is no lineage, no vote, and no amount of money that can control us. People in power are in power because we say they are in power," said the man with a conspiratorial smile. "A world that has lost its will and its way do not care about details. You have been chosen for the reasons already stated. To put you in power will be no more difficult than finding you a new pair of shoes."

"I've heard enough to know that if half of what is written is true, then we don't fair too well in the end. That's why I sought the calamus," said Yalad.

"Our history has not been written yet. It has only been presumed," replied Kaden. "Your dream has always been our dream—to ascend to the most high. You will not be ruled. You have seen the foolishness of mankind and you have tasted the power and rightness of our way. We are not interested in righteousness. We are however interested in righting a wrong and not abdicating our power to those who are underserving. You deserve this and it is yours for the taking."

The stranger put his hand on Yalad's arm and patted it once. He gave a slight, somewhat detached smile.

"Either way, you have a choice. You're dying. With us, you not only have a chance to live forever but to rule in the manner you have always dreamed. Someone will rule. Until now, our minds, yours and ours, have always been aligned. We have sought the same outcome. It is only our methods that have differed. Our master is more patient than you have ever been."

Kaden paused as he looked at one of his nails, "Besides…if it's not you, it'll be someone else. You can either return to the dust or rise to rule the heavens."

Yalad looked out the window at the world he had tried to outlive and had wanted always to rule. He could taste death in his mouth and feel it for the first time rotting his bones, as if in a moment he could turn into dust and be blown away by the wind. He hated Benedict. He despised the way of Benedict. There was no going back, and there was no standing still. He turned to face the creature called Kaden and in an instant Kaden knew that Yalad would be the one that they were waiting for. Kaden leaned forward slightly and spoke to the driver.

"Now we are ready to leave. We have much to do. Let's start with some new shoes."

The End

Ingram Content Group UK Ltd.
Milton Keynes UK
UKHW040610210323
418905UK00001B/58

9 798886 164626